Back

To

Newark

A Novel by Len Serafino

Author's Note

This book is a work of fiction. Names characters, places and incidents either are the product of the author's imagination or are used fictitiously. Any resemblance to actual persons living or dead, business establishments, events or locales is entirely coincidental.

For
Nancy Karen

Chapter 1

On what was to be the last full day of his life Carmine Cifelli made a mistake that would cost his best friend, Phil Falco a small fortune. Phil's dreams of relaxing under the Florida sun, enjoying early morning golf rounds, would evaporate like the dew on the fairway; all because Carmine acted on impulse. That afternoon, not yet aware of what was heading his way; Phil Falco was in a good mood. As he waited at the US Airways baggage claim carousel he pondered his future and was happy. He was in a good mood, thinking about his future plans. Another two or three years and he would be living his dream.

Carmine was picking him up at the airport. Phil grabbed his overnight bag and headed for the passenger pick up area. Carmine pulled his Cadillac up to the curb just as he walked through the revolving door and stepped outside. Right on time. He dropped his bag in the back seat, sat down, slammed the door shut and slid into the front seat next to Carmine. The guy looked terrible.

"Great timing Cifelli. Exactly how cold is it here?"

"It's twenty degrees Phil. The Weather Channel said it was seventy-three in Orlando. Welcome home, pal."

"Home? Are you serious? I haven't lived in Newark for thirty years. "Twenty degrees," he said, shaking his head. "Any questions about why I left?"

Carmine laughed. "Yeah, it's cold."

"When did you buy the Caddy?"

"I leased it last month. It's a CTS. You like it?"

Phil nodded. "Black with black interior. What a surprise."

"Don't be such a wise ass. You know black was always my favorite color. So, you got your divorce from what's her name,"

Carmine said.

"Tracy. Three months ago."

"One more and you'll be even with me. What time we gotta be in Toms River?"

"We have time. The closing's at four o'clock in my lawyer's office."

That beautiful Victorian style home where he spent so many fabulous summers brought back fond memories. Nestled just two blocks from Barnegat Bay in Toms River, he recalled crabbing with his father early in the morning and heading to nearby Ortley Beach in the afternoons. Now he was selling it. His parents bought the home years ago. He spent the month of August in that house every year from the time he was six years old until he graduated from college. So many fond memories of those long, hot days and summer nights by the bay. "Carmine, do you ever think of those summers we spent at the shore?

Carmine smiled and nodded. "All the time. You invited me every year."

Phil laughed. "I didn't have a choice. I wanted to invite Ralph or Gerard, but my mother always made me pick you."

"That's what I thought," Carmine said. "You know your mother left you the house at the last minute. She used to tell me she was going to leave it to me, not you."

"My mother really liked you but not that much."

He rented the house out during the season for a few years after his mother died but it was annoying, him living in Florida and dealing with a property management service. Lot's of calls and always about a sink needing to be fixed, a stove that had to be replaced. Anyway, he needed a nest egg now. Always careful with money, he was shaken by how little he actually had left after his divorce. For one thing he was still paying alimony to his first wife Arlene. And now he was divorced again. Of course Tracy was awarded a settlement that cut what little assets he had in half. At least she didn't ask for alimony. Still, what he had left wasn't

2

nearly enough to retire on. Being careful with money wasn't much help after two divorces.

Now, with one transaction, he would fix his financial problem. He would have a decent nest egg to go along with his pension and Social Security when the time came.

Carmine turned toward him for a second: "So how much you figure to make on the house?"

"When all is said and done just under five hundred."

"Thousand? Like five hundred thousand?"

"Carmine. The house is paid off. You know what real estate goes for at the Jersey shore."

Carmine shrugged. He started to say something but he was interrupted by a coughing fit. The entrance to the Garden State Parkway was just ahead. It was only one o'clock but the skies looked dark and now snow flurries began to fall.

"So, what are you going to do with the money?" Carmine looked over at him.

"Try to hold onto it for a while,"

"Then whatever you do, don't get married again," Carmine had a big smile on his face.

"You should know Carmine."

Carmine nodded. "Three marriages. Who would have thought? All those Catechism classes Tuesday afternoons too."

Phil looked at his friend. He knew Carmine hadn't really done a lot with his life. No children, he didn't own a home, and no savings. Fortunately, he had a decent retirement from working for the New Jersey National Guard. He retired a year ago as a Master Sergeant after twenty-eight years. Now he supplemented his retirement income working as a waiter in an Italian restaurant in Newark's north ward. Phil wondered about that. At 57, Carmine was still good looking with a full head of black hair but he had the look of a guy who had worked his way through too many Italian cheese cakes. In fact, looking at him Phil thought his color was off. Carmine really did look terrible. He had seen that look plenty of times working in the hospital. "Carmine, you feel okay? You look, I don't know, tired maybe."

"I am tired Phil. I got bronchitis for Christmas. I'm still not a hundred percent. Really, what are you going to do with all that loot?"

"I don't know. Sometimes I think I should retire like you did. That crazy bitch Tracy still works at the hospital. I think she's trying to get me fired. Every time I see her I get a headache. You know she's seeing one of the doctors. Did I tell you that?"

"Yeah, you told me. But really, what did you expect? Nine, maybe ten years ago that was you. You left Arlene for her right?"

Phil nodded. He wasn't sorry he left Arlene but he had regrets over the way it happened. "Tracy snuck up on me. Before I knew what was happening I was sleeping with her. One thing led to another and we got married. Now here I am fifty eight years old and I can't decide what to wear when I get up in the morning."

"How could she get you fired? She's a secretary and you're a vice president. That's got to count for something, right?"

"Hospital politics are not like office politics." He explained the situation to Carmine. It was true that he was vice president of purchasing but physicians that admitted lots of patients to a hospital had a lot of pull. The doctor Tracy was seeing was probably the most influential physician on the medical staff. And, his divorce from Tracy was painful, and within the confines of the hospital, public. In spite of the fact that she was the one having an affair and not trying too hard to be discrete, it was Phil who would suddenly find that Mercy Medical no longer needed his services. A doctor like Tracy's boyfriend got what he wanted. If Tracy decided she was uncomfortable having Phil around, he was expendable.

Carmine listened but kept his eyes on the road. When Phil took a breath he said, "I hear what you're saying but half-a-mill should ease the pain a little."

The two men rode in silence for a while. Phil stared out at the snow flakes. Off in the distance he could see the sorry looking houses that stood guard on the perimeter of the Parkway, some of them still adorned with Christmas decorations even though it was the end of January.

Phil loved Carmine since they were kids running around on the streets of Newark. They had been inseparable, attending the same schools, walking to church on Sundays, double dating and singing in a rock group with two other kids from the neighborhood. But things changed after high school. Phil left Newark for college, leaving Carmine behind. He remembered arguing with Carmine about going on to college but Carmine wouldn't hear of it. Carmine skipped college and joined the Guard to escape Viet Nam. When his six year commitment was up he took a full time job at the local armory.

"How's your sister Marianne doing?" Phil asked.

Carmine glanced at Phil. "All things considered, not bad. Her boy Ricky's a piece of work. The kid looks like Haystacks Calhoun, but other than that Marianne's okay,"

Phil laughed. Haystacks Calhoun had been a well known 600 pound professional wrestler during the 1950s. "Haystacks Calhoun was great wasn't he? Is the kid really that big?"

"No, but the kid likes to eat."

"She still teaching?"

"Oh yeah. And get this: She's taking acting classes in the City."

"You're kidding." From what Phil could remember of Marianne, she was a shy, quiet girl. He couldn't imagine her standing in front of an audience. "What's that all about?"

Carmine shrugged. "Who knows? I think maybe after Hank left she just needed to do something different. She took the divorce hard. The bastard drained her good."

"What do you mean drained her?"

"Took her money and then left her for another woman."

"When was that?"

It was 2001. He left her the day before 9/11." Carmine said.

Phil nodded, remembering the story now. Although he had quit smoking years ago, Carmine's cigarette looked good. "Let me have one of those."

"No," Carmine said. Then, shaking his head, he handed him his pack of Marlboro's and Phil took one. He lit it using the car's lighter.

"Don't get ashes all over the seat."

They rode down the Parkway and they talked about old times. Carmine zipped along in the passing lane, driving fast just the way he did when they were teenagers.

"You know," Carmine said, "we should have cut a record. We were good."

Phil laughed. It was an old refrain. They had been good as a neighborhood quartet but certainly not good enough to turn professional. They reminisced about the places they played and the girls they met. To change the subject, Phil mentioned the Yankees. Carmine shared his passion for baseball and the Yankees. They remembered well the championship teams of the Fifties and early Sixties. Phil and Carmine would try to outdo one another as they tried to remember the names of the different players of the era.

"Do you still have your four finger Andy Carey glove?" Carmine asked. Andy Carey had been a Yankee infielder during the Fifties.

"Somewhere, assuming Tracy didn't get it in the divorce settlement." At least he could laugh.

Just then a dark blue BMW in the middle lane pulled alongside Carmine and blew his horn. Both men looked at the guy in the other car. When he had their attention, he gave them the finger and sped ahead of them swerving into the passing lane Carmine occupied. It was a near miss.

"You mother fucker," Carmine shouted. He hit the gas and gave chase.

"What the hell is going on?" Phil asked. "Do you know that guy?" Carmine's Cadillac was nearly doing a hundred miles an hour now, in hot pursuit.

"No. What an asshole. Wait till I catch him."

"Carmine! Slow down. I have business to attend to, remember?" It was the only thing Phil could think to say. They were up to 110 now. Carmine was staring intently at the BMW ahead. He was gaining on him but as soon as the driver saw he was being chased he hit his accelerator too.

"Carmine, really, knock it off."

Carmine relented. "Fucking asshole."

To get Carmine's mind on something else, Phil concentrated on Marianne. "So does Marianne go out or has she given up on that?"

The two men talked about Marianne's situation for a few minutes. Carmine told Phil about Marianne's marriage to Hank. She was thirty-nine by the time she married him. He was a loner who said he had been married once before. It was Marianne's second marriage too.

"After Danny died I figured she would get married in a year or two. It took a lot longer than I thought for her to get hitched again."

"How long were they married before he died?"

"Two years. Then he gets nailed on the New Jersey Turnpike. And she was pregnant with Ricky when it happened."

Carmine went on. "Now, here's Ricky, twenty years old and still trying to find himself. He's got a tattoo on his neck and earrings in each ear."

"That's still young, only twenty," Phil said.

Carmine waved him off. "The kid's okay but he's lazy."

Marianne had waited ten years to marry again. Apparently, it wasn't worth the wait. She got a nice settlement when Danny died. It was enough to ensure Ricky could go to college. If she invested wisely it would have afforded her a comfortable retirement. Now the money was gone. Hank took care of that. At least she managed to cut Hank off from access to her pension. That, plus she took back her maiden name of Cifelli. Fortunately, she would get a nice pension one day from her job as a teacher in Newark's school system. She had been teaching high school English for years. According to Carmine she only went out occasionally now, never seeing the same man for very long.

"How's your daughter Lisa doing?" Carmine asked.

"Who knows? Ever since I divorced her mother we don't talk much."

"After all these years things aren't better? Sorry to hear it Phil."

Phil shrugged. He didn't want to talk about Lisa. He lost her when he married Tracy. Maybe he could start over with Lisa but he knew it would be painful for both of them.

Carmine put his blinker on and guided the car toward the Toms River exit. "Good old exit 82," Carmine said, "When we were kids it seemed like we would never get here."

"Is Seaside Heights still a good place to spend a week?"

Carmine laughed. "Not unless you're skin color is even darker than ours."

Phil ignored him. "What are you going to do while I'm at the closing?"

"I got a girlfriend that lives near here," Carmine said, "She works at Falzone's. If she's working tonight maybe we can eat dinner there."

"Even if she isn't working tonight we should eat there. Good food as I recall. They've been around for years. I can't believe they're still in business," Phil said.

"Oh yeah, good as ever. But if she's not there I have other plans for us tonight."

Phil didn't feel the least bit nostalgic about giving up the old house. In fact, Carmine had asked him if he wanted to swing by the place one last time.

"Let's drive by the old place and have one last look. Remember what your father used to say every year as soon as we got here?"

"If you guys don't behave…"

Both men finished together. "It's baaack to Newark."

They enjoyed a good laugh but Phil didn't want to drive by the house. He didn't need to see it again to remember the glorious summer vacations he spent in that house. The closing went off without a hitch. The buyers didn't even attend. Their attorney handled all the paperwork. When the title agent handed him a check for four hundred and ninety-seven thousand dollars, he was happy. Now he could really start over.

The attorney who represented Phil's interests was standing next to him staring out the window, looking out at the traffic on Route 37. The office was a storefront in a strip mall, small but perhaps just right for a lawyer in solo practice.

"Mister Falco, do you need a lift?"

"No, I'm just waiting for a friend to pick me up."

"Do you expect him soon? I'd like to close up shop for the day. I always try to close early on Thursdays. I play poker every Thursday night."

"Any minute," Phil said.

"Well, I don't want to be a prick but I need to get going. Does he have a cell phone?"

Phil really looked at the guy for the first time that day. He stood about six feet tall, a full five inches shorter than Phil. He had a stocky build and was especially thick around the middle. Phil had carefully maintained his athletic build over the years. The lawyer had a smug, self satisfied look on his face.

The temperature was in the low teens. Phil wasn't keen on standing outside but he had had enough of this guy. He pulled out his cell phone and called Carmine. As he did this he brushed past the attorney, forcing him to take a step back. He stepped outside. The attorney followed and locked the door behind him.

Once outside the two men faced each other. Neither spoke. The lawyer started to say something and then thought better of it. He headed off to his car.

After five long rings Carmine finally answered his cell. "I'm two blocks away."

"Well hurry up. I'm freezing."

The car had barely pulled to a stop and Phil was reaching for the door handle.

"Just take me to the airport. I can't stand the cold weather," Phil said.

Carmine laughed. "How'd you make out?"

"Okay. What do you want to do now?"

"We're going to Atlantic City," Carmine said.

For some reason that set off alarm bells in Phil's head. "Whoa, what do you mean we're going to Atlantic City? I'm flying out of Newark early tomorrow morning, remember?"

"Look, we're more than half-way there already. We'll put a few bets down, play a little roulette and head back tonight."

"That's a hell of a long ride to lay down a few bets isn't it?"

Carmine had another coughing fit, apparently still plagued by bronchitis. When it stopped he said, "I do it all the time."

"You ever win?" Phil asked.

"Oh yeah. I feel really lucky right now."

"Why? You get laid this afternoon?" Phil asked.

"I wish. She wasn't there. It's her day off. How about this: we'll stop and get a sandwich or a pizza and then run down there. I'll have you back in plenty of time, I promise."

Against his better judgment, Phil agreed. He had to admit that the idea of running around with Carmine again was appealing. The more he and Carmine talked the better he felt. Anyway, he wasn't in a hurry for his little adventure to end. Riding on the Parkway with Carmine, near the Jersey shore with some money in his pocket, reminded him of their youth. He had about four hundred dollars in cash on him. The big check was safely tucked into his wallet. Why not have a little fun?

Phil hadn't seen Atlantic City for years. He was still living in New Jersey when casino gambling was voted in. He had been against it. He even worked on a campaign to persuade voters to reject the proposition, the one time in his life when he could describe himself as an activist. He had enjoyed the experience but once the campaign ended, he drifted back into the familiar routines of work and family obligations. Well, he had to admit he had been wrong. Maybe the casinos didn't really help the city but they did create jobs and they were a good source of revenue for the state.

They shared a pizza at the Bayville Pizzeria and Deli, reminiscing some more about old times. Carmine also told him about his job as a waiter. He said he hated it but couldn't think of what else to do. Then they jumped back on the Parkway and headed south. It was getting dark now. It was almost six o'clock. It was snowing again and there was now some accumulation. Phil was beginning to fret about his decision to go all the way to Atlantic City. He really did have an early flight the next morning. "Are you sure we'll get back there tonight? I don't want to be stuck in the snow."

"It's just flurries."

CHAPTER 2

An hour later they pulled into the Branford Hotel and Casino. It had stopped snowing. Phil noticed that Carmine was visibly excited, moving fast and behaving like a man who knew how things worked in the peculiar world inhabited by gamblers. "We'll just play a little roulette," Carmine said. Maybe we'll get lucky right away and then we'll get out of here. We could be in and out in twenty or thirty minutes, Phil."

Phil doubted that but he went along. He had come this far so why not? Still he had a nagging feeling about being in a casino. It was his first time ever. Since he had been so vocal in his opposition to casino gambling, he always worried about being seen in one. Although seen by whom he couldn't say.

Walking into the dimly lit casino was a revelation for Phil. Carmine led him past endless rows of slot machines, blackjack tables and craps tables. Phil heard cries of joy and shouts of anguish, punctuated by bells and buzzers. The sights and sounds gave him goose bumps. They finally came to a stop at the roulette tables. Carmine had no trouble finding them. He really did know the terrain.

"Carmine, who are you looking for?" Phil asked. The room was crowded, or at least it seemed so to Phil. Did Carmine plan to meet someone here?

"I'm looking for a croupier. Name's David. He's usually here on Thursday nights."

"Why him?"

Carmine smiled. "He's good luck." "There he is, he's just coming on," he said, pointing off to his right. "Let's go Philip."

Phil followed Carmine to the roulette table. "I know you don't gamble, so just watch me for a while," Carmine suggested.

Carmine pulled three one hundred dollar bills out of his wallet. He gave them each a kiss and placed them all on red. The wheel spun and the ball bounced around until it settled on number fourteen; a red number. Carmine had doubled his money. He let it ride. Another spin and red came up again. With twelve hundred dollars on the table, Phil figured they would quit. But Carmine had other ideas. He let it ride yet again. And again he won. He was jubilant, pumping his fist in the air. "Maybe you're my good luck charm," he said to Phil. Then his broad smile soured. He looked at Phil, about to say something. Instead he started coughing, a violent spasm this time. He struggled to catch is breath.

Phil grabbed his arm. He thought Carmine might swoon, he was coughing so hard, but Carmine waved him off. Instead, Phil turned and reached for the chips, now worth twenty four hundred dollars and started to hand them to Carmine. He would ask Carmine to take him back to Newark now. Only he never got the words out of his mouth. A tall, husky man of about thirty grabbed his wrist and said, "I need to talk to you guys." With his other hand he took the chips from Phil.

His coughing fit over, Carmine's face turned an even deeper shade of red. "Bucco, what are you doing here?"

The guy named Bucco let go of Phil's wrist, fully aware that others were watching. He smiled a friendly smile but his eyes suggested otherwise. "Let's have a drink Carmine. Introduce me to your buddy."

Carmine stood mute. The big man smiled. It was a malevolent smile. Then he looked at Phil.

"I'm Phil Falco. I'm a friend of Carmine's from Florida."

The two men shook hands. Phil was no slouch. He had played football and baseball in high school. He worked out enough to stay in decent shape for a man his age. But when Bucco grabbed his wrist, he knew instinctively that he was out of his league. Bucco's strength and confidence were readily apparent.

They made their way over to the Horizons Lounge, the hotel's night spot.

"Yo, Doofus, you want to talk business with your friend here or do you want to ask him to take a walk for a while?" Bucco asked.

Carmine looked at Phil, embarrassed in front of his friend.

Phil said, "I'm not going anywhere. Do your business."

Bucco looked at Carmine who just shrugged and said, "What's up Bucco?"

"You know what's up. You owe Mister Florio some money. You're behind on your payments. This will help a little," he said pointing to the chips parked in his breast pocket.

"How much does he owe?" Phil asked.

Bucco whirled around to face him. "You planning to take over the payments?"

Phil froze. Once again he felt out of his depth. How did Carmine ever get involved with this guy, he wondered?

"Stay the fuck out of it my friend," Bucco said.

"Come on Frank. He didn't mean nothing. We been friends for a long time."

"Never mind him," Bucco said. "Where you been?"

"Right where I always am. I'm not that far behind. Is Dennis here?"

"Dennis? Dennis Florio? Is that the Florio you're talking about? I know Dennis," Phil said. "We played ball together," he looked at Carmine for confirmation. The three of them had been friends, playing baseball in high school. Carmine, Phil and Dennis all came from the same Italian American neighborhood in North Newark. For some reason, the mention of Florio's name didn't click with Phil immediately. It all came together now. Of course he had heard all about Florio's crime family connections. He knew about that when they were kids. He wondered why he didn't make the connection until Carmine said Dennis. He wondered why Carmine never mentioned Florio on their ride to Atlantic City.

Bucco turned to look at Phil. Only now he was just a bit less certain of himself, trying to calculate whether he needed to be more careful with this guy. "Yeah, he's here. Hold on a minute. Don't go nowhere." He pulled out a cell phone and speed dialed Dennis. They spoke for a minute. Then he pointed at Phil. "What's your last name?"

Phil sensed the tide had turned. "Did you forget? It's Falco."

Bucco repeated it into his phone. He listened for a minute and then snapped the case shut. "He wants to see you both. Follow me." He led them to a bank of elevators. He pressed the button for the 48th floor. On the ride up he said to Phil, "You shoulda told me you knew Mister Florio."

Dennis Florio wasn't a well know organized crime figure. At least he wasn't a public figure like some of the dons who had actually played to the TV cameras. A throwback to earlier times, he religiously avoided the limelight, preferring to operate beneath layers of captains and lieutenants allowing him to adopt a profile of a respectable businessman. He had inherited the family business, nominally a trucking company, from his father. His real business was gambling and loan sharking plus an occasional interest in high jacking the goods carried by trucks, including some of his own. Officially, within the crime family, he was semi-retired. He spent most of his time in Orlando, Florida now. In fact, unbeknownst to Phil, he lived only about five miles from the hospital where Phil worked.

The suite he currently occupied at the Branford was plush by any standards. Overlooking the Atlantic Ocean, the suite's décor was French Colonial. Florio was sitting behind a smallish writing desk, talking on the phone when the three men entered the suite. As soon as he saw them he hung up. "It is you," he said smiling at Phil. He rose to greet them. He was wearing a charcoal gray suit with a white shirt, no tie. He looked for his shoes and saw they were under the desk. "Bucco, get my shoes for me will you?"

Bucco complied, reaching under the desk for the shoes and then laying them down at Florio's feet.

"Dennis," Phil said, sticking out his hand. "It's been a long time."

"You still hanging around with this bum?" he said pointing to Carmine.

"What can I say?" Phil answered.

Dennis Florio signaled Bucco to leave. The big man said, "See you later Carmine." He dropped the chips on Florio's desk and looking at Florio, said, "twenty-four hundred." He nodded toward Phil before making his way out the door.

The three friends from the old neighborhood moved to the suite's living room. Florio poured each of them a healthy portion of Scotch, no ice. He motioned for them to sit down and handed each of them a drink. "Salute," he said. They all took a good gulp of the whiskey.

Phil couldn't help noticing that Dennis Florio had not maintained his athletic build. He was grossly overweight. Even his face looked puffy. For the next few minutes Phil and Dennis brought each other up to date, both men genuinely surprised that they were practically neighbors in Florida.

Florio, always curious about people, asked, "So Phil, what brings you to Atlantic City? You here on business?"

Before he could answer, Carmine spoke up. "He made a big score today before he ever got to A.C. Sold his ole man's house in Tom's River."

"That so?" Florio said, turning to Phil for confirmation.

"Yeah, I closed on it today," Phil answered.

"So you came here to blow your wad at the tables?"

Again before Phil could answer, Carmine said, "Not him. He's cheap as ever. Still squeaks. He'll take his half-mill down to Florida with him."

Florio smiled, properly impressed. He picked up his glass, nodded toward Phil and said, "Risalute"

Then Florio got down to business. "Let me apologize for Bucco.

He's a little too eager to please sometimes. Plus he's young. He still likes to show off his muscle. But, Carmine, you know I give you more room than most guys because we both come from the old neighborhood. I don't usually handle matters like this myself. Where have you been, Carmine?"

"I apologize. Right now I'm a little stretched," Carmine said.

"That's not a good answer Carmine and you know it."

There was a pause in the conversation. Each of the men took a sip of their drink. Phil pondered asking the same question he had asked Bucco. He was concerned for Carmine but he wasn't sure he wanted to get in the middle of something he didn't really understand. Still, he sensed that Carmine was in serious trouble. Florio's next words confirmed Phil's suspicions.

"You know Carmine, there are things I sometimes have to allow to happen even if I would prefer not to, capece?"

"Jesus, Dennis, I'm good for it. You know that." Again he started coughing.

Florio ignored Carmine's plea. Instead he turned to Phil. "I'm sorry you have to hear this Phil but I blame Carmine. I would like to believe he was hoping for a little score in the casino. Something he could give me so I wouldn't think he forgot me. Then again, maybe he figured with you here he wouldn't have to face the music."

"You know I'm good for whatever I owe," Carmine said.

"I get clowns coming in here almost every night. They have a small roll in their pockets. They owe me money and they're behind in their payments. Do they pay me? No. Instead they decide to play their games, blackjack roulette whatever. And you know what? They all say, 'I'm good for it.'"

"Dennis, can I ask a question?" Phil said.

"Shoot."

"How much does Carmine owe?"

Florio laughed. It was sad laugh. "That is a bad question Phil."

"I understand. And believe me I wish I was sitting in the airport right now waiting for my flight to Orlando. But I'm sitting here and my best friend seems to be in some kind of trouble."

"He is indeed. Carmine; okay if I answer Phil's question?"

Carmine, head down, merely shrugged his shoulders.

"Let's take a look," Florio said. He struggled up from his seat on the couch and waddled over to the desk. He turned the page of a ledger he had sitting there. "It's forty-seven grand and growing every day the interest isn't paid."

"What do you bet on?" Phil asked, turning his attention to Carmine.

"Ballgames mostly."

"Carmine, how the hell could you get in that deep on ballgames?" Phil asked.

Carmine looked up. "I fucked up. Okay?"

Phil stood up needing to stretch his legs. He walked over to the window and looked out at the ocean. The wind was whipping up the waves and carrying sand onto the boardwalk. He looked at his watch. It was almost eight o'clock. Then he turned to Dennis and asked the question he knew he had to ask. "Dennis, can't you just let Carmine off the hook for old time's sake?" He walked back over to his chair and sat down again.

"I could do that. But in six months this shit head will be right back where he is now."

"Not if you refuse to take any of his bets or lend him any money."

Carmine stood up now. "Hey. Why are you calling me a shit head? I'm tired of you guys always calling me names. You make your living off guys like me. I'm a fucking customer. Besides that, we go way back. I get a little behind and suddenly I'm a shit head? Fuck you Dennis."

Dennis gave Phil a knowing look, not unlike what might have passed between them when they were kids dealing with a punk who couldn't back up what came out of his mouth.

Phil said, "Carmine, do you have the money?"

"I can get it."

There was a long pause. The next move was obviously up to Dennis. "Tell you what I'm going to do. I have a package here that I need to get delivered to New York. You two drive it up there for me and maybe I'll cut the nut in half. For old times sake"

Carmine shook his head no. He looked over at Phil and shook his head again.

"What's in the package?" Phil asked.

"That's another bad question Phil."

"Don't you get it Phil? The big shot, Mister Florio asks the questions," Carmine said, jerking his thumb toward Florio.

Florio took a moment to take it all in, Carmine's defiance, his inability to pay, all of it. His face flushed with anger. "You know what? Now I want it all, forty-seven grand in forty-eight hours." He turned his head and fixed Carmine with a look. "Fuck you Carmine."

CHAPTER 3

The atmosphere in Dennis Florio's suite at the Branford Hotel had grown chilly. No one spoke. Florio got up again and refilled his and Phil's glasses.

Finally, Carmine said, "Dennis, I'm sorry. I guess I was out of line. Look, I can make the payments if I stop gambling. Just give me another chance."

Florio smiled. He looked at Phil and then back at Carmine. "Let's get something to eat," he said.

By now Phil realized he probably would be taking a later flight back to Orlando He doubted he would make the morning flight. Maybe he could get a seat on the afternoon flight. At the moment he didn't care. It was just beginning to dawn on him that his problems back in Orlando were small. He had half a million sitting in his wallet. In spite of his concern about Carmine's situation, he was intrigued by what was unfolding. In fact, it was the most interesting thing that had happened to him in a long time. Plus he knew that if necessary, he could square Carmine's debt and let Carmine pay him back instead of owing the money to Dennis Florio. He considered doing just that but on some instinct he decided to hold back a while.

"Where's the best Italian restaurant in Atlantic City?" Phil asked.

"Dante's Inferno. It's right on Pacific Avenue.," Florio said.

"Can we get in?" Phil asked.

"You don't just ask bad questions, you ask dumb questions too," Carmine said, wanting to show he wasn't bothered by Florio's outburst. It worked. Florio laughed and agreed, acknowledging the compliment.

When they got to Dante's they were seated immediately. The maitre de welcomed the three men and gestured for the wine steward to bring a bottle of wine. The label said Antinori, which Phil recognized as a good wine.

The steward opened the bottle and handed the cork to Florio who glanced at it and set it down on the table. Once the wine was poured, the maitre de stepped forward and looked at Florio. "Do you want menus?"

"Nah. Bring us an antipasto for the three of us. We're going to share some linguine marinara and then give us each a porterhouse."

Carmine and Phil were impressed. "I hope this isn't the last supper," Carmine said.

Florio smiled. "You guys have a long night ahead of you. You got to drive to New York and deliver my package."

The men sipped the wine. No one spoke for a while. Finally Phil spoke up. "How about if I just write you a check to cover his losses?"

"That's fine if you want to do that. You can fly to Orlando from here tomorrow morning. I'm leaving too. It's too damn cold here. I'm getting old; I can't take the cold weather anymore."

"It will take a couple of days for the check to clear but I'm good for it," Phil said.

"I know you're good for it. You were always a stand up guy. I don't know why you hang around with this shit head, but that's your business," Florio said, gesturing toward Carmine with his head.

The antipasto arrived. Carmine, whose face had turned beet red, didn't reach for anything. In fact he had been munching on a piece of bread. He put that down too. "Phil, thank you. I'll pay you back. Count on it buddy. I think I'll let you guys catch up on old times. Phil, I'll get your bags out of my car and leave them with the bellman at the hotel."

"Where the fuck do you think you're going?" Florio asked.

"I'm going home. We're square thanks to Phil."

"First of all I just ordered you a steak. If you didn't want it you should have said so. And, you little prick, you're gonna take care of my package tonight. Did you forget?"

"I thought we resolved that," Phil said, suddenly not so intrigued by the adventure.

"Phil, may I give you a little advice?" Florio said.

"Sure."

"Shut the fuck up. This doesn't concern you. Eat your dinner; write me a check and tomorrow morning we'll fly out of here. Capece?"

"I guess I just don't understand why he still has to make the delivery."

"Because I want him to. Let's leave it at that."

Phil looked at Carmine and shook his head. He was beginning to understand. Carmine was always a little wild but when they were kids he had been able to keep Carmine on a short leash. Carmine looked up to him, probably because he had been such a good athlete. Over the years they stayed in touch of course but living 1,100 miles apart, family and work obligations, plus the simple passage of time made it impossible to stay as close the way they once were. Obviously there were things he didn't know about Carmine's life.

Yet, through the years, Phil genuinely appreciated Carmine's loyalty. More than once Carmine was there to help him when he needed it. For one thing, Carmine did some serious hocus pocus to get him into his National Guard unit only days before he was expecting to receive his draft notice, something akin to a Houdini's magic according to Carmine. Then Carmine got him an easy job as company clerk. Phil's time in the Guard turned out to be easy duty. More importantly, it kept him out of Viet Nam.

Another time he borrowed money so he could lend it to Phil. The job Phil thought he was taking when he moved to Florida fell through. Here he was in Orlando with a new house, a family and no job. It took Phil six months to find one. He didn't find out until three years later that Carmine had borrowed the money. And he found that out not from Carmine but his sister Marianne at one of Carmine's weddings. The money had been a godsend.

Now it sounded like his buddy was mixed up in some kind of organized crime activity. Gambling might be just the tip of the iceberg.

The linguine arrived with more bread. The waiter filled the wine glasses and asked if he could do anything else.

"More water," Florio said.

The three men were sitting there, sullen looks on their faces. If for no other reason than to get through the meal, Phil decided to change the subject. "Dennis, remember the time we beat East Orange after a rain delay? I remember you were soaked from head to toe."

"Yeah, with all that catcher's gear. I remember that game. What was the guy's name that pitched for East Orange?"

Phil shrugged.

"Doesn't matter. Gallo hit one out and the guy started crying. He was pitching a shutout before the delay and suddenly he's losing three to one."

The two men traded stories for a few minutes between bites of pasta. Phil was trying to figure a way to square things for Carmine. He had no idea what was in the package but he was sure Carmine knew or had a good idea. Whatever it was it sounded like a risky proposition. Florio seemed to read Phil's thoughts.

"Phil, I'm not trying to be a prick here. Carmine understands that. The thing is I really need him to make that delivery for me. There's no alternative. Unless you want to do it," he said.

"If he makes the delivery did you mean what you said about cutting the debt in half?" Phil asked.

Florio waved his hand, half in disgust and half in resignation. He was losing interest in their little reunion. "Yeah."

"Do I have your word?"

Florio stared at Phil, this time looking at him the way he looked at Carmine.

"Another bad question?" Phil couldn't help it, he was laughing.

Again Florio shook his head. "Yeah," he said, trying to suppress a smile. "You going with him?"

Phil looked at Carmine who was about to protest. Before he could say anything Phil said, "I'm going with him."

Carmine and Phil were on the road by 10:30. After dinner they had headed back to the hotel to pick up Carmine's Cadillac. Florio had Bucco get Carmine's car. The three men went back to Florio's suite. Phil wrote a check for twenty-three thousand five hundred dollars to something called Harter Management Inc., probably one of Florio's shell companies. The check was post dated a few days to give Phil time to deposit his check.

When they stepped outside the hotel lobby, Bucco was waiting for them, standing next to Carmine's car. The package, tightly wrapped in brown paper, was sitting in the back seat. As soon as they pulled out of the casino's parking garage, Carmine said, "You know I'll find a way to pay you back Phil."

"I hope so Carmine. Can you stop gambling?"

"I don't think it's going to be a problem. But I'm serious; I'll pay you back."

"That's a lot of money Carmine. You'll be paying me for years."

"We'll see. Let me ask you something. Why did you do it? Why did you pay that asshole Florio? You've always been tight with money."

"I was afraid they were going to kill you, I guess."

"Really? Not likely. But it's nice to know you give a shit about me. Nobody else ever did."

Phil laughed. "What the hell are you talking about? Your mother and father were always good to you and now your kid sister; isn't she there for you?"

Carmine shrugged. "Sure. I feel so lousy; I'm just feeling sorry for myself. Anyway, I'm not in any danger. As long as I make payments on the interest plus a little on principal, they'll ride with me. I'm like an insurance annuity thing for them."

"But you weren't making your payments," Phil pointed out.

"I've been sick. They should worry about that."

"Yeah but they also have you by the balls. Would you be making this delivery if you didn't owe the money?"

"I've done little jobs for them here and there. I never got into anything heavy. Mostly deliveries like this," Carmine said.

"Did you ever get paid for making a delivery?"

"Oh yeah. I got two grand about a year ago for flying some papers out to LA."

"Papers?"

"Forget it. No big deal."

The men found their way to the entrance to the Garden State Parkway. They rode for a while and then stopped to get some coffee to go. They drank in silence. The Cadillac offered a smooth, quiet ride. Carmine had the speed set at 65 miles per hour to make sure they wouldn't be stopped for speeding. He kept chewing on breath mints too in case they were stopped.

"What's in the package?" Phil asked as they passed the Toms River exit.

"I'm not sure. But even if I was, I wouldn't tell you. Its better you don't know. If there's any kind of trouble you don't know anything. Understand? You don't know where I got the package and you don't know what's in it. You don't know where we're taking it either. In fact I'm dropping you off at the airport. You can stay at the Marriott tonight. Tomorrow morning I'll make the delivery."

Saturday morning, the phone rang, jolting Phil out of a sound sleep. He had been dreaming. In his dream he was a croupier standing at the head of a craps table taking bets. Bucco and Carmine were standing at the other end of the table winking at him. In his dream, Phil was somehow in on a scheme to cheat the casino. The phone's ring was a welcome rescue from the dream.

"Hello."

"Phil? Is this Phil?"

"Yeah, it's me. Who's this?" The voice didn't register.

"It's Dennis. What, were you sleeping?"

"I was. Uhm, Dennis. Dennis Florio?"

"Right Phil, Dennis Florio. I want you to meet me at noon at The Bread Company in Winter Park. You know where that is?"

"I know where it is. I've eaten there a lot. Good hamburgers. What's this about?"

"Just be there at noon. It's important," Florio said. Then he hung up.

Phil looked at the clock radio on the night stand. It was 8:30. He sat up in bed and looked around the room. His suitcase was still sitting in front of his closet. He hadn't bothered to unpack yet.

He had arrived back in Orlando late Friday morning, less than twenty-four hours ago. He had thought about stopping by the hospital but decided to get some things done around the apartment instead. His first stop though, was the bank. He went into his local branch and asked to see the manager. She was a bespectacled woman not quite middle-aged but dressed to look younger, with a very short and tight leather skirt. Her face betrayed her advancing years. She was pleasant but she seemed distracted, at least until Phil told her what he wanted. Until then she hadn't even invited him to sit down. Now she wanted to get him a cup of coffee and asked if he would please follow her to her office. She was suddenly all charm.

He couldn't resist. When they sat down Phil said, "Money is really attractive isn't it."

The woman blushed but she was up to it. "It can make anyone seem interesting, at least for a while," she said.

Phil deposited the check the agent from the title company gave him for $497,000 in his passbook savings account. He would transfer the money he needed to cover the check he wrote to Florio as soon as the check cleared. Of course the bank manager wanted him to set up money market accounts, IRAs, and mutual funds. He said no. "I don't know what I'm going to do yet. I'll need time to think about it," he said.

He spent the afternoon getting groceries and going through his mail. Friday night he went out to a bar that had a band and a large dance crowd. He drank a couple of glasses of wine and watched people dance. Then he went home to his apartment and watched the final minutes of the Orlando Magic game. He didn't really care for basketball on TV but there wasn't anything else on. One of the things he hated about winter, even in Florida, was that there was no baseball. Phil still loved the game. He opened a bottle of wine and drank another couple of glasses. The apartment was depressing. Built twenty years ago it had the feel of a motel with a narrow kitchen that could barely squeeze in a three piece Dinette. The living room with his couch, a recliner, an end table and lamp often made him feel claustrophobic. At least he could buy a decent place to live in now. That would be a priority.

Florio's call was a big surprise. A bit hung over from all that wine, he stood in his bedroom trying to make sense of it. He decided to shave, take a quick shower and get dressed. Before he hopped in the shower he made some coffee. Once he got cleaned up he would call Carmine and see if he had any idea what Florio wanted. Anyway, he meant to call Carmine to thank him for the ride but never got around to making the call.

After slipping on a pair of jeans and Polo shirt, he poured a cup of coffee and picked up the phone. There was no answer at Carmine's apartment. Next he tried his cell phone. No answer there either. Maybe he was at the restaurant. It was probably too early but under the circumstances it was worth a shot.

"Veneto's, can I help you?"

"Is Carmine Cifelli there?"

There was a long pause. "Who is this?"

"This is Phil Falco, a friend of Carmine's."

"You the guy he picked up at the airport the other day?"

"Yes. Is he there?"

"I hate to tell you this pal, but Carmine's dead."

Phil was stunned. "What are you talking about? I just saw him Thursday night. What do you mean he's dead? Did he have a heart attack or something?" Tears were welling up in Phil's eyes and his throat got tight. He immediately thought of Florio. Did he already know about this? If he did why didn't he say something? The implications were frightening.

"Who is this again?"

"Phil Falco. Carmine and I have been best friends since we were little kids. What the hell happened?"

"I'm sorry pal. Tell you what, maybe you should talk to somebody in his family. Do you know his sister?"

"Marianne? Yes, but I don't have a phone number for her."

Another pause. "Hold on. I'll get it for you."

Phil called Marianne Cifelli. They had not spoken since the last time Carmine got married. She was hysterical, having trouble getting her words out. As far as she could tell, Carmine had been in a car accident. He had been on an icy back road near the Meadowlands. His car must have skidded and hit a telephone pole. The coroner was confident he had been killed instantly. The car had been moving at a very high rate of speed. It was demolished.

"Exactly when did this happen," Phil asked.

"They think it was maybe three-thirty or four in the morning, Friday," she said.

"I'm so sorry Marianne. I can't believe this." Phil was crying too. "Have you made any arrangements yet?"

"I'm going to do that this morning. He'll be laid out at Pegaros starting Monday. Will you be there?"

"I'll be there. I have a few things to clear up here but I'll fly up there tomorrow. Marianne, when did you find out about this?"

"I got a call yesterday morning, Friday around 7:30. A cop from Hackensack called me. I can't believe it Phil."

Phil arrived at the Bread Company early. He was wary now, afraid that Florio or one of his men had something to do with Carmine's death. But why he couldn't imagine. Did Carmine make the delivery? What if he didn't? And what was in the package? Phil had a sinking feeling in the pit of his stomach that Carmine had made some kind of mistake, had gambled and miscalculated the odds.

Dennis Florio walked in wearing Bermuda shorts and a florid Tommy Bahama shirt. The shorts were stark white, a color generally reserved for the warmer months. They made Florio look even bigger around the middle than he already was. The unlaced sneakers with no socks on his feet completed the picture. Only the look on the man's face and the deliberate way he walked would warn off anybody who might be tempted to mock his attire.

"You here long?" Florio asked.

"Ten minutes." Phil had decided not to play any games. He considered waiting to see what Florio knew about Carmine but decided against it. He was out of his league. "Carmine's dead." His voice choked again. He took a deep breath. "He was in an accident. Hit a telephone pole and was killed instantly Thursday night- I mean Friday morning around three o'clock."

"I heard," Florio said, "Lucky you weren't with him."

"He dropped me off at the airport as soon as we got to Newark."

"Did you go to New York with him first?" Florio asked.

"No, he wouldn't let me. He said I had nothing to do with the package thing. I should forget it ever happened, he said. He apologized for getting me involved in the first place, the stupid bastard."

Florio nodded. He looked hard into Phil's eyes. "That delivery never got made, Phil."

Phil just stared back at Florio, waiting. The significance of

Florio's comment didn't immediately register. All he knew was that Carmine was gone. The waitress stopped by and handed them menus. Both men ordered Cokes. Phil half-expected Florio to order for them again.

"You have any idea where the package is?" Florio asked.

"Not a clue Dennis. I assume it's with his personal effects. I don't know if he was brought to a hospital or the morgue but that's where the victim's things usually wind up."

"That's been checked out already. No dice," Florio said. The waitress took their orders. As if they were back in high school together, sitting in a diner, both men ordered a hamburger and fries to go with the Cokes.

The two men chatted aimlessly for a while, Florio biding his time. They talked about Florida living and tried to remember who taught them Latin in junior year. Neither man was eager to talk about Carmine's death. The whole time they talked though, Florio never took his eyes off Phil, searching for clues. But Phil hadn't caught on yet.

Finally, Florio addressed the issue directly. "You know we have a problem here Phil."

"What's that?" Suddenly it dawned on Phil. He felt his body tingling right down to his fingertips. Now he had a good idea where this was going. "Listen Dennis, I don't have the package and I don't know where it is. Like I told you I don't even know what was in it. Carmine wouldn't tell me."

Florio looked around to make sure no one was sitting close by. Actually the place was almost empty. "Money," he said in a low voice. "A lot of money in that fucking package Phil. I hate to say this, I really do but if you have it Phil, now would be the right time to turn it over."

Fully aware of the implications now, Phil said in a deliberate tone, "If I had it I would have given it to you already." For a moment he considered asking how much money but he knew better now. The waitress came over to the table with their Cokes.

Florio looked him over, assessing the man and his words. He took a sip of his Coke, buying time. "I'm going to tell you something Phil. Guys like Carmine, God rest his soul, think they understand what's going on but they don't. They only know what they see. They see me in a nice big suite at the Branford and they figure I'm the boss. And I am the boss of some things. But there are other people, bigger than me that I got to answer to. Capece?"

Phil nodded.

"That money, four hundred and fifty grand by the way, didn't belong to me. The people I work for don't care what happened. They just want their money. If they don't get their money there will be consequences. You catching my drift here?"

The two men sat quietly, eyeing each other. Florio was patient. He had learned long ago to go slow in a situation like this. Phil fiddled with his napkin. When the waitress brought their hamburgers over, Phil was grateful for the distraction.

Phil picked up his hamburger, about to take a bite. Then he thought of something. "How can you be sure Carmine didn't make the delivery?"

Florio took a big bite of his hamburger, juice running down his fingers and onto his wrist. He put his burger down and wiped his mouth with his napkin. "First of all it wasn't the first time Carmine made a delivery. He did it without a hitch for two years until I switched him out for another guy."

"Why did you make a change?" Phil asked.

"Florio shook his head, not really having the patience to instruct Phil on what he thought was obvious. "Its simple Phil. Guys get ideas. To be honest Carmine did it a lot longer than anybody else because we went back a lot of years. In the end it's just smart business."

"He never did anything stupid before. Again, I have to ask, are you sure he didn't make the delivery?"

Florio grimaced. "You're suggesting that someone in New York took a walk. That's not possible. The credentials on the receiving end of the transaction are impeccable. Now it's possible that the State Troopers or the local cops found it in the car. Once they got hold of it who knows? Maybe they turned it over to the Feds and maybe they kept it. Either way, the people in New York don't care."

"I see. So where does that leave us? Are you suggesting that maybe he gave me the money and I killed my best friend? Is that it?"

"Well, stranger things have been known to happen, but like I said it don't really matter. He could have given the money to just about anybody."

"Well I don't have it," Phil repeated.

"Neither do I."

The two men sat in silence again. Florio ate as if it was just a casual lunch. Phil barely touched his food. He told Florio he would be going back to Newark the next day to attend the wake and funeral. He had to fight back tears one more time. In the last few months he had been teary eyed several times for no apparent reason. Phil had one now. Carmine was dead and he was in trouble with the mob. Before they left the restaurant Florio laid it all out for him.

CHAPTER 4

Phil met Tracy Palmer in 1996, when she came to work as an administrative assistant, working for the nun that ran the nursing staff. Although he found her attractive enough, he was still married to Arlene so it was merely an observation at that point. Since his duties in the purchasing department required that he consult with nursing administration on new products designed for patient use, he spent a lot of time with Sister Janice. As a result, he also saw a lot of Tracy. At first they just made small talk while he waited for Sister Janice. Tracy was recently divorced, having moved to Orlando from Pasadena to get away from her ex-husband. The guy was good to her until he was in a motorcycle accident. His injuries left him with chronic pain so severe that even oxycontin didn't help. He alternated between being needy and argumentative. According to Tracy she tried to work through the problems but when he started threatening to beat her, she left.

Phil invited her out to lunch because, as he said, they seemed to have a lot to talk about, and never enough time to finish a conversation. In hindsight he realized that he was putting a move on Tracy but when he asked her to lunch he wasn't consciously aware of it. Of course they had a delightful time. Maybe it was the fact that she was fourteen years younger than he was. He never saw her coming. His marriage to Arlene was far from passionate but on a day to day basis it worked. After twenty-two years he had more or less settled in. He and Arlene had their daughter Lisa and that was worth something.

Until he met Tracy he had not strayed. Arlene had been the one to step out. She had had a brief fling a year after they relocated to Florida. Phil learned of the affair only because their daughter

Lisa, then only a three year old, let it slip that a man came to visit mommy one afternoon. He moved out of the house but only for a week. Arlene begged him to forgive her. He relented because of what she had been through. Eighteen months before the incident they lost a child, a baby boy, to crib death, just two months after he was born. Both of them had been devastated by the loss but Arlene took it extremely hard. Even having Lisa to take care of couldn't distract her from her grief. Phil hoped that moving to Orlando would help. At first it seemed to work but after her affair, Arlene let herself go. She gained weight. Once a casual smoker, she started smoking two packs a day. A trained nurse who once specialized in health education, she seemed to be doing the very things she had spent years doing her best to discourage.

Not having much of a life beyond his routines at work and home, Phil found in Tracy, an oasis, an escape from a life that felt more and more to him like drudgery. He had even given up golf, a game he excelled at. The life he was living was certainly not the life he imagined as a young man.

Tracy was tall, thin and pretty. She had the blond good looks of a girl raised on the West Coast, the kind that Jan and Dean and the Beach Boys sang about. That she was a social climber who needed the things money could buy was lost on Phil. Only later, when it was too late, would it become painfully obvious.

Their affair started in earnest after their second lunch date. She said she wanted him to see her apartment. He didn't hesitate. The sex was everything he imagined. It didn't help that he had just turned fifty. The only thing he gave himself credit for years later was that he had never kidded himself. He knew there was absolutely nothing unique about their romance. It was a common event happening to thousands of men his age. He didn't care. Tracy made him happy. She made him feel young again. Their romance didn't have to include overtones of a Greek tragedy where they cursed their bad luck at not having met their soul mate sooner. The way Phil saw it that kind of drama was nonsense.

Tracy changed him or at least she tried. When they first got together he took her to the movies or ballgames. It didn't take long though for her to persuade him they should be going to concerts where the headliner was a classical pianist. She even persuaded him to stop wearing a New York Yankees baseball cap everywhere he went. Phil had worn a Yankee cap for years, even dressed in a suit, he had one on. It was something he had done as a kid. His whole family, including uncles, aunts and cousins teased him about the Yankee cap.

"We never see that boy without that Yankee cap on," someone was likely to say.

He finally abandoned the cap when he went off to college. But a year or so after he joined the workforce, he bought a new cap and started wearing it every day again. Some guys wear bow ties. Others wear suspenders, wanting to set themselves apart or maybe just to hold on to a bit of the rebelliousness they felt as kids. With Phil it was the Yankee cap.

It was on their honeymoon that Tracy told him the hat made him look ridiculous, that the entire hospital staff snickered behind his back. To please her, he stopped wearing his beloved cap.

As soon as he realized this wasn't going to be a short term affair, he told Arlene he was leaving. She didn't seem surprised. At first, both felt a sense of relief but then as is almost always the case, pride kicked in and Arlene gave Phil a hard time. She also turned their daughter against him with a vengeance. He caught a lucky break though when Arlene decided to move to Phoenix to be near her sister. That meant Phil could keep the house, a good piece of real estate in Winter Park. Arlene got almost all of the money, in part, as a payoff for her share of the house.

Of course the settlement included monthly alimony and child support payments of fifteen hundred dollars until such time as Arlene remarried. Still, Phil was happy. He was free to marry Tracy and that was all he cared about at the time. Their daughter Lisa, who was a rebellious seventeen year when her parents divorced, had taken her mother's side but Phil was confident that in time Lisa would come around. Eight years later he was still waiting for her to come around. It was heartbreaking for Phil. He and his daughter had once been close. Now she would speak to him only rarely and then she wanted something.

It didn't take that long for Phil to grasp just how much his fling had cost him. Happiness with Tracy lasted two years. At first she was impressed, being married to a college graduate with a vice president's title. Their combined incomes made it possible for them to live well by middle class standards. The first sign of trouble occurred during the second Christmas of their marriage. No one would ever accuse Phil of being a romantic. He bought Tracy a fancy food processor and some costume jewelry for Christmas. There were a few other things as well, including a pair of shoes and a skirt. She gave him a Brooks Brothers suit, expensive shoes and two tickets to ten Orlando Magic basketball games. On top of that she bought each of them a set of top of the line golf clubs, plus a thousand dollars for lessons with a top pro in the area. Phil felt all of this was beyond their means. Always careful with money to begin with, he didn't need this and said so. Tracy was miffed both by what she found under the tree and by Phil's reaction to the gifts she had given him. They had a serious fight, one that didn't really get resolved until well after the Holidays.

Later on Phil would point to that Christmas as the starting point of the sure and steady downward slide of their relationship and marriage. He tried to please her in other ways but he was clumsy. He had a way of letting her know that even his romantic gestures like sending flowers set him back a few bucks. He did agree to send her back to school to get her degree. He hoped that more education would make her more grounded in life's realities. Of course, the hospital had a generous tuition reimbursement plan that kept the cost down to a minimum.

Still, as the months and years passed, Tracy pressured Phil to upgrade everything. First it was bigger, more expensive cars.

No more Chevy's. They had to buy a Lincoln Navigator, which Tracy finally settled for when Phil said a Lexus 430 was out of the question. Then they had to hire a decorator to redo the house. Phil went along for a while but he put his foot down when he saw that Tracy planned to spend three thousand dollars on pottery for the foyer. He put a stop to the entire remodeling project which caused some long and tiresome arguments. When Tracy couldn't persuade Phil to do the remodeling, she decided they should sell the house and move into a better neighborhood. Again Phil put his foot down. They would not be moving anywhere. She pouted for three months after that, a tactic that often worked but Phil stood firm.

She wanted the moon but beyond her considerable good looks, Phil didn't see what she brought to the table that could give her the lifestyle she dreamed of. Foolishly perhaps, it never occurred to Phil that Tracy's looks were good enough to take her farther than he could possibly hope to go. And going to school not only didn't change her perspective, it fueled her desire for a more cultured existence. One night they were sitting by the pool in their backyard enjoying the warm air and a full moon.

"It's nice to sit here with you," Phil said.

"Uh huh." Tracy seemed lost in thought. "Phil?"

"Yes?"

"I need something more than this. I'm tired of living such a quiet life."

"What do you have in mind?"

"I don't know. I wish we could travel. Go to Europe or maybe China. Wouldn't it be nice if we could live like the doctors at the hospital do?"

They had been married almost six years by then. At that moment, tired of all the bickering and the constant demands for more, Phil sensed it was over. It took six months to play out but he knew it was over. Sitting there by the pool that night he remembered something she said at their first lunch together. How did she put it? "I'm not going to settle for some quiet life in the suburbs, stuck in the middle of the middle class. I want excitement and adventure."

He had answered saying, "You mean like James Bond?"

They both laughed. "No not like that. I just don't want to be ordinary."

Tracy Palmer-Falco had a different perspective. She genuinely liked Phil and even fell in love with him for a little while. She really appreciated his encouragement about going back to school. But he was a man obsessed with saving money. The odd thing was he didn't have much money in spite of his penny pinching. To Tracy, he was a man that liked to plan and scheme. He was constantly preparing and updating the household budget. He looked for ways to cut household expenses. He was a bargain hunter who haggled with everyone to get a better price. But, as fast as he could save it, Tracy could find a way to spend it. And why shouldn't she spend it? If she didn't spend it his snotty daughter would. She had a treasure trove of sob stories that her father would swallow.

The poor guy was naïve really. He let Arlene take him to the cleaners but learned little if anything from the experience. He never asked Tracy to sign a pre-nuptial agreement. When she asked him to put her name on the house he did so without hesitation. He didn't even seem surprised when Tracy and her attorney took him to the cleaners again, just like Arlene did. Tracy got the house in Winter Park. She felt she earned it. Living with Phil was an exercise in futility. He had no passions, unless you considered his love of sports. He watched pro sports on TV constantly. He wasn't interested in much else. She desperately wanted to travel but he always came up with some excuse, usually suggesting they put that off until retirement. Tracy didn't buy it for a minute. Phil would never want to travel even after he retired.

She understood that Phil loved her but that wasn't enough. He was an adequate lover but certainly not inspired. Besides, he was getting older and she had reached a point in life where she could see what the future might hold. She wasn't about to give up the best years of her life only to spend endless days and maybe even years feeding him pabulum if he had a stroke or some other hideous ailment. The one thing she couldn't get her hands on, the prized possession, was the house at the New Jersey shore. It didn't matter. Her soon to be third husband, an orthopedic surgeon, was loaded.

Once it was over, she had nothing against Phil but having to see him at work every day was a problem. Her boyfriend didn't much like it either. She had heard that Phil had paid a visit to human resources inquiring about retirement benefits. For a while she was hopeful. But after a couple of months went by with no indication that he might call it quits, she began to fret. She was uncomfortable having him around. They would bump into one another in the cafeteria. When he visited Sister Janice of course she would be right there sitting at her desk. Twice he got on the elevator she was already riding in. Neither said a word the first time. The second time she tried to make light conversation.

"How's it going Phil?"

He simply made eye contact with her as if to say drop dead and then looked away. That was the day she decided he had to go. The good doctor could put enough pressure on management to make them do something about Phil.

For his part, Phil was fully aware of the risk he faced under the circumstances. He hadn't survived in a large hospital system all those years without having finely tuned antenna. A month before he left for New Jersey to close the deal on the shore house, he had a meeting with his boss, John Tiger.

"John, with everything that's happened to me over the last six months, do I have anything to worry about?"

"Not that I'm aware of. What's this all about?"

"Tracy or more to the point her boyfriend, Doctor Hansen could make it hard for you to keep me."

"I haven't heard any major complaints Phil. Sam Hansen is always complaining. You know that. Are you really worried?"

"He puts a lot of patients in our beds. And I know what Tracy is capable of. Sure I'm worried."

"Well, if I hear anything I'll let you know. Just keep doing your job Phil," John said.

But there was a problem. The way Doctor Hansen approached it was that he started complaining about the hospital's surgical product formulary. He insisted that the hospital wasn't buying the right surgical kits and they were cutting corners on sterile gauze and bandages. The sutures were cheap and so were the materials used to make casts. Everyone was aware of Phil's reputation for driving a hard bargain. Now Doctor Hansen was doing his best to turn it against him. And it was working. Phil's boss John knew the doctor was making trouble but he was hoping it would blow over. That's why he told Phil not to worry. Then, unexpectedly, it got worse. Just two days after his meeting with Phil, the hospital system's president was asking John questions about Phil's performance. The day before Phil was scheduled to go to New Jersey his boss called him into his office.

"Phil, something has come up, kind of along the lines we talked about last week. I need you to go over your contracts with all our orthopedic lines and make sure we are buying the right things."

"Right things? What the hell does that mean John?"

"I'm getting complaints from a couple of the doctors about the quality of the instruments and pads, things like that," John said.

"Listen John, let's make this easy on everybody. Offer me a decent package and I'll go quietly. Otherwise I'm going to make this really uncomfortable for a lot of people. This is just what I told you about last month."

"Phil, I understand how you might say something like that for dramatic effect, but take it easy. Go to New Jersey and take care of business. When you get back you can give me what I asked for and I'll take it from there."

John's office was located within a suite of offices reserved for senior management. Since that was where Tracy worked Phil decided to pay her a visit. He planned to confront her but when he saw her standing over a copy machine he didn't know what to say.

"Hello Tracy."

She stared back it him, a nervous look on her face. "Hi Phil. Is there something you need?"

"No, I think you've done enough don't you?"

He said this without affect. His face was expressionless but he held her gaze an extra beat before turning on his heel and walking away.

She called after him but he didn't respond.

CHAPTER 5

After his lunch with Florio, Phil went back to his apartment and packed his suitcase again. He booked another flight to Newark for Sunday afternoon and then kept himself busy doing little chores around the apartment. He stopped by his office at the hospital and went through his mail. Before he left he sent a voice mail to his boss John explaining why he wouldn't be back to work that Monday. Momentarily he wondered if he would hear from Tracy with some acknowledgement of his loss. She had met Carmine but only the one time. Naturally, she hated him on site. As Phil remembered it, the feeling was mutual. Carmine had been his best man when he married Arlene. Just before his marriage to Tracy, he decided to ask Carmine to do the honors again. Carmine had refused, saying only that maybe it would be bad luck. He never actually said he didn't like Tracy, of course, but his refusal to stand up for Phil was telling.

When he got to Newark he made his way over to the rental car counter and picked up a van, the only thing available on short notice. He wasn't happy about having to pay a higher rate but then he figured he might be able to help chauffeur people around. The weather had warmed up to the low thirties, not quite enough to satisfy Phil but it was better than the Artic air of a few days ago.

He thought about calling Marianne but he felt funny about it for some reason. He hadn't seen Marianne for a long time. He remembered she was a pretty girl. Somehow the look on her face, even when she was a kid, seemed to suggest that she always knew exactly what she was doing. He knew if he called her she would invite him to her house. Rather than help, he might be a burden at a moment like this. Carmine's parents were dead but Marianne would probably have plenty of help from all her aunts, uncles and cousins. He decided to call her later.

Instead he took a ride up Bloomfield Avenue through his old neighborhood in the North Ward section of the city. For many years it had been populated mostly by Italian immigrants and then their sons and daughters after that. By the time his generation grew up and began settling down, the neighborhood was changing. Most of them fled to the suburbs in the Sixties and Seventies. Remnants of the old neighborhood remained, with a few bakeries and a grocery store that carried Italian specialty items. The only other holdovers that served as a reminder of what once dotted Bloomfield Avenue were a couple of the names adorning the storefronts and rooftops; Gianotto's Pharmacy and Di Vincenzo's Tires. These were the remnants of what was once a thriving Italian American community. He stopped at a traffic light and saw Veneto's Restaurant, where Carmine worked. Veneto's was one of the few surviving Italian restaurants in the old neighborhood. He was hungry so he decided to go in.

Even though it was only seven o'clock, the restaurant was almost empty. An elderly woman approached him. "Would you like a table?"

"Can I get service at the bar?" he asked.

The woman didn't answer. She handed him a menu and pointed him toward the bar. The bartender was a woman who looked to be in her late thirties. She had on a name tag that said Fred.

Phil almost asked her about the name when she walked over to him but then he realized that she probably got that question a lot. She was good looking, obviously Italian, but the bleached red hair and excessive makeup made her less so.

"She smiled. "Hi! What can I get you?"

"A Cabernet would be great." He glanced at the menu and ordered. "I'll have chicken marsala with a side of spaghetti."

"Consider it done."

Phil took a good look around the place. It wasn't quite the

typical neighborhood Italian restaurant he remembered. The dining room, which was off to the left, offered a hint of upscale dining with indirect lighting and a muted color scheme. Even the tablecloths, traditionally either white or red and white check, were a pale blue instead. Each table was carefully set as if the patron was expecting the mayor and other dignitaries to walk in momentarily. Yet, the prices were moderate and the menu was mostly standard Italian fare; with pasta dishes, chicken, veal, fish and the usual appetizers.

Fred the bartender placed the wine Phil ordered in front of him. "You look familiar," she said. "Have you been in here before?"

Phil took a sip of wine. "Yes I have but not for a couple of years. The place has changed some since I was here last."

"New owners bought it a couple of years ago."

Right, I remember now. My friend Carmine worked here."

"Oh. You knew Carmine? I guess you heard about what happened."

"He had an accident. Hit a pole, right?"

She nodded. "That's what they say." She was about to say something else but a soft buzzer caught her attention. "Be right back," she said.

But she didn't come back right away. When he saw her again she was carrying his meal. She looked like a rookie. She was having a hard time balancing the plates on her left arm while carrying a bread basket in her right hand.

"Have you been working here long?" Phil asked.

She laughed. "You might think I just started but no, I've been here three years now."

"So you knew Carmine pretty well then."

"I knew him very well. He was a good guy, just all screwed up if you know what I mean." She picked up Phil's glass and walked down to the other end of the bar to get him a refill.

"How did you know Carmine?" Fred asked.

"We were friends for more than fifty years."

"Oh, you must be Phil, right? Carmine talked about you all the time. You're his friend from Florida."

"That's me. What did you mean when you said, 'That's what they say' about the way he died?"

The buzzer rang again. She turned and left. This time she was back quickly. "I just think Carmine had a lot of problems. Who knows?"

Phil let that sink in for a minute. Again he thought about Florio and that goon Bucco. "Well, if it wasn't an accident what are we talking about here? Murder? Suicide? Come on, Carmine?"

"Like I said, he had problems. I think we should change the subject. How's the chicken?"

"It's fine." Phil finished his meal in silence. When Fred cleared the plates away he ordered a cup of espresso and a Sambuca. It was almost nine o'clock. The restaurant was empty. He called for the check. On impulse he said, "Fred, how would you like to join me for dessert and a nightcap at some other joint?"

Fred laughed. "You look like you need some company. Since you were such a good friend of Carmine's I feel like I know you." She paused for a minute, thinking it over. "I bet I can trust you. Sure, let's go. I need about ten minutes to wrap things up here." She took a quick look around. "This place is dead."

Two hours later they were in her apartment, a walk-up in Bloomfield, one of Newark's many suburbs. They stood in the kitchen and chatted a while, mostly about Carmine. Although she never said it, Phil wondered if Fred and Carmine had something going on. There was something about the way she talked about Carmine, with a familiarity that suggested more than a simple friendship based solely on working together. The thought made Phil nervous but on the other hand, it had been months since he had been with a woman. He was ready now but not sure how to proceed.

Fred seemed to sense Phil's timidity so she made the first move.

She guided him over to the couch and sat down close to him. He put his arm around her and she moved toward him actually pushing him down with her body as she leaned over to kiss him.

They lay there kissing for a few minutes, not talking. Then she sat up and taking his hand led him to her bedroom. She removed his shirt and trousers. ""I'll be right back," she said, "why don't you finish what I started."

Phil stripped off his socks and underwear and climbed into her bed. When she came back she was naked and her hair was down. She slid into bed next to him.

The next morning Phil awoke with a start. He searched frantically for a clock, petrified that he had overslept. Fred, whose real name was Phyllis, wasn't in bed. He jumped up and grabbed for his watch. It was only 7:15 a.m. He had plenty of time to get ready and head over to Marianne's.

He got dressed and walked into the kitchen. Fred was sitting there sipping coffee.

"Good morning. You really know how to show a girl a good time."

Phil smiled. "That's not something I'm used to hearing. I guess maybe it depends on who you're with."

"I'll take that as a compliment."

"I hope so. I'm not too good at that." Phil saw his car keys sitting on the kitchen table where he left them the night before. "I have to go down to my car and get my suitcase. I left it in the car last night. I didn't want to be presumptuous."

"Smart man."

Okay if I take a shower?"

"Of course."

Phil got his suitcase and picked up the morning newspaper he found lying on the front stoop. He dropped the paper on the table, gave Fred a quick peck and headed for the shower, giving himself some time to think. His first impression of Fred was that she was an old school Italian girl of a certain type who liked to flirt but would be slow to come across. And then when she did, she would be very modest. He had been wrong on both counts. She was wild even by his standards. After being with Tracy he never expected to find a woman who could outdo her in bed. Fred was more than equal to the task. At some point during the night she confessed that she and Carmine had a thing, once upon a time. That was how she said it. Phil didn't probe too much. He really wasn't that interested, and anyway, it would have felt creepy to discuss it given that Carmine's body was now lying in Pagaro's Funeral Home.

Freshly shaved and showered, Phil put on a white shirt, dark suit and a charcoal gray tie. He was ready for Carmine's wake. He walked back to the kitchen and saw that Fred had made a quick run to the bakery on the corner and picked up some rolls to go with the coffee she made. They ate in silence. It was almost comical, each of them reading the morning papers as if they had been together for years. Finally it was time for him to go. He had to see Marianne. "Will you be at the wake tonight?" he asked.

"Yeah. See you there I guess."

"Why do you say it that way?"

"Carmine's sister and I didn't hit it off too good," Fred said. "Really? Why?"

"She didn't like me. I never did a thing to her either. But she was like this mother figure to Carmine or something, always telling him what to do even though she was younger than him."

"I never saw that," Phil said, picking up one of Fred's cigarettes. "So you don't think you'll be comfortable going to the wake?"

"I'm going but that bitch better not say nothing to me. I'll smack her in front of Carmine's coffin."

"Right," Phil said. He couldn't help it he was laughing.

Fred poked him in the ribs. "You know what I mean."

Phil nodded, still smiling. "By the way, when was the last time you talked to Carmine?"

"It must have been Tuesday night. I was off Wednesday. Why do you ask?"

Phil shrugged. "No reason."

On his way over to Marianne's, Phil checked his voice mail at work. There was a message from John asking him to call him as soon as he could. He said something about being sorry for Phil's loss but repeated that he needed to speak with Phil right away. Phil dialed John's number. His assistant answered and said John was in a meeting. She put him into voicemail. Two minutes later John called him back.

"We have some problems here Phil. When do you expect to be back?"

"Well the wake is today and tomorrow and the funeral is Wednesday. I have a flight back Thursday afternoon. It was the only flight available on short notice."

"That long?" John said. "Will you be here Thursday then?"

"I get in around five. I won't be in until Friday morning. What's up?"

"Not on the phone Phil. Just come see me when you get in."

"Hey John, am I fired?"

"Let's just say there are some things we need to clear up."

"You didn't answer my question."

"See you first thing Friday," John said. With that he hung up.

Phil sat at a traffic light pondering the conversation. It sounded like he was about to be fired but John's comment about clearing things suggested it might not be a sure thing. Try as he might he could not think of a thing that might need clarification. Well, he would have to deal with that later. Right now he had to figure out how to handle Carmine's sister Marianne.

He had called her right after his lunch with Florio. He told her he had something important to discuss with her. At first she said something about seeing each other at the wake. Phil said no. He needed to talk with her privately. If necessary, it could wait until the funeral was over. Of course she wanted to know what was going on. Phil just said it was something involving Carmine's personal effects. His head finally on straight, he downplayed the problem, saying only that it would keep until after the services.

Florio had made his position clear. As far as Florio was concerned, Carmine gave the money to Phil or his sister Marianne or maybe somebody else. It didn't really matter, he said. Phil was his first choice but he said things could get tough for Marianne too. Then Florio pulled out his heavy artillery.

"Phil, if you don't have the money I hope you can get Marianne to come across with the dough. Otherwise I'm going to have to get it from you."

"Where would I get that kind of money?" Phil had asked, his tone pleading.

Florio laughed. "Yo, Phil. You just made a big score. I had your real estate deal checked out."

"Dennis, you wouldn't do that. We've known each other since we were kids. That's my retirement. I can't give you that," Phil said. "Look, I don't have your money. Honest."

"Talk to Marianne. Call me when you get back. I want my fucking money."

Phil pulled in front of Marianne's house. He was hoping she would be alone but there were cars in the driveway and no spaces nearby. No doubt Carmine's relatives, aunts, uncles and cousins were all there to support Marianne. He found a spot around the corner and walked back to the house. It was getting colder again and his jacket wasn't warm enough. The wind blew right through him. How he hated this weather.

Marianne's house, the one she and Carmine grew up in, was situated in the middle of the block on Twelfth Street in Newark. It was a small cape cod with dormers that allowed for two small bedrooms and a bath upstairs. The outside of the house was covered with a dull gray siding. He rang the bell and a young man who looked to be in his early twenties opened the door. The kid fit Carmine's description of Marianne's son. He was heavy but not as big as Carmine said he was. He stood about five feet ten inches tall and weighed maybe 225 pounds.

"You must be Ricky," Phil said.

"Yeah. Who are you?"

I'm Phil. Is your mother here?"

The kid pointed to the kitchen. Phil walked in and was immediately greeted by a chorus of hellos. Someone said, "It's Phil Falco."

Marianne quickly moved over to greet him. She hugged him tight and said, "Thanks for coming Phil. You want something to eat?"

In spite of the circumstances, Phil couldn't help noticing that Marianne was a very attractive woman. Of course he had known her for years but maybe because she was Carmine's sister, he avoided thinking of her in those terms. Five feet, seven inches tall, she had jet black hair, cut short. She had that classic olive skin and unlike many women who grew up in the neighborhood, she wore little makeup. For just a second he wondered if Fred had it backwards. Probably Fred didn't like Marianne rather than the other way around.

Carmine's Uncle Mike handed him a shot of Seagram's which he accepted gratefully. He got reacquainted with Carmine's family. Most of them he hadn't seen in years. None of them had attended Carmine's last wedding ceremony. But some of them remembered stories about the way Carmine and Phil behaved when they were little boys and then later when they were teenagers. Everyone was relieved to have something to talk about other than what had happened to Carmine. They were desperate for good memories.

Carmine's Uncle Joe talked about the time the boys stole a cake from the old Dugan's Bakery truck, about how they got caught behind Carmine's father's garage by Carmine's mother. She made them throw the barely eaten cake away and then gave them money to take to Dugan's to pay for it. Just then, one of the aunts handed Phil a piece of cake, getting a few laughs. Someone had to explain to the woman why everyone laughed. She didn't get it. She was just being polite and chose that moment to give Phil the cake.

One of Carmine's cousins, Ann Marie, a girl they had teased mercilessly, reminded Phil about how the boys spent summers looking in empty lots for bottles that had a deposit on them, only to spend the pennies on baseball cards and candy. Listening to the stories was actually hard on Phil but he didn't dare cry. It would have ruined what was probably the one light moment these people had in days. Sensing he was struggling, Marianne rescued him.

"Phil, would you do me a favor please? I need more ice. It's on the back porch. I'll show you where it is." The porch was a small room in the back of the house with ancient wood paneling, enclosed by storm windows.

"He just got here and you're putting him to work already?" said Jimmy one of the cousins.

"Give him a minute to breathe, will you Jimmy?"

Once they were on the porch Marianne walked him over to an old freezer. There were a couple of bags of ice inside.

"Phil, you said you needed to talk to me. Something about Carmine. What is it?"

Phil realized that this wasn't the time to have this conversation but Marianne was looking at him intently. He decided to ask her a couple of questions and see what happened. He had so much at stake. "Marianne, when was the last time you saw Carmine?"

"It was Thursday morning. He said he was picking you up at the airport that afternoon. Why?"

"Are you sure? This is important."

"Of course I'm sure. What are you asking me Phil?"

Phil raised his hands, palms out as if asking for a time out. "I'm sorry Marianne." He tried again. "Are you sure you didn't see him Thursday night, late? Did he by any chance give you something to hold?"

"No. But if he did what business would that be of yours?" Marianne was getting angry now.

"Let me tell you what happened that night. Then you'll know why I'm asking."

Phil explained the situation, how they went to Atlantic City and gambled a little, how they met Dennis Florio and how Carmine owed him money. Then he told her about the package. Apparently, it was missing and Florio wanted it back, he said.

Marianne listened to everything without saying a word. When Phil finished she finally spoke. "Phil, I don't know anything about a package. But I wouldn't worry about it if I were you. I remember Dennis Florio too, even though I was just a kid in those days. I doubt if he's a big time operator, although I hear he's really big."

"He seemed dead serious to me, Marianne."

"Carmine thought he was jerk," she said, "and I think he was right."

"Yeah, probably, but what makes you think Florio won't come after us?"

"What good would it do him? I don't have his package do you? What's in it anyway?" Marianne asked.

Phil decided not to tell her what was in the package. If Carmine had given it to her, she already knew the contents. And, if she really didn't know anything about it, the less she knew the better. "Marianne there was a package but I never saw the contents. So who knows? You think I should just tell Florio we talked and neither one of us knows where the package is?"

"Yeah Phil. That's exactly what you should do."

Phil thought about it for a moment. "Okay, I'll give it a try."

He picked up the ice and they turned to walk back to the kitchen. Suddenly Marianne grabbed his arm. "Phil there is something I want to tell you. I haven't said a word to anybody." She rolled her eyes toward the kitchen where everyone was waiting. "Carmine might have committed suicide." She started crying. She quickly grabbed a tissue.

"Suicide? Why would he do a thing like that?"

"The autopsy showed he had an advanced case of lung cancer.

He had no more than six months to live."

"Oh boy. Isn't that how your father died?"

Marianne nodded, "He was a smoker too."

"You think he deliberately ran the car into a telephone pole to get it over with?"

"Maybe. He was acting funny the last couple of weeks. One day he said, 'I wish I had more to leave you when I'm gone.' I asked him what that was supposed to mean but all he would say was 'pay no attention to me.' Phil, he looked so tired I got scared. I told him to go back to the doctor and get another prescription for that cold."

"He did have a horrible cough. He said it was bronchitis," Phil said.

"Phil, please don't say anything to anybody."

"No, I won't say anything."

CHAPTER 6

The funeral parlor was crowded. Seeing Carmine looking so peaceful gave Phil some peace. The casket was surrounded by floral bouquets and white candles. He had been nervous about seeing his old friend, worried that he might lose his composure. It had been a long afternoon. Out of respect for Phil's long and faithful friendship with Carmine, Marianne had asked him to sit next to her. Old friends, people he hadn't seen in years streamed in, all of them there to pay their last respects to poor Carmine. The women cried and the men offered handshakes and grim faces. Phil figured Carmine must have stayed in touch with a lot of them over the years. A few of the faces looked familiar but Marianne had to reintroduce him to most of the people that stopped by. Ricky stood next to his mother, looking bored.

At 4:30, the family, including Phil, took an early dinner break. No one said much while they ate. Anyone looking at these people could easily see the strain on their faces. They trudged back to the funeral parlor and took up their positions again, ready to face the evening crowd. As the night wore on, Phil grew restless. He found himself thinking about his own mortality. When he died, how many of the people he knew years ago would show up to pay their respects? Never mind that he had been a star athlete all those years ago in school, a neighborhood kid that knew his way around. That was a long time ago. Once he left Newark, these people became part of his past. He knew the answer to his question. When he died not one of them would show up to say goodbye to him. The thought depressed him. Then Fred walked in giving him something better to think about.

As soon as they made eye contact, Phil smiled at her but she shot him a warning look: Her expression was clear. We don't know each other. Phil wondered what was wrong with her. He couldn't think of anything he might have done to offend the woman. As it turned out Phil had little time to concern himself with Fred's attitude.

Carmine's first wife, Gloria, who had been standing in the back of the room, finally made her way to where Phil was sitting. She went out of her way to be nice. Gloria reminded him about the band he and Carmine were in. Actually, Phil, who played the guitar, organized the group around Carmine who had the uncanny ability to sing like Frankie Valli, the lead singer of the Four Seasons. They called themselves the Four Suits after the number of suits in a deck of cards. For a while, they were much in demand at high school dances and even managed a few gigs at mixers sponsored by local colleges.

Gloria and Carmine got together at one of the mixers. Of course they knew each other from the neighborhood but other than running into each other at local hangouts, they never paid much attention to each other. Things changed when Gloria heard Carmine sing. Gloria often said she was mesmerized by Carmine's beautiful falsetto voice. They were married a few years later. The marriage lasted seventeen years, a fact Gloria brought up standing in front of Carmine's casket. Phil wanted to get away from Gloria, mostly because she went on about the Four Suits and how they should have pursued a recording contract and how they should have been famous by now. He realized that she was probably nervous and certainly dealing with grief on some level. Still, her talk made him feel uncomfortable. Everyone close to Carmine was struggling with his death. He had had his fill of talking about old times earlier that day at Marianne's.

Another thing that bothered him about Gloria was his suspicion that she had had a crush on him when she was dating Carmine. He found her attractive back then but there was absolutely no chance that he would pursue her even if Carmine had dumped her. Neither he nor Gloria ever acknowledged the chemistry between them but Phil was always glad they didn't spend much time together after Carmine and Gloria got married. Now, so many years later, her brilliant silver hair cut short, Phil thought Gloria was still attractive. That thought made him uncomfortable what with Carmine's body lying less than ten feet away, but there was no denying it. She was still good looking.

Phil looked around for Marianne hoping she might rescue him. He caught her eye but she ignored him. She was chatting with a well dressed man Phil didn't recognize but the body language between Marianne and the stranger suggested they were interested in each other. Phil turned his attention back to Gloria. He excused himself, saying he needed to stretch his legs. He would see if he could find Fred and maybe have a word with her. He walked into the main hall that separated the various viewing rooms. He didn't see Fred. Then he felt a tap on is shoulder.

"Phil, right?" It was Florio's henchman, Bucco.

Phil nodded.

"You talk to the sister yet?" Bucco asked.

"Bucco, right? This isn't the time or place for this," Phil said, remembering Marianne's suggestion that this was all a bluff. He did his best not to act surprised or show any fear.

"Is that right? Okay. I'll wait outside." Then he leaned closer to Phil and squeezed his arm. "I don't have all night, dickhead," he whispered.

Unsure of what to do next, Phil decided to face the music. He followed Bucco out the door and into the cold night air. The two men walked about twenty paces down Bloomfield Avenue. The avenue was well lit from store fronts and the line of cars going up and down the street. Bucco spoke again. "What did Carmine's sister say?"

"She doesn't have the package either."

"Then I got a message for you from our friend. You got forty-eight hours to come up with the money."

"Well, Bucco I got a message for your friend. He needs to look elsewhere. I don't have it."

"Elsewhere?" Bucco laughed. "Are you a fucking moron?"

But he spoke to Phil's back. He was already walking toward the funeral parlor. Under other circumstances Bucco might have made him suffer for that. But he was under strict orders. Not here. Not now.

The next couple of days were a whirlwind of hushed conversations with people who wanted to express their condolences to the Cifelli family. Although Phil still couldn't place people, a lot of them remembered him through Carmine. Apparently, Carmine kept Phil's membership alive in the extended group of friends and family from the old neighborhood. Phil had to listen to the same stories repeatedly about the things he and Carmine did years ago. He was gracious but he was relieved when the funeral service was finally over late Wednesday morning.

Marianne invited him to eat with the family at Veneto's after the service. Fred was working the bar. As soon as he could get away he left the table and went to the bar.

"You and Marianne look kind of cozy together," She said.

Phil didn't answer other than to ask for a Coke. She placed it on the bar and started to slide away. "Fred, can I ask you something?"

"What?"

"Why didn't you say hello to me at the funeral parlor?"

"Should I be honest?" Fred asked.

"By all means."

"You had a stupid grin on your face. Anybody who saw it would have got the whole picture in two seconds if I even said hello."

"I guess I was just happy to see you," Phil said.

"I guess."

Phil's plane was late arriving to Orlando. There had been a delay in Newark and then air traffic control instructed the pilot to circle Orlando for about thirty minutes. Phil was awakened from a nap by the pilot's announcement that they would be landing in fifteen minutes. That gave him some time to think about his last conversation with Marianne at the restaurant. She had thanked him for being there and helping her get through the ordeal. She said she decided not to say anything to anyone about the cancer or Carmine's suicide, if that's what it was. What good would it do? Let Carmine rest in peace she said.

Phil debated whether to say anything to Marianne about his run in with Bucco. He felt he had to say something in the event she might be in danger.

"Before I go, I need to tell you I had a conversation with one of Florio's boys at the wake the other night."

"At the wake? I didn't see Florio there." She had an annoyed look on her face.

"It wasn't Florio. It was some guy named Bucco. He had a message. They want the package."

"Oh please. My brother just died. Listen Phil, he can drop dead as far as I'm concerned."

"Marianne, I know you said you don't know anything about this. And all I know is Carmine had the package when he dropped me off at the hotel. But somebody knows where it is. The thing is I'm not as sure as you are that Florio is bluffing."

Marianne was beginning to tire of the conversation. "Florio is just a blowhard. Don't worry about it," she said with a dismissive wave.

"I wish I could be as sure as you are about this," Phil said.

"God Phil, you were a tough guy when you and Carmine were kids. What happened to you?"

"I'm not a kid anymore, I guess."

Phil's face flushed when he said this. They said goodbye to each other. Marianne kissed him lightly on the check and told him again not to worry so much.

Finally on the ground, Phil hustled over to the remote parking area to pick up his car. When he finally got to his apartment he couldn't wait to jump in the shower. As soon as he opened his door though, he knew something was radically wrong. He flipped the light switch on and saw that his place had been ransacked. Instinctively he knew it had been Bucco's work. They hadn't done a lot of damage to the place. The seat cushions were strewn around the room but none were ripped open. One of the lamps had been knocked over. Everything else was in place. He performed a quick check of his bedroom too. That was a mess with clothes all over the mattress and floor. In the kitchen there were a few broken dishes. Nothing serious; he assumed they weren't expecting to find anything. They just wanted to send a message. As he bent down to pick up one of the broken plates he heard a voice.

"Where's the money shithead?"

Phil had left the door wide open. He stepped back into his living room. Bucco must have been waiting for him. There was another guy, a real bruiser standing behind Bucco.

"I told you, I don't have it."

Bucco took a step closer and said, "I don't think you're listening to me." With that he backhanded Phil with a closed fist hitting him hard on the right side of his face. Phil's reaction was pure instinct. He had been an athlete after all, and a damn good one and Marianne's comment about him being a tough guy was still bothering him. He hit Bucco with a right cross, the best shot he could muster, landing squarely on Bucco's jaw. And nothing happened. Bucco didn't even flinch. His superior strength and his youth were simply too much for Phil's aging body. He said, "Do you want to take another shot before I kick the living shit out of you?"

Phil took a step back. He shook his head. "No," he said, "sorry."

Bucco took a look at the guy with him. The guy was laughing. Then he turned to Phil. "Listen old man, you been catching a few breaks here because Mister Florio and you go way back. Now

I don't know and I don't give the slightest fuck if you took the money, or that asshole Carmine's sister took it or the fucking Pope took it. You gotta pay. You'll be making an investment in one of Mister Florio's businesses."

"What if I say no? Suppose I just go to the police?"

"Suppose Carmine's sister gets beat up so bad she looks like her asshole brother when we're done?"

"You guys have an honor code. Even I know that. You never involve, what are they called, civilians right?"

Bucco shook his head. "That was the good old days Phil," he said in a mocking tone. "Times have changed. Meet me at the Denny's on I-4. The one on Lee Road, tomorrow morning, nine o'clock. Bring a check for four hundred fifty Gs. We'll tell you who to make it out to when you get there. I'll have some papers for you to sign."

"Listen, I need more time than that. I have to go to work tomorrow. Can we meet at five-thirty tomorrow afternoon?"

Again Bucco looked at his partner. "This guy really is a fucking idiot." Then he turned back to Phil. "Tomorrow morning at nine." With that he hit Phil in the stomach, bringing him to his knees. The two men left, closing the door behind them.

Phil spent several hours cleaning up his apartment. It gave him time to think things over. Maybe he wouldn't meet Bucco the next day. Instead he would call Florio and see if he could talk him out of taking his money. The whole thing was crazy. After all, he wasn't even supposed to be in Atlantic City that night. How could he have even had time to plan a heist- if that's what Florio thought it was? But then he realized that Florio might not really think he took the money. Phil just represented an easy way out of a jam. Thanks to Carmine's big mouth, Florio knew about his real estate transaction. Phil also wondered whether Florio might be in trouble himself. Was he in danger of being executed if he didn't come up with the money soon? Was it possible that if he, Phil stalled long enough, the problem would go away? Of course if he guessed wrong, they might rough up Marianne. Maybe he should just go to the authorities. And he would have done that already if not for his concern for Marianne.

In spite of growing up in an area that had a long history of organized crime, Phil had no idea of how organized crime really worked. Like everybody else he watched The Sopranos but that was the extent of his knowledge. What if going to the authorities was a mistake? Sure they could protect Marianne and him for a while but what about later?

He finished sweeping the kitchen floor. He was exhausted. He knew he needed to get some rest before going back to work in the morning. He had been so caught up in Florio's attempt to extort money from him that he hadn't given any thought to his job situation. There was no doubt in his mind that he was about to be fired. The thought depressed him but in one way at least he had to admit that getting away from the hospital and from Tracy could be a refreshing and even healthy change. In spite of everything, he had a sudden thought that made him smile. Maybe he could ask Bucco to give Tracy's Doctor Hansen a stiff beating.

The next day, a Friday, he was back at work. He made sure he got into his office early. He was at his desk by 7:30. Not that he got any work done. He didn't see the need. He was more certain than ever that this would be his last day at the Mercy Health System Rather, he concentrated on his problem with Florio. He thought about what Marianne had said. Her opinion that Florio was just trying to scare him stuck with him. He clung to that thought as he pondered his options. He wanted to believe that Marianne was right, that if he just refused to bend, Florio would move on to other interests. Still, his apartment had been turned upside down and his jaw still ached. He wasn't ready to fork over half a million dollars but he didn't have a lot of confidence in Marianne's point of view either.

By six that morning, standing in front of his bathroom mirror shaving, he had made up his mind. He would go to the hospital and settle that score first. Then he would call Dennis and explain that he had just lost his job. That should buy him some extra time to figure out how to play out the situation. Anyway, even a goon like Bucco wouldn't be stupid enough to make a scene at the hospital just because Phil didn't show up for breakfast at Denny's.

Promptly at 8:30 a.m., he got a call from his boss, John. Could he meet him in the executive conference room? If Phil had any lingering doubts about what was going to happen before he got to work, he had none now. He knew from the countless war stories he had heard over the years that people summoned to a meeting in the executive conference room rarely if ever left the meeting still employed. The vice president of human resources would be there seated next to John. He would be fired. The only question was how much severance pay he would receive.

"Phil, please have a seat. I assume you know why we're here."

"I'm getting the humanitarian award?" Phil said this without a trace of humor, keeping his delivery deadpan. He knew what was coming and he wanted to get a few licks in on his way out the door. He sank into one of the tan, leather, swivel chairs. He was confident he would be taken care of; be paid for months. His pension was untouchable. And, he had his bankroll if he could manage to hold onto it.

"I wish that was why we were here Phil but let's be serious. We have to let you go," said John.

Even though he knew it was coming, the words, once he actually heard them, surprised Phil. "Why?" Phil asked staring at John.

John reached for the water pitcher and poured himself a glass. He was normally unflappable. Now he seemed unusually nervous. He tugged at his tie and looked at the vice president of human resources. Even on her best days, she seemed nervous.

"As I told you there have been some complaints about your performance. I don't think it serves anyone's interest to go into too many details. Suffice it to say that some of the doctors aren't happy with what you buy in spite of repeated requests that you change vendors."

"Now John, you and I have spoken about this many times. I thought we were fully in agreement that controlling costs was our number one priority."

The VP of human resources broke in. "Be that as it may, there is another problem."

Phil looked over at the woman. She was a short, pudgy lady with brittle hair who in spite of a perpetual nervous look on her face always appeared dignified. "What are you talking about Marilyn?" Phil asked. He had known Marilyn for many years and he liked her.

The woman hesitated. She looked at John. If this was rehearsed, Phil thought, it was in need of a re-write.

"Phil, one of our most important vendors has charged that you solicited him for a kickback in exchange for giving him an exclusive contract," John said.

Phil's head snapped back. "What? Say that again."

"A vendor has informed us you solicited money from him."

Phil was quiet for a moment. He sat there, drumming his fingers on the table, trying to contain his anger. "Okay, which vendor made that accusation? I have a right to know."

"No, you don't have a right to know Phil. However, the man who represents Alford Surgical Instruments has informed us that you asked him to send you to Europe for two weeks."

"Oh my God! That was a joke. He knew that. In fact he was telling me about the purchasing director at another hospital that actually did ask for a trip. The guy wanted to go to Hawaii, and I said, 'I'd rather go to Europe.' We both laughed."

Marilyn and John exchanged glances. "Well," John said, "he thought you were serious."

"I don't believe this. You know what? I think we all know what this is really about. An important physician and my ex-wife are uncomfortable having me around. Fine, I'm willing to go, but under no circumstances am I going to listen to any nonsense about a kickback. That's a lie." He looked from one to the other squarely into their eyes. He let his words sink in before going on. "Just tell me how many months severance I'm getting and let me get out of here."

Marilyn and John shuffled in their chairs. The sound of squeaky leather punctuated the clearly uncomfortable mood.

Marilyn spoke. "Under the circumstances Phil, we don't usually pay any severance."

"The circumstances?" Phil asked. He leaned forward. "I've worked here for more than twenty years with no problems. Someone makes an unwarranted accusation and we're talking about circumstances? Here's a circumstance for you. I want six months severance. If I don't get it, I'll sue both of you personally and I'll sue the hospital system. It will make a great story for the Orlando media."

"Calm down Phil," John said. "We are going to give you a severance but it isn't what you just asked for. We can give you three months, take it or leave it."

Ten minutes later Phil signed the paperwork necessary to terminate his relationship with the hospital. Of course he got to keep his pension and he was allowed to resign rather than be fired. He had been ready to fight them for the additional three months. But before he could respond to John's offer, his cell phone rang. He didn't recognize the number but he picked it up if for no other reason than to give himself a moment to think. The caller said just five words before hanging up. "Phil, your apartment's on fire."

Phil didn't recognize the voice that delivered the chilling message, but he knew what happened. His first instinct was to jump up and get home. But then he realized that there was nothing he could do about his apartment. If what he had in that dinky three room apartment was burning up, let it burn. He turned back to the matter at hand, accepting their offer. He had bigger problems to worry about and it didn't look like he was going to have the time or the stomach to wage war on his soon to be former employer. He signed the papers. He needed to talk to Dennis Florio. That was his number one priority.

Marianne Cifelli was tired. She had spent her entire day in her brother's apartment cleaning out his things. His clothing would go to charity. The furniture, pots, pans, dishes, his TV and CD player she would give to her son, Ricky. The kid was still struggling but at least he was working and he said he was almost ready to move into his own apartment.

Now she was home getting ready to take a hot bath so she could soak away the aches and pains from her day's labor. The doorbell rang. She wasn't expecting anyone but wasn't entirely surprised. It might be another neighbor who prepared a meal for her as a way of expressing her condolences. Once a common ritual in the neighborhood it didn't happen as often in recent years as the old guard, second generation Italian Americans, left or died. She opened the door to find a man standing there. He was young, maybe twenty-five and he was solidly built. She wouldn't have thought anything of it really had it not been for Phil's warning. She grasped the situation immediately.

"How can I help you she said?"

"I hear your brother gave you a package to hold before he died. It's mine. Can I have it?"

Marianne stepped outside and closed the door behind her. It was twilight so they were visible to anyone who might be watching. "I don't know what you're talking about. Did my brother know you?"

The young man smiled. "Do the right thing. Plastic fucking surgery is expensive and I hear it hurts. I'll be back in a couple of days. Have the package ready." With that he turned and walked away. Marianne stood there momentarily paralyzed with fear. Then, regaining her senses she yelled, "Hey."

The man stopped and turned around.

"Whatever it is you're looking for, I don't have it. If my brother had any secrets he took them with him to his grave," she said.

The young man spoke deliberately, his voice powerful. "You heard what I said Marianne," emphasizing with his voice that he knew her name. He turned around again and kept walking. Marianne watched him until he turned the corner.

An hour later she heard the front door open. It made her jump but then she remembered Ricky was due home. "Is that you Rick?"

"Hi mom. Got anything to eat?"

Marianne had completely forgotten the time. She completely forgot about her bath too and now she had nothing ready for dinner. She had spent the hour thinking about what she should do about the visitor and his open threat. It was one thing to tell Phil to ignore those hoodlums. Now, she wasn't so sure they were only trying to scare them. Maybe they were serious. For several years she had been suspicious of her brother and how he made his money. He really worked just three nights a week at Venetos. She had questioned him but he just laughed, making jokes about being a Godfather.

Ricky walked into the kitchen. "Mom, did you make supper tonight?"

Marianne looked up at her son. "No, I'm sorry Ricky, I guess I just lost track of the time."

"Well, I guess I gotta go out then," he said.

"Where?"

"Just out mom. You want me to bring you something?"

Marianne didn't answer.

"Yo, mom, what's wrong with you?" Ricky asked

She smiled at her son. "Nothing. Go out to eat. You need some money?"

"What do you think?"

She reached for her purse and pulled out two twenties. Ricky took them and headed for the door. Marianne decided to take that hot bath. She went up the stairs, gathering a few things along the way that her son had left that morning. It didn't take long to get the tub filled. She stripped, dropping her jeans, sweater and undergarments in the hamper. She stepped in and started soaking. The heat felt good right away but she couldn't relax. The truth was, her brother Carmine was always a problem, even when he tried to do something nice.

An hour later the phone rang. She had just put on flannel pajamas. Marianne had lived a very quiet life after Hank left her. She didn't get a lot of phone calls. When the phone rang, her first concern was Ricky. He was a good son but like his uncle Carmine, he often lacked judgment. He was easily led astray in her opinion. But this call turned out to be a problem solver. "Hello Marianne. It's Phil Falco."

"Hi Phil, how are you?" she said. She was about to tell him about the visitor she had but before she could say anything, Phil spoke.

"I just wanted you to know that the problem I told you about is solved. I spoke with Dennis and he understands that we can't help him."

"When was that?" She asked, mindful of the hoodlum who frightened her just a couple of hours ago.

"I just talked to him. We had a drink together."

"And that's it?"

"Yeah. Problem solved."

"Did he find what he was looking for?" Marianne asked.

"That I don't know, but you and I are off the hook."

"That's great news Phil." Marianne could feel the tension floating out of her. "See, I told you there was nothing to worry about."

"Did anybody else contact you about this?" he asked.

Marianne wasn't sure what to say. She decided to keep it simple. "No."

Marianne didn't press him for details about his conversation with Florio which was a relief for Phil. They chatted about Carmine for a few minutes.

Toward the end of the conversation, Phil said, "By the way, I've decided to come back to New Jersey for a while, so maybe I'll see you around."

Phil lied when he said he had a drink with Dennis Florio. He did meet Dennis Florio's associates for a drink late that afternoon. The day before that, he called Florio on his cell phone. There was no answer. But an hour later, standing in front of his burned out apartment, Phil got a call. This time he recognized the voice. It was Bucco.

"Falco, you're standing outside your apartment right?"

"I am."

"Looks like you had a problem. I hear your friend up north could have the same problem as you if my problem isn't solved. Maybe I can help you out. You interested?"

Phil said he was. They agreed to meet on Saturday afternoon at Vito's Chop House on International Drive in Orlando. Bucco just told him to be there at five o'clock sharp. He also told him to bring his checkbook.

Phil was worn out. Fired from his job, no place to live, his clothing and personal effects in charred ruins, he felt helpless. He would have to give up his stash, the one thing he had counted on to help him live in peace during his later years. When he turned over a check for four hundred and fifty thousand dollars in exchange for meaningless stock in a Florio owned company, he would be left with a measly twenty-one grand to start over. He would have to find work until Social Security and his pension kicked in, no question about it.

Of course he again considered going to the authorities but even if that got Florio off his back, he would probably spend years looking over his shoulder wherever he went. In the end it wasn't worth it. And suppose they set fire to Marianne's house? What if she or maybe her son were home at the time? It was too risky. He had the money to make it go away and he would do that.

The idea to go back to New Jersey hit him when he was talking to Marianne. The words popped out of his mouth. Marianne simply said something about how it would be nice to see him more often. Phil figured she was just being polite. Anyway, once he said it, it sounded right. Even if he had to endure the cold weather, he needed time to think; time to plan his next move. Why not get back to his roots? Thanks to Tracy, Florida no longer felt like paradise.

When he met Bucco at the chop house, the idea of asking Bucco to rough up Tracy's boyfriend came to mind again. The thought shamed him. Then he wondered if that's how Carmine got started. Maybe he asked for a favor. Bucco made a comment about Carmine as they were leaving the restaurant. He said, "Your friend Carmine was a real dumb ass. He had the idea he was a tough guy. For a little while I thought maybe you were as dumb as he was, God rest his soul."

Phil shrugged, acknowledging the fact that Carmine wasn't the smartest guy in the world. He felt numb.

"By the way, Falco, you can tell Carmine's sister that the visit she got was a false alarm."

"What the hell does that mean?"

"One of our associates dropped by to talk to her. It was too late to call it off."

"Talk? Was that it?" Phil asked.

"Just a conversation. He was under strict orders."

Phil nodded his head. He wondered why Marianne didn't mention the visitor when he asked her about it. Possibly she was embarrassed because she had been so dismissive of him when he expressed his fears. That bothered Phil but Bucco was about to get in his car. Phil had some questions for Bucco and now was the time to ask them.

In his years of negotiating purchasing agreements he had learned that people who got what they wanted were often willing to say more than they would under other circumstances.

"Carmine's gone now so maybe you wouldn't mind telling me something. How involved was he in your line of work?"

"He did odd jobs for us. Nothing heavy, deliveries mostly."

"Did he know any of the New York people?" Phil asked.

"They would know who he was but that's about it," Bucco answered, a bored look on his face.

"Does Dennis really believe I took the money?"

Bucco stared at Phil, interested now. Wanting to choose his words carefully, he took his time. He looked around to be sure no one could overhear what he was about to say. "I think you got a good deal for old times sake. I know he wants to think you didn't take it. Somebody else wouldn't be so lucky if you get my drift."

Chapter 7

After another long day of driving, Phil was almost home. After so many years it seemed unnatural to call New Jersey home, yet, when he conjured up fond childhood memories, it did have the feeling of home. But then, as he pulled his 2001 Nissan Altima off the New Jersey Turnpike and onto the Garden State Parkway North, he felt a sudden and overwhelming sense of panic. In fact he had to admit that he had been fighting it off since he crossed the North Carolina border into Virginia. The closer he got to New Jersey the more he worried. What would he do for a living? Where would he live? When he had crossed the Delaware Memorial Bridge into New Jersey, he momentarily contemplated whether he should head to Atlantic City to try his luck. He imagined winning big at roulette, having a tremendous run that would almost even the score. Of course he knew better. He knew he needed to spend what was left of his drive time thinking about realistic alternatives.

Marianne and Fred were his only contacts in New Jersey, not much to go on. He hardly knew Fred. After he left New Jersey so many years ago, he abandoned his connections. Carmine was the exception. Of course he visited his parents once or twice a year until they passed away but even during those visits he made no effort to contact old friends. Now he wondered if that was a mistake.

When he wasn't worrying about his future, he alternated between being angry with Carmine and feeling pity for himself. What had he ever done that something like this should happen to him? As the miles ticked by, he felt worse and worse. When he approached the Union County toll plaza, a short five exits from the motel he would be staying at, he was in such a state he could barely focus on the road. He managed to get through the toll booth. Then he headed for the rest area. The sub-freezing weather added to his misery. It was cold outside, in the low teens that night.

He stepped into a convenience store, shivering so hard he wondered if he had a fever. Instinctively he pulled a tall can of beer from the refrigerator, grabbed a package of corn chips and started toward the register to pay for it. Then he noticed the coffee pots a few feet to his left. That was more like it. He set the beer on the counter and poured himself a large coffee. Then he exchanged the chips for a package of white powdered donuts. Usually, he drank his coffee black but for no reason at all he decided to add some milk. Then he saw a rack of baseball caps. There were Yankees and Mets caps to choose from. He pulled a Yankee cap off the rack and his mood brightened a little. Then he headed for the cashier. A huge display of instant lottery tickets caught his eye. Here was a game of chance he could afford. He bought a few of those too. As soon as he got back into his car he put his new Yankee cap on. He took a sip of coffee, trying to shake off the cold air that assaulted him as soon as he stepped outside. He pulled out the lottery tickets and grabbed a quarter from the ashtray. He came up empty. He was about to open the window so he could throw the tickets on the ground, something he wouldn't think of doing in Florida. He caught himself and laughed out loud. New Jersey, he thought. He started his car and got back on the Parkway. It would all be better in the morning, he told himself. One day at a time.

The next week was bitter cold. Perfect weather for the way Phil was feeling. The wind whipped through him, giving him aches and pains that made him feel old. After living in Florida for so long he wasn't used to this. On top of that he caught a nasty cold. He was forced to ask the local pharmacist to recommend a doctor. Still, he managed to find himself a small two bedroom apartment on Franklin Street in Bloomfield after just a week living in a motel. The apartment had been empty so he took immediate occupancy.

He gave the owner the first month's rent plus a two month security deposit. The woman had him fill out an application. Under current employment he wrote, 'healthcare consultant.' That satisfied the landlord.

He went to a discount furniture store and bought the bare necessities: a bed, including mattress and box spring, a nightstand, dresser, lamps, a kitchen table, two chairs, a love seat and a recliner. He was able to arrange delivery of the heavy stuff the following morning. He went to the local Wal-Mart and got himself some towels and sheets, a shower curtain, a few plates, utensils and pots and pans. He also bought a decent television set and an alarm clock.

After the fire, the American Red Cross had supplied him with enough clothing to get through about a week without having to do laundry. During his week living in the motel he filled out his wardrobe, even buying a suit and tie in case he got an interview.

He hadn't bothered to get apartment insurance in Orlando so he was out of luck as far as collecting anything there. He was beginning at ground zero. He opened a checking account, and called the human resources vice president at Mercy to tell her where to send his checks for the next three months.

Two weeks later he was ready to emerge and face the world. He awoke on a late February Saturday morning to find that the cold snap had finally broken. By that afternoon the weather had turned unseasonably warm. For the first time since he got to New Jersey he was ready to go out for something more than grocery shopping or laundry. His first stop was Venetos for dinner. He got there at 5:30. He was delighted to see Fred standing behind the bar. He didn't bother waiting for the hostess. He found a seat at the bar and waited until she turned in his direction. She smiled at him, a good sign. He smiled back. He thought it was probably the first time he really smiled since he hit the Garden State.

"Well look what the cat dragged in," Fred said.

"That's me Felix the cat."

"I can't believe you're back so soon. Did you miss me?" Fred asked. She handed Phil a menu. "Cabernet, right?"

Phil nodded. He picked up the menu, trying to remember what he ordered the last time he sat at the bar. He was afraid he would order the same thing. He didn't want to seem like a creature of habit, fearing Fred would interpret that as him being an old man set in his ways. She brought the wine over. "Fred, what do you recommend tonight?"

"Everything's good here. But I like the broiled salmon."

"That's what I'll have then with a side salad. Why don't you join me?"

She gave him a look. "I must be okay huh? I get dinner instead of just dessert before you take me home." She was smiling.

"Do you have to work tonight?"

"Saturday's my big night. How I do tonight is the difference between a good week or a bad week."

"When do you get off?"

"My shift ends at ten. Why?"

"I thought maybe we could do something."

"So that's why you came in here. I'll bet you flew all the way from Orlando just to see me again."

"It would be well worth the trip but actually I just moved here a couple of weeks ago."

Fred's face showed genuine surprise. She went into the kitchen to put Phil's order in and then hurried back to ask him what he was talking about. He gave her a brief explanation about going into semi-retirement and wanting a fresh start after his divorce. Of course he told her nothing about what had happened to him after Carmine was found dead. By the time his dinner came out, the bar had become busy. Fred couldn't linger. He could see that she was obviously popular with both men and women patrons. She had a knack for keeping the men guessing while at the same time putting the women at ease. She had a compliment for every woman she saw. One woman's hair looked stunning, another's dress was to die for and the jewelry yet another one was wearing was a perfect match for her outfit. Fred was good at what she did. That was something Phil appreciated.

He ate his dinner slowly, trying to decide whether to sit around until Fred could leave or maybe go home and watch one of the basketball games. He could come back later. He decided on the latter. For one thing it would be cheaper, something he always took into consideration but all the more so now. He also realized he would probably drink too much if he just sat there. So, he paid his bill, leaving Fred a generous tip in spite of his financial worries. "I'll be back later, okay?"

"Whatever," she said.

He almost asked her what that meant but he remembered the way she was at the funeral home. She was probably just being cautious. When he got back to his apartment rather than turning on the television, he picked up the phone to call his ex-wife Arlene. He had been putting off making this call since he returned to New Jersey.

The phone rang five or six times before she answered.

"Hello?"

"Arlene, its Phil."

"Oh." There was a long pause. "What's up?"

"Well, I just wanted to let you know that I'm living in New Jersey now."

"What? When did this happen?" Arlene asked.

"Two weeks ago." Phil told her about his retirement –that's what he was calling it- from the hospital and his divorce from Tracy. She listened without saying a word until she heard that he was divorced. She laughed out loud.

"I'm sorry Phil. I didn't mean to laugh."

"Don't worry about it. How about you? How are you doing?"

"Never mind how I'm doing," she said. "Retirement must be nice. Am I correct in assuming you have sufficient resources to meet your obligations?"

Now it was Phil's turn to laugh. "You're covered, Arlene." Now that Lisa was out of the house she got a grand a month. Phil would never renege on something like that.

"Good Phil. That's what I wanted to hear." There was no trace of caring in her voice. Whatever she might have felt for him once had been fully replaced with layers of bitterness. "Have you heard from your daughter lately?" Arlene asked, her tone suddenly worried.

"No, I haven't. She must be working."

"Oh Lisa's working alright. Maybe you should call her and let her tell you what she's doing."

"Arlene, let's not play games. Why don't you tell me?"

"Not this time Philip. She has to tell you. I've said all I'm going to say."

Phil could hear her exhale. She was still a smoker. He gave her his new phone number and address. His divorce decree required that he notify Arlene of any permanent changes in his whereabouts. That was the purpose of his call. Now that he had done so he was eager to get off the phone. At times like this he wondered what he had ever seen in Arlene. Being an honest man though, he had to acknowledge that once upon a time, he was crazy about her. Now he only thought of her when he had to.

Phil picked up the phone to call Lisa but he hesitated long enough to reconsider. His relationship with his daughter was tenuous. He had to be in the right frame of mind to call her. She could be difficult, having inherited her mother's talent for biting sarcasm. If she was doing something crazy, a contentious conversation wouldn't help. He loved his daughter and he would do anything to help her. Over the last few years though, whatever he did seemed to cause more damage. He would call her but he needed a little time to prepare himself.

At 9:30 Phil backed his Altima out of his parking space and headed for Bloomfield Avenue. His apartment wasn't far from Venetos. He got there in just ten minutes. It had turned cold again.

The car's heater barely had time to warm things up. He was shivering as he jumped out and walked over to the restaurant's entrance. The warm afternoon had dissolved into a cold evening. The place was practically empty but there were a couple of guys seated at the bar. Fred was having what appeared to be a light hearted conversation with the two men. She saw Phil come in and smiled again. Phil hoped that was another good sign.

"Hey, this is the guy I was telling you about," she said pointing to Phil. The two men turned to look in Phil's direction. Fred introduced them to Phil saying, "He was Carmine's best friend."

The men shook hands with Phil. They chatted for a while, talking about what a nice guy Carmine was. One of the men had served in the same Guard unit with Carmine. The other guy said something about how some people thought Carmine was a boss in the family, meaning Mafia, of course. Fred looked at Phil and rolled her eyes. She knew better but why spoil the customers' good time? Neither she nor Phil said anything. They both understood that their silence would actually reinforce the guys' suspicions. Finally the two men got up to leave. Phil was relieved. He had been worried that they might outlast him; that Fred would have to close up and head for home without company. There was no way she would be seen leaving with Phil or any other man for that matter. She had a simple rule about that. She demanded discretion and she got it. Ten minutes before closing time, she said, "take a long ride around the block or something. Do you remember where I live?"

Phil nodded. He remembered.

"Meet me at my apartment and I'll make you a cup of coffee."

Later in her apartment, Phil said, "You would have left me standing alone in the parking lot if those guys didn't leave when they did."

"You got that right. All I need is for the men who come in there to think they can score with me."

Phil understood. The rest of the night and the following morning were a repeat of their first time together only better. Fred was terrific in bed.

Neither of them got much sleep. During the night Phil told her a little bit more about his situation. He admitted that he had been fired, explaining how Tracy and Doctor Hanson arranged things. Of course he didn't say a word about the money Carmine had cost him but he let on that he would need a job before long.

"Really, Phil, why did you come back to Jersey? Fred asked.

"I'm not sure to be honest about it. I guess I could have stayed in Florida, maybe even moved farther south closer to Miami, but when I was here for Carmine's funeral, I realized that maybe I was missing something, all those years away."

"Missing something? Like what, shoveling snow? Shitty people?"

Phil laughed. "Okay," he said, "you have a point about winter, I'll grant you that, but there are shitty people everywhere."

Phil didn't want her to know that one reason he came back was to search for the money. If there was one chance in a million that Carmine hid it or gave it to somebody, perhaps his sister Marianne, he could only find it on Carmine's turf. He figured it would be best to change the subject and talk about her.

"This is where you're from right, Phyllis?" He called her by her proper name just to get a rise out of her.

"Phyllis? Are you serious? Please, it's Fred," she answered.

Phil waited. "Yeah, this is where I'm from," she said.

"Ever think of leaving?"

"All the time."

"But you don't," he said, "Why not?"

"Where would I go? Another bartending job where I don't know anybody would be lousy." She snuggled closer to him then.

"I don't think you would have trouble meeting people but I see your point," he said.

"For what it's worth Phil, I'm sort of glad you decided to come back to Jersey."

He smiled. "This is where I feel like I need to be right now. I just need a job."

"Why don't you take Carmine's job? They still need a waiter three nights a week."

Phil laughed. "I was thinking about something more substantial," he said.

"Oh, substantial; excuse me," Fred said, turning away from him. She pulled the covers around her body.

"You know what I mean. Tell you what though; now that you bring it up, it might be alright. I don't know how long I'm going to be here anyway. You think I could do the job?"

Fred turned back toward him. She looked into his eyes; wanting to be sure he wasn't being sarcastic before she answered. Satisfied, she said, "Carmine did it. Why can't you?"

Two weeks later Phil was already an accomplished waiter. He mastered the job his first week. The thing that surprised him most was that he made decent money on tips. The restaurant paid minimum wage but the people who frequented Veneto's tended to be decent tippers, leaving anywhere from fifteen to twenty percent. On his first Saturday night he netted nearly three hundred dollars in tips. He was pleased. He had felt a little awkward asking for the job, but Fred had tested the waters with Jerry, the guy who owned the restaurant a couple of hours before Phil approached him. The guy was willing to give Phil a try. He had seen him around, talking to Fred and he thought Phil, a tall, good looking guy, had the look of Italian royalty that fit right in with the ambiance he was trying to create.

Of course Phil was a bit nervous about running into people he might know but as Fred pointed out, he hadn't lived in that neighborhood in more than thirty years. Who would recognize him? Well, Marianne Cifelli for one. She walked in on Phil's second Saturday night on the arm of a man Phil remembered seeing at the funeral parlor. His instincts had been right. As it turned out the guy was one of the teachers at the school where Marianne taught.

When Marianne saw him, she had a shocked look on her face. "Phil, what are you doing here?"

"I told you I was moving back to New Jersey." Again Phil was struck by how pretty Marianne was. She was dressed in a pink sweater and a long black skirt and high-heeled boots. She looked great.

"How long have you been back? And why didn't you call me?" She asked. Marianne said this standing near the bar, waiting for a table. Fred overheard. She made a face at Phil.

"I wanted to get settled a bit first. I haven't decided what I want to do yet."

"It looks like you have a job already. Can we sit at your table?"

The hostess seated Marianne and her friend at one of Phil's tables. Marianne introduced her friend to Phil. It was obvious that they were dating but Phil guessed that it was only the second or third time they were together. Phil was embarrassed to have Marianne see him in his waiter duds, with the black bow tie and pale blue cumber bun underneath a black jacket. "I'm new at this," he said as he took their order, "and I don't think I'll be doing it very long." Phil did his best to keep his eyes riveted to his order pad.

"Carmine did it for a couple of years, but I think he just needed to stay busy," Marianne said. Her voice trailed off and she stared hard at her menu.

Phil walked back to the bar to order their drinks. "Fred, I need a Cosmopolitan and a Bombay Martini with a twist, both up."

"Is that for the witch and her friend Dracula?"

Phil nodded. "Why do you hate her so much? I noticed she said hello to you as soon as she saw you."

"She's a phony. And don't think I didn't see you get three inches taller as soon as you laid eyes on her."

CHAPTER 8

Lisa Falco did have a job in Los Angeles. Only twenty-five, she was still trying to find herself. Her job in the front office of a small movie studio in Chatsworth, California seemed to agree with her. She wore her hair stylishly short with powerful red highlights that complemented her skin color and she kept the number of earrings she wore to a minimum, at least in the world she inhabited. When her father called her to see how she was doing she was happy to hear from him. She was surprised when he told her he had moved back to New Jersey. She didn't entirely buy his story about moving back to New Jersey to plan his next move. If he was thinking about retiring, why not stay in Florida? That got her attention though. Right away she wanted to know if he had enough money to retire.

Phil sidestepped that question but she pressed him, asking if he was moving into the house at the Jersey shore. He told her he sold the house but he quickly added that he had invested the proceeds in a business venture. Technically it wasn't a lie. He had the stock certificates to prove it. But mostly he wanted to make sure Lisa didn't get any ideas about borrowing money. He was always a soft touch for Lisa but now he couldn't afford it. As soon as he could he turned the conversation to her.

"So, your mother tells me you have a boyfriend out there. What's his name?"

"It's Riley. I think you would like him Daddy." As she said this she rolled her eyes. She was sitting by the pool in her apartment complex. Riley Rivers sat next to her holding her hand. The guy was in his early thirties. He was tall and he obviously worked out on a regular basis. He was solidly built, his skin was tanned bronze. In other words he looked like the stereotype of the

Southern California beach bum. Only he made good money in the movie business, producing low budget, pornographic films. Many of the people in the porn business hoped to move on to legitimate films. Not Riley. He was happy where he was.

Phil asked Lisa about her job.

"I'm kind of a manager for the front office," she said, "but I'm thinking about what I want to do next too, just like you daddy."

"I see. Well, your mother seemed worried about what you're doing. Is there any reason to be concerned?"

"Not in the least."

"What's the name of your company?" Phil asked.

"It's Double R Productions. My boyfriend owns it."

"I see. What does Double R do?"

Riley was stroking Lisa's thighs now and grinning at her. He knew this would drive her crazy. She pushed him away. "It's a movie production company, daddy. They make films for mature audiences."

Phil's jaw dropped. He gripped the phone tight now. "You mean pornography?"

"Oh no. It's not hard core stuff or anything like that. These movies have plots. Complicated story lines. It's not just about sex."

"I see," Phil said. But he didn't. He would have to go to Los Angeles. At that moment he felt like he could strangle Arlene. How could she have been so coy? Their daughter was in trouble, no doubt about it. He knew enough not to rush right out to California. His experience with Lisa over the last few years told him he would need a more subtle approach. A few years ago she had wanted money to buy into a franchise that specialized in over the counter nutrients for pets. She said she needed $25,000 to purchase a forty percent share of the business with an acquaintance she knew in college. Phil had been immediately dismissive of her request. He berated her for her lack of business knowledge and told her the idea was foolish. She would be wasting his money.

They fought about it over the phone a couple of times. Phil had been merciless, in part to keep Tracy happy. She had made it clear that she would walk away if he gave Lisa a dime.

In a fit of anger, Lisa sold her car, borrowed money from a few friends and managed to come up with most of what she needed to join her friend in the business. Just as Phil had predicted, in less than a year it failed miserably. Later, when he was thinking more clearly, Phil realized that had he taken his daughter seriously and worked through the numbers with her, she might have made a wiser decision. Instead, she was determined more than anything else to prove him wrong.

He wasn't going to make that mistake again. As concerned as he was, he simply suggested that he would like to see Lisa. Trying to sound casual, he asked if she might have plans to come back east any time soon. She told him no.

"Well, maybe I can visit you then. I haven't been to LA in years."

"Sure," she said. "When do you want to come?"

"I would give anything to get away from this cold weather for a while. Maybe in a couple of weeks?"

"I would like that daddy. I want you to meet Riley anyway."

So they agreed that Phil would come out during the third week of March. Phil figured he would have enough cash by then to spend a week out there without having to dip too far into his savings. He consoled himself with the thought that Lisa wasn't acting in these films, at least not yet.

Phil started spending weekends with Fred as soon as he went to work at Veneto's. The sex was great and Fred was easy going. Her company helped him through the misery Phil felt from the lingering winter. They would get cozy after a long night of work on Friday nights and then spend the day Saturday going to one of the malls or a matinee. Of course they worked Saturday night too. They quickly developed an enjoyable ritual of showering together when they got back to Fred's apartment, steaming off the residue of marinara sauce, fried fish, broiled chicken and cigarette smoke from their bodies. Afterward, they would make love. Friday nights were usually torrid. They were eager for each other and quickly spent.

Saturdays were different. They would make love in the afternoon a couple of hours before their shift, much more deliberate in their movements. Everything slowed down. They would make love again on Sunday mornings before Phil left for his apartment. Fred always went to her mother's for lunch on Sunday before her shift. At that point she had no desire to introduce Phil to her family. And that suited Phil just fine. So Phil headed off to his apartment to do laundry and maybe take a quick nap before going to work.

But then just as he was getting ready to leave her apartment one Sunday morning he asked Fred if she wanted to go to LA with him.

"Hey, Freddie," he said, "Would you like to go to LA with me next week?"

"Sure. But I don't have the money for a trip like that."

"I know. I'll buy your ticket. My treat. I have to pay for a room anyway. Maybe you could cover a few meals while we're out there."

"I don't know Phil. I would miss work too, don't forget."

"Well, you said you wanted to see California some day. If not now when?"

"Let me think about it okay?"

"Sure, I'm leaving next week." Phil smiled and pulled her close. He kissed her forehead. "I want you to go with me."

With that he left her apartment. Driving up the avenue he wondered what possessed him to invite Fred to go with him. Sure, their lovemaking had been especially tender but what of it? He wasn't really sure he could handle a full week with her. And for that matter, he wasn't so sure she could stand him. Plus, if they were comfortable together over a longer stretch, she might get ideas about a future together. In spite of her denials, Phil was certain that Fred would like to be married. The subject came up a few times, once when they were watching a documentary about marriage in the third world and then again when Phil, without thinking about it, asked her if she wanted to be married some day.

Phil's question about the trip was typical of the way he operated now. No longer so cautious, he now lived in the moment, saying and doing what felt good at the time. The bigger picture, whatever that was, didn't enter into his thinking; at least not often enough. Asking Fred to go with him to Los Angeles was a case in point. It wasn't a vacation. Rather, he had serious business to take care of, namely the well being of his only child. His impulsiveness made him feel foolish. Offering to buy her a ticket was even worse. He didn't have that kind of money.

Now, when his life should be settled, when he should be positioned for a soft landing into a secure retirement, his life was at a crossroads with nothing settled. He began to get depressed about his bad luck. He felt he could trace it all back to Tracy. Not that he was blaming her. The decision to leave Arlene though, now seemed like the catalyst for all that followed. If he never left Arlene surely he would have taken her with him to the closing that fateful day when Carmine's stupidity sent Phil's life into a downward spiral. He never would have gone to Atlantic City had Arlene been with him.

He steered into the tiny parking lot where his apartment was. He felt tears of frustration welling up inside him. Tears began streaming down his face. He knew he had to stop or he would be sobbing. Quickly, he pulled himself together, wiped his tears, took a deep breath and climbed out of his car. He managed to distract himself watching television for a while. Sleep was another matter. He spent most of the night fighting off the tears and cursing his fate. He didn't fall asleep until after four in the morning.

But, after an agonizing night, a pity party to end all pity parties, he had had enough. He woke up with a new outlook. If bad luck could come unexpectedly, good fortune could happen just as easily. If he didn't quite believe it, that was okay. He would be optimistic. What choice did he have? He had to get his head on straight to handle his trip to Los Angeles. Of course he wasn't sure visiting Lisa would help him remain optimistic about the future. But then he realized that focusing on Lisa's problems instead of his own might help him to put his own situation into perspective.

A week after his crying jag, he hopped an early morning flight to Los Angeles. The flight gave him time to think things over. One of the first things Phil felt he had to do was stop playing games with Fred. As it turned out, she made it easy on him. When Fred didn't mention the trip to LA the next time he saw her, he let it drop. When it was time to leave work that night, he told her he was going home. She acted as though she was hurt but Phil caught her first reaction, the briefest of expressions. She was relieved. Starting the very next night, they were cordial toward each other at work, just good buddies. They both acted as if nothing had ever happened between them. It was weird certainly, but at least no one had been hurt. In no time, Fred went back to being her old self with the men who stopped in for a drink. She had stopped being even mildly flirtatious with male patrons out of respect for Phil. Now she was back to her old self. Her tips got better too.

On the night before his trip Phil made another decision. He told Jerry, the restaurant's owner, he would not be back to work. The guy was disappointed. In the short time he was there Phil had developed a following. People would come in for dinner and ask if they could sit at one of Phil's tables. Phil was a good conversationalist. He had a good memory too which allowed him to remember names and recite each parties preferred drink even before they sat down. Well, Veneto's would have to find someone else. Phil wasn't going to live in the moment anymore. He might not have a master plan but he was going to think things through before he acted.

As the plane sailed high above the Midwestern plains, he spent some time contemplating his future. Where should he live? What did he want to do for a living? But constantly his thoughts came back to one question: Where was the package Carmine was supposed to deliver? That was the missing piece to the puzzle, the thing that drove him back to his home town. He could not bring himself to let go of his irrational fantasy that he could find the package and recover the money he lost; the one thing that could solve all his problems. The thought of losing all that money made him miserable again but he managed to catch himself before he fell back into a depression. One step at a time he told himself over and over again.

The flight was bumpy. The weather was miserable all across the country it seemed. The guy sitting next to him provided some unexpected entertainment. To take his mind off his worries, Phil engaged the guy in conversation. He introduced himself as Clark, telling Phil he sold oxygen conservers.

"I travel to the west coast twice a month. That's where our headquarters are located," Clark said.

"What is an oxygen conserver?" Phil asked.

Clark pulled out a picture and handed it to Phil. It was a donut shaped device that fit around an oxygen cylinder. The device made the oxygen in the cylinder last longer. Anybody with emphysema could get extra oxygen through a cylinder. Phil was beginning to lose interest but then the flight attendants came down the aisle with the drink cart. Clark asked for a tomato juice.

As soon as the attendant handed it to him, Clark took a serious gulp. He frowned. "This isn't right. Tastes like tomato soup, not juice."

Phil nodded as he reached for his water.

"Yo, stewardess," Clark said, "Can you take this back. It's no good."

The flight attendant gave the passenger a withering look. "I can't right now," she said, "Hold it until I can get back to you. I have no place to put your drink right now."

Clark was fuming. Forcefully, he put down his tray table and said to Phil, "Ten-fifteen years ago you know what I would have done?"

Phil stared at the guy, keeping his face blank.

The guy looked around to make sure the flight attendants weren't listening. "I would have poured this shit on the floor. Then when they were cleaning it up I would say something like, 'Sorry you got stuck doing that. Too bad you didn't take the cup when I asked you to. Maybe it wouldn't have happened then."

Phil nodded. "You've matured a lot I guess." Their conversation over, Phil took a quick nap.

He was very relieved to be landing at LAX. Lisa and her boyfriend would be waiting for him at the baggage claim carousel. Caught up in his own turmoil, he had spent very little time thinking about Lisa's situation. Anyway, what could he do? After all she was an adult. Maybe it wasn't as bad as it sounded. He loved his daughter but he had to admit he felt a little bit of resentment toward her. She had sided with her mother in the divorce. Even when the smoke cleared she steadfastly refused to spend time with her father. In fact, he was surprised when she sounded so agreeable to his proposed visit. That set off a few alarm bells of course. Did she want money? Was she hoping to hit him up for a big wedding? Whatever it was, at the moment, Phil didn't care. He was just glad he would get to spend some time with his daughter. Maybe they could begin to thaw the ice and rebuild their relationship.

Lisa and Riley met him at the baggage claim carousel. Phil was just picking up his bag when Lisa walked up to him. One look at Lisa and his heart melted. Whatever resentment he might have been feeling could not stand up to her radiant smile. She was a pretty girl and she looked so innocent notwithstanding the way she was dressed in a short black skirt and low cut top tenuously clinging to thin spaghetti straps. The guy standing next to her gave

Phil pause. For a split second he hoped he was wrong but when he focused on the guy who put his arm around Lisa as soon as the two men made eye contact, his moment of hope was dashed. Here was a young man for whom the term grease ball was coined. Thinning blond hair slicked back, gold jewelry on both wrists a diamond stud in his left ear, he had managed to combine the Southern California look with a Mafia persona that just might make Bucco jealous.

"Hey Phil, how are you? I'm Riley Rivers. Ooops, I guess Lisa just said that."

Lisa had already hugged her father and introduced Riley to him.

"Nice to meet you Riley. That's an unusual name. Is it yours or did you create it to fit in out here?" Phil asked.

Riley smiled. "It's mine. I'm from Charleston, South Carolina originally. It's a family name."

"I see. Well it certainly suits you."

"Come on Daddy, let's get out of here. I'm starving. Did they give you lunch on the plane?" Lisa gently pushed Phil toward the exit.

They rode in separate cars. Phil picked up a low budget rental car and followed them to the restaurant. They found a Mexican place not far from Lisa and Riley's apartment on Topanga Canyon Boulevard in Chatsworth. "I know it's not much to look at daddy, but the food is incredible here," Lisa said.

"Good. I've been eating mostly Italian since I got back to New Jersey," Phil said. The waiter stopped by with menus, salsa and a basket of tortilla chips. "So Riley, I understand you're in the movie business."

"Uh-huh. I am. Right now I'm doing B movies but I hope to produce a major feature film with an independent studio soon." This was a lie but Riley sensed he was better off telling Lisa's old man what he wanted to hear. It was easier that way all around.

"Well I don't know anything about your business but I'm curious about it. I'd like to know how you move up to the A list.

Maybe we can talk later." It was Phil's way of signaling that he wasn't buying that B movie nonsense.

Lisa was fidgeting with the menu. "Riley has to go back to work as soon as we finish eating. He gave me the rest of the day off so we could spend time together."

"Is that right? How nice." There was no hint of kindness in his voice.

Lisa rolled her eyes. "Daddy cut us some slack will you?"

Riley stood up. "You know what? I really have to get ready for a meeting. I'll take the car baby. Your daddy can give you a lift to the apartment. I'll catch up with you later."

He reached down and gave Lisa a long, hard kiss. He turned to Phil and stuck out his hand. Phil took it. "See you later man," Riley said.

"Jesus daddy did you have to be so mean? What did Riley ever do to you? I haven't seen you in I don't know how long and already you're fucking up my life."

"First of all, if you ever use that language with me again it will be even longer before you see me again. Second, who is this guy? He looks like someone who came out of that movie, Pulp Fiction. Where did you meet him?"

"I met him at a party. He asked me out. He's not like you think he is daddy. You haven't even given him a chance."

Phil sat silently for a while. The waitress approached and took their order. They both asked for frozen margaritas to go with the taco and bean burrito special. "Okay, maybe I'm not being fair. Here's the thing, Lisa. Your mother seems to think your job is dangerous or maybe unsavory. From what you told me, I'm worried too."

"There's nothing to worry about."

"Good. So what do you do working for Riley?"

"I'm his assistant mostly but I run the office too. We have nine employees."

"Okay. Do you act in any of these movies?"

"Not yet but I want to."

"Have you taken any acting classes?"

"How could I afford that? Do you want to pay for them?"

Phil ignored her. "Lisa, what kind of movies is Riley making?"

"Oh, so that's what this is about. He makes adult movies. What about it?"

Phil had to use every reserve in his body to restrain himself. Lisa's words were bad enough but her tone was sickening. He again reminded himself that his daughter was an adult. He told himself again to go slowly. "Are you telling me you would be willing to appear in one of those films?"

"Maybe. A lot of successful actors got their start in the adult entertainment industry," she said.

"I wouldn't know."

Lunch arrived but Phil wasn't hungry. Instead he ordered another margarita. After a few quiet moments Phil changed the subject. They talked about Arlene and how she was doing. He filled Lisa in on his divorce from Tracy offering very few details. He mentioned the apartment fire too, but made it sound like an unlucky accident. Lisa asked about the house in Toms River again but he just told her it was still there, having it both ways. She seemed satisfied. Since she didn't mention needing money, Phil wondered if maybe she had matured some or maybe she was doing well enough not to need anything. That thought worried him. Under the circumstances he would have felt better if she needed money.

They rode over to her apartment still making idle chit-chat. Once inside, Phil was impressed by what he saw. Here was an apartment that was beautifully decorated. It was a three bedroom affair with a large kitchen complete with copper pots and a solid oak table already set with obviously good China. The living room had a wide screen TV. Lisa informed him it had a sixty-five inch screen. The furniture was rich white leather with a matching thick white carpet. "Am I right in assuming that this apartment didn't come with any of this?" Phil asked.

"Oh no. Riley bought it all when we moved in."

"Why doesn't he own a place?"

"He doesn't want to be tied down to real estate just yet."

Phil let that one go. His daughter had looked away when she said it. The implication wasn't lost on her.

"We have room if you want to stay here with us," Lisa said.

"That's okay honey. I think I would rather stay somewhere else. I got a room at the Comstock Inn."

"Okay. Why don't you go over there and get settled. I'll give you directions. I should get a few things done around here anyway."

That night Phil returned to the apartment his daughter was sharing with Riley to have dinner. The mood was somber. Phil was sure his daughter and her boyfriend had some kind of a fight. He made no attempt to lighten the mood though. Why should he? He hoped his daughter would break up with this character. Instead, as soon as dinner was finished he decided to bring his feelings out into the open.

"Riley, I think you're making pornographic films instead of what you referred to as B movies. Am I right?"

Riley gave Phil a long appraising look. "Yeah, that's right. Porn is big business now. You have any idea of how many of these movies get made a year?"

Phil shook his head.

"I'll tell you. It's about ten thousand pictures a year, about ten times what it was ten years ago. Hey man, it's a ten billion dollar a year business. It's gone mainstream."

Phil had no idea that the business of pornography was anywhere near that big. He grew up in a time where that kind of thing was relegated to back alleys and seedy movie houses in questionable neighborhoods. Of course he had been to a few smokers when one of the guys he went to school with had managed to get his hands on a silent, black and white film. He knew things had changed over the years, of course, but what he was hearing now was staggering.

Riley went on to explain how major, otherwise well respected corporations were now, making millions from enterprises specializing in erotica.

"There's like almost a hundred million x-rated video rentals a year now. And, at least half of all people staying in hotels rent one of our films during their stay. Can you believe it?"

Phil said he couldn't believe it. Riley went on. He told him how the industry was run like any other business now, employing thousands of people and paying taxes just like any other business venture. What he didn't mention was that most of the young women who agreed to make such a film, never did it again because they found it degrading and humiliating. Nor did he mention that there were more than enough studies suggesting that pornography often led to divorce, domestic violence and even murder.

Phil listened in silence. He couldn't help noticing that Lisa was stroking Riley's arm while he talked. Finally, Phil had heard enough.

"My daughter tells me you are thinking of putting her in one of your movies."

Riley looked at Phil, a look of contempt on his face. "People come out here and right away they pass judgment. Can I ask you something?"

Phil nodded his head.

"You ever watch a porn flick?"

"I have seen a porn film, yes."

"I'll bet you have. And I'll bet you liked what you saw. Were the women in the film from outer space or were they human?"

"What's your point?" Phil asked, knowing full well where this was going.

"My point is the girls in the movies you saw had fathers too. Just like Lisa. Why was it okay to watch their daughters perform but not okay for them to watch yours?"

Phil stood up. He got his jacket and put it on. Then he turned to face Riley. "I don't know about the fathers of the women that appear in your films. Maybe these women have fathers and maybe they don't. But Lisa here has a father. If my daughter appears in a porn movie you will answer to me." He looked directly into Rivers' eyes to be sure he got the message. No one said a word. He kissed Lisa goodbye and left.

Phil spent the night in his hotel room, unable to sleep. He was dead serious when he threatened Riley but he had no idea of what form his wrath would take. He still hadn't forgotten the fiasco he endured when he punched Bucco. He felt helpless lying there. Maybe Rivers, who seemed cocky, would worry anyway. How could he be sure that Phil wouldn't back up his threat?

Phil thought about calling Arlene but he knew she would only make him feel worse. He considered calling Fred but that didn't feel right either. So he tossed and turned. At day break he called the airline and got on the standby list for the ten a.m. flight back to Newark. When he got to the airport he called Lisa at her office.

"I decided to go back to New Jersey. I'm on standby for the ten o'clock but if you want to come with me I'll wait for you."

"Why would I want to come with you to New Jersey? My life is here now, daddy."

"You don't have a life here Lisa. You're on a destructive path. Look, I'll borrow money if I have to. You can go back to school. It's not too late."

"Oh please. You just don't want me out in the real world. Well don't worry. Thanks to your comment last night, Riley won't let me act in one of his pictures now. He's afraid you're a mafia guy or something."

"Maybe I am."

CHAPTER 9

For the next month Phil kept mostly to himself. He stayed away from Veneto's mostly because he wasn't sure he could stay away from Fred. He did call Arlene but he minimized his concerns about Lisa when he talked to her. As Phil saw it, there was no sense in worrying Arlene. Lisa wouldn't listen to her mother any more than she listened to him. Anyway, he was confident now that what he had said to that Rivers character slowed down his daughter's dive into oblivion. He needed time to think things through. Obviously he couldn't command his daughter to do anything. That wouldn't work. He would have to find a more subtle way to get her away from Riley.

It didn't take long for Phil to establish a routine. Most mornings he spent an hour or two looking for work. While his coffee was brewing he checked the local want ads in the morning paper. Then he went on line to see what he might find. Getting a computer and Internet service had been his first move when he got back from LA. He bought the cheapest desktop he could find. It turned out to be an excellent investment. The Web turned out to be a faithful companion, capable of warding off loneliness when things got really bad.

To help with his job search he forced himself to learn more about the Web, familiarizing himself with search engines and sites that focused on job opportunities. He also got an eyeful working his way through the different dating services. He spent a lot of time browsing through Yahoo personals, checking out the profiles of women living in Northern New Jersey and Manhattan. He was tempted to register but he couldn't bring himself to complete a profile. What would his moniker be? Unemployed and living day to day? No, none of that for him.

Neither the newspaper nor the on line want ads offered much to get excited about. He saw several ads for hospital purchasing jobs but he didn't answer them. That would be the easiest course to follow but he could feel his stomach churn at the thought of going back to that kind of work. He believed he was a top notch professional before he was fired. And, while he really believed Tracy had set him up, he worried that somehow he had contributed to his own demise. Had he been too familiar with the vendors who sold to him? Sure he had kidded with that one guy about a trip to Europe, but it was a joke after all. Looking back now, he was forced to admit that even the joke, however innocent his intentions, had been over the line. His confidence was shaken. Deep down he knew he had slipped. He was bored with that kind of work anyway. It was time to move on.

His biggest problem at the moment was coming up with enough money to pay his alimony and still be able to get by on what was left.

He realized he could make his life a lot easier if he could just find a job in purchasing somewhere but he wanted to do something different. Since he still had another month's severance coming from the Sisters of Mercy he was determined to wait things out a little longer. Something would come to him if he used his head. Still, every morning he woke up feeling a little bit more nervous than the day before.

His other big problem was loneliness. At least at Veneto's he met people every day. He joked with the other waiters, the chef and the dishwashers. And of course, he enjoyed being with Fred. Three weeks into his self imposed hermitage Fred called him to see how he was doing. They had a nice chat. Fred hinted around about getting together but he passed. Phil surprised himself when he ignored her hints. He felt good about having the willpower to keep his distance but ten minutes after he hung up he wished he had played it differently. Whether he was just horny or he actually missed her he couldn't say.

Six weeks later any distinction between liking Fred and just being horny didn't matter. He was overwhelmed by loneliness. And, he hadn't done even one thing to find what happened to the package Bucco had placed in Carmine's car that fateful evening. He might as well go back to Florida, he thought. But that money had to be somewhere. His resolve weakening, he finally called Fred. She didn't pick up. He was about to leave a message but didn't know what to say. The truth was he felt funny about saying anything. He had no job. He had no prospects. He worked with executive recruiters; he continued to search on line job sites and hospital web sites looking for work. Now even purchasing sounded inviting. But the same thing happened over and over again. He would get a nibble and then the hiring party would find out he was closing in on sixty. Opportunities vanished. He was collecting unemployment now and dipping into savings to cover the difference.

Now that it was spring and the baseball season was underway, he put his demons to rest watching the Yankees or the Mets and sipping jug wine until he fell asleep. More than once he woke up the following morning to cartoons, still stretched out on the recliner. He also kept the phone close by in case Fred called him. One night, when neither the ball game nor the wine was giving him peace, he gave in to temptation and took a ride over to Venetos.

Fred saw him as soon as he opened the door to the restaurant. She looked great. Her hair was cut shorter and so were her nails. He had teased her about the way her long nails looked more like claws. Once in a serious moment he suggested that a little thing like that really did matter. For one thing it affected the type of man who might be attracted to her. At least that's what Phil believed.

The smile on Fred's face when she saw Phil brightened his mood considerably. It was too late to order dinner. Besides he had already eaten. Instead he ordered a piece of cheese cake, an espresso and a glass of red wine. They chatted amiably for a while, just catching up on what they had been doing.

Fred finally broke the ice. "I've missed you Falco."

Phil didn't hesitate. "I've missed you too. Somehow you got under my skin."

"Just like the song. Sorry."

"I'm the one that should be sorry, Freddie. Anyway, it's good to be here talking to you now."

Naturally they went to her apartment that night and made up for lost time. Later they talked things over.

"How's the job search going?" she asked.

"It's not going. I'm having trouble even getting an interview these days."

"I know you don't want to hear this but I'm sure Jerry would take you back if you wouldn't mind being a waiter again for a while. All the time he's talking about how good you were."

"Freddie, I have to be honest. I'm at my wits end. I never felt like I was the victim of discrimination or anything like that. To be honest, I used to think minorities just weren't willing to try hard enough. But discrimination, including age discrimination, is real and it sucks," Phil said, talking to himself more than to Fred.

"Well, there is a job at Veneto's and if you work five nights a week you can make decent money. Why don't you come back? You can keep looking during the day, right?"

"I guess."

He lay back and she started gently rubbing his chest. Within just a couple of minutes they were making love again. "I know at least one area where you ain't over the hill," Fred whispered.

The next morning he told Fred that he would take the job if Jerry would have him. He did some figuring and he was sure he could clear at least a thousand a week and maybe more working five nights. Veneto's was always busy. Money would still be tight, but he could probably make it stretch far enough so he wouldn't have to dip into his savings too often. And, Fred was right, he could still look for work during the day.

Phil was back to work at Veneto's the very next night. The owner was so excited he put the words, "Phil's Back!" on the marquee that stood in the parking lot near the street. Only a handful of customers really had any idea who Phil was but it made Phil feel good anyway. Three nights later Marianne Cifelli came in again with the same guy she was with the last time. Again she berated Phil for not calling her.

Fred, who was standing behind the bar, gave Phil a knowing glance. She mouthed the word bitch. Phil ignored her. He led Marianne and her friend to a table near the huge picture window. The sign announcing Phil's return was in full view.

He took their drink and their meal orders. They both knew exactly what they wanted.

"Marianne, I'll give you a call next week. Maybe we can meet for lunch or something," Phil said.

Marianne's friend gave him a funny look. Marianne smiled and said, "Sure Phil. Call me next week." She was laughing as if to show she didn't take Phil's promise seriously.

Phil settled into an enjoyable routine. He was no longer worried about appearances. The money was decent and the work was steady. After a few half-hearted attempts, he stopped looking for another job. Jobs for guys nearing sixty years old and looking for something close to a hundred thousand a year were a long shot anyway. In any case, once he relaxed, he found that he liked working in the restaurant. Too, he had once again fallen into a comfortable relationship with Fred. Finally, considering everything that had happened to him in the last six months, Phil thought that maybe it was a good time to take a breather. Careful planning was getting him nowhere. He would take each day as it comes and let the future take care of itself. Somehow the right path would be laid out for him.

On a sunny Saturday morning just before noon he saw Marianne again. This time he ran into her at a supermarket. They chatted for a few minutes but quickly ran out of conversation. He started playing around with cantaloupes just to keep his hands busy.

"It's almost lunch time," Marianne said, "You want to get a bite to eat?"

"Sure," Phil answered, grateful for the opening.

They kept it simple, enjoying a nice chat over a couple of slices of pizza. She told him a little bit about the guy she was seeing. It was nothing serious she said.

"And how about you? Are you dating the woman that works the bar at Veneto's?"

"Yeah. How did you know?"

"I can see her shooting daggers at me every time I walk in the place. You do know that Carmine dated her for a while, don't you?"

Phil nodded. "It's not serious. For one thing she's too young for me."

"That's what I tried to tell Carmine. Not that it mattered. He was two-timing her anyway. He had a girlfriend that worked as a receptionist in that restaurant down the shore, I can't think of the name of the place," Marianne said.

"Falzone's?"

"That's it," Marianne said, "Did Carmine tell you about her?"

"Not by name. He mentioned stopping there to see an old girlfriend. He never said her name," Phil said.

"Her name is Angela. Are you sure he said 'old girlfriend?'"

"Something like that, why?"

"Nothing I guess," Marianne said. "If they broke up it would have been just before he died. He was with her on Christmas Eve at my house."

"I wonder if she knows where the package is," Phil said.

Marianne didn't answer right away. She got up to leave and Phil followed suit.

They dumped their paper plates into the trash receptacle and headed out the door. As they approached their cars, Marianne turned to Phil and said, "About the package Phil, exactly how did you convince Florio to leave us alone?"

Phil hadn't expected that. When he mentioned the package he was merely speaking a private thought out loud. "It wasn't easy. I think he suspected you as much as me. Maybe more. Anyway, the idea that I might take the money didn't add up."

"So it was money?"

"I don't really know. It could have been anything really. I never actually saw the contents and Carmine wouldn't tell me what it was," Phil said, backpedaling, "Maybe it was money or maybe betting slips or who knows it could have been securities of some kind."

Marianne nodded. "Well, why wouldn't it make sense for Florio to think you took whatever it was?"

"A lot of reasons Marianne. For one thing, I couldn't know that Carmine would turn up dead unless I killed him. Florio knew we went way back together so there's no way that would happen. So, if I took the package and Carmine was alive, I would be putting him in a terrible spot. No way that would happen either."

"But I still don't know why he let us off the hook," she said.

Phil shrugged. "Like I said it didn't add up. Once he saw that he let it go."

Marianne stood there, her eyes riveted on Phil. Her face suggested she wanted to say something but she remained silent. Phil leaned toward her and gave her a kiss on the cheek. Momentarily, he considered asking her out. The thought paralyzed him. He sensed she would turn him down and he didn't want to deal with that. Instead, they made their usual promises to stay in touch.

Phil spent the rest of the afternoon wondering about Angela. He remembered that Carmine said he didn't get to see her the day of the closing. Something about her being off from work that day. Maybe Carmine did see her. But then, how could he have given her the money? They made no stops between Atlantic City and Newark Airport. Still, he wondered whether Angela might have some clue about what Carmine might have done with the package. He knew he should forget about it but half a million dollars wasn't the kind of thing anyone, and certainly not Phil Falco, could or would forget.

He decided to take Sunday off and head to the Jersey shore. He wanted to find this Angela woman. She probably didn't know anything but he had to find out. Fred wouldn't mind. Anyway she rarely gave up a shift. She was always running short of cash.

Falzone's was well known for its terrific Italian food and the bar was well known in Ocean County as the place to be on Friday and Saturday nights. It was huge, actually larger than the restaurant was and always packed with people who wanted to hear a live band and drink away their miseries. A lot of those same bar patrons turned up on Sunday afternoon with kids in tow for a Sunday dinner of spaghetti and meatballs or veal cacciatore.

Phil arrived at two o'clock. Rather than head right for the restaurant seating area, he stopped off at the bar. It was much quieter on Sunday afternoons. He ordered his usual, a glass of cabernet. The bartender, a guy in his mid-thirties sporting a full black beard, placed the glass in front of him. He noticed Phil's Yankee cap and said, pointing to the television, "the Yanks are losing six nothing."

"What inning?"

It's only the third."

"Is Angela working today?" Phil asked trying to sound casual.

"Who wants to know?"

"I do," Phil said, in a matter of fact tone.

"And who are you?"

Phil laughed. "My name is Phil Falco."

The bartender nodded. "She doesn't work here anymore. She quit a couple of weeks ago."

"Do you know where I might find her?"

"She lives right here in Toms River. She shouldn't be too hard to find."

"Yeah, but I don't remember her last name."

"I guess you're shit out of luck pal," the bartender said.

Phil sipped his wine, wondering if he could slip the guy a few bucks and get the information. He laughed at the thought. The bartender fancied himself a tough guy. Phil had had all the tough guy stuff he could handle. Instead he reached for his cell phone and called Marianne. In less than a minute he had what he needed. According to Marianne, Angela's last name was Dearborn. She even had her phone number. Of course she wanted to know why Phil wanted to know. Just tying up loose ends was all Phil could think to say. Marianne let out a sigh of frustration and hung up.

Angela Dearborn wasn't home apparently. Phil realized he probably should have asked Marianne for her address too but he didn't dare call her again. He would simply have to wait. To kill time he ordered a meal. As soon as he finished, he tried Angela again, still no answer.

To kill more time he took a ride to Seaside Heights, a popular summer resort town on the ocean. It was early in May so the boardwalk wasn't crowded. A lot of the shops and stands that offered games of chance were open. Others were working feverishly to get ready for the season. The smell of the ocean, mixed with the aroma of steak sandwiches and fried sausage with onions, brought back fond memories for Phil. He walked the length of the boardwalk and back again. Along the way he bought fresh lemonade to quench his thirst. He decided to try Angela one more time. This time she picked up the phone.

"Angela, my name is Phil Falco. I was a friend of Carmine's."

"I know who you are," she said. "Barry said you were looking for me. What do you want?"

"Who's Barry? Oh, never mind. That would be the bartender at Falzone's right?"

Sherlock Holmes I'm talking to here," Angela said.

"Not exactly," Phil said, stifling a nervous laugh. "Angela I would like to meet you. I'm sure you know all about Carmine's death. I just need someone to talk to about it."

"He was a good friend of yours right?"

"He was."

"And you throw me a line like that? What did he tell you, I was some easy piece?"

"Oh boy, no, no, Angela, absolutely not," Phil said. "I really do have some questions and nothing more than that. Anyway, to be honest, he didn't tell me a lot about you at all."

"What exactly do you want?" she asked.

"To talk. I would rather meet you someplace."

"You can come here if you want. Do you know where I live?"

"Do you live in Toms River?"

"No I'm one town over in Beachwood." Phil laughed. The bartender's antenna must have gone way up as soon as he saw Phil.

She gave him directions and Phil headed for her house, not sure of exactly what he would say to her.

Angela Dearborn lived in a very nice split-level home in one of Beachwood's better neighborhoods. Parked in the driveway was a new beige Cadillac. One question Phil wanted to ask was how a restaurant hostess could afford the big house and a Cadillac.

"Hi Angela, I'm Phil Falco." Phil thought he might recognize her from the wake or funeral services but he couldn't place her.

"Come on in. You want a cup of coffee?"

"That sounds good. Thank you."

Angela led Phil into the dining room. Her home was tastefully decorated in a Mediterranean style. Sitting on the dining room table was a plate of Stella D'Oro cookies. Next to the plate were some photographs. Phil took a seat while Angela went into the kitchen to get the coffee.

"Very nice home you have here. Have you been here long?" Phil asked.

"About seven years. I bought it after my husband died. He left me pretty well off I guess you could say."

Phil took a good look at Angela. He guessed she was in her mid-forties. She had brown hair cut short with blond highlights. She was maybe ten pounds overweight but she wore it well. Wearing jeans and tight sweater, she was still pretty in a perky sort of way. She also wore a lot of jewelry.

"So you and Carmine were close according to his sister Marianne," Phil began.

"We were, although I must say I don't know how Marianne would know that. I only met her one time."

"Christmas Eve?"

"Right. What else did she tell you about me?"

For a moment Phil felt like saying, "she told me Carmine two-timed you," but that would serve no purpose. It was a perverse thought and it made him smile. "Not much else. Did you know Carmine and I were together the day he died?"

The woman nodded. She reached for the photographs. There were four of them. Each one was a picture of Angela and Carmine together, taken at various parties. The last one was from Christmas Eve. Looking at them it was easy to see how much Carmine's appearance had changed by Christmas. Obviously the woman wanted to talk about Carmine too. She really cared for him.

"Carmine was a very handsome and charming man. Maybe he wasn't smart in a lot of ways but he had style and I really liked that," Angela said. She had tears in her eyes. Phil found a box of tissues and handed it to her but the moment passed quickly.

"Did Carmine ever tell you he was sick?" Phil asked.

Angela frowned. "He didn't have to. I worked in a doctor's office for years, an oncologist no less. He was sick alright. Did he say something to you?"

Phil shook his head no. "When was the last time you saw him?"

"Are you a cop or something? Maybe I should ask for ID," Angela said.

Phil pulled out his wallet and flipped it open showing his driver's license. "Far from it," he said. "I was Carmine's best friend."

Angela seemed to really look at Phil for the first time. "Were you the guy that was selling that big house in Toms River?"

Phil nodded.

"Well, Phil, the last time I saw Carmine was the day he drove you to the closing."

"Are you sure Angela?"

"Of course I'm sure. We did it right over there on the couch. He was in a hurry," she said, just a trace of a smile on her face now.

"I see," Phil said. "Funny but for some reason he told me he looked for you that day but you were off from work or something."

"Maybe he didn't want you to know how good I am."

CHAPTER 10

Lisa Falco stood in the dressing room, a converted supply closet in a modest warehouse, waiting for the director to call her. She would be in her first scene of her first movie any minute now. For a moment she thought of her father and how he almost derailed her career before it started. She had to do some fast talking to convince Riley that her father was all talk. Still, to play it safe, Riley insisted that she play the part of the innocent young girl who would refuse to play along with others at a wild party on the beach. It was only a cameo role actually. The purpose of her part was to offer some redeeming moral value that would get the film past censorship laws. Not that Riley Rivers was really worried about running afoul of Federal obscenity laws. Ever since porn moved from movie theatres into living rooms, it had become much harder to prosecute and win convictions in such cases. Still, there was always the threat that a prosecutor wanting to make a name for himself, would pick on a little company like Double R and try to make an example of them.

The set was cheap: A simple twenty by twenty space made to look like the interior of an oceanside bar in the tropics. She would have two lines. She practiced them over and over. When one of the men who was wearing a skimpy European style bathing suit approached her, she would say, "No thank you," when he asked her to dance. Then another guy would come up behind her and whisper something in her ear. She was supposed to spin around to face him. Then slapping him in the face, she would say, "Every woman you see isn't your plaything." Then she would give the actor a shove and walk off. There would be one final shot of her leaving the bar with her head held high.

The scene took seven takes. She said 'thank you' instead of 'no thank you' on the first two takes. She was mortified to blow such an easy line but she was extremely nervous.

Afterward, she ran into Riley's arms, desperately wanting his approval.

"How could you fuck up a simple line like that?" Riley asked.

"Oh I know. I was so nervous. Did I do okay after that?"

"I don't exactly see a Golden Globe in your future."

Lisa let go of Riley then. She could feel the tears coming. She walked back to the dressing room to change. Still in tears, she drove back to the production company offices.

That night when Riley got home he found her sitting on one of her suitcases. She was crying. "Can you give me a ride to the airport?"

"You're not going anywhere baby," Rivers said.

"I'm going home. I'm leaving tonight."

With a malicious grin Riley Rivers knocked Lisa off the suitcase she was perched on, hitting her with a force that wouldn't cause major damage but would send a message.

"Get your clothes off, go in the bedroom and wait for me," Rivers commanded.

Phil Falco was putting his shorts back on. Sex with Angela Dearborn had been as advertised. She was good. Maybe not wild like Fred, but good nevertheless.

"I never expected that," Angela said.

"It must have been the Stella D'Oro cookies I guess."

Angela swatted him gently on his behind. "So, before we were so rudely interrupted, you said you wanted to ask me something about Carmine. What was it?"

Phil sat back down on the bed, pulling up alongside Angela who was still naked.

"Carmine and I went to Atlantic City after the closing. We gambled a little but then we ran into some Mafia guys."

"Dennis Florio I'll bet," Angela said.

"Right. Do you know him?"

"I've seen him around. Carmine did some work for him now and then. He was real secretive about it but he didn't mind me knowing he was connected and stuff."

"How connected was he?" Phil asked.

"Not very, if you ask me. I think he was more of an errand boy who got roped in because he gambled too much."

"Beyond his means?

"Way beyond his means," Angela said. She reached down to the end of her bed and grabbed her robe. She pulled back the sheet she was under and slipped it on. Phil reached over and cupped her breast one last time and gave her a light kiss. She smiled.

"Carmine ever talk to you about mob money?"

"What do you mean?"

"I was under the impression that sometimes he made deliveries to New York. He ever say anything about that to you?"

Angela shook her head. "Never about delivering money. One time he said he had to deliver a package to the City. He asked me if I wanted to take a ride. I told him I couldn't because my niece was coming over."

"But he never said what was in the package."

"Absolutely not. At the time I figured it was drugs which was the real reason I wouldn't go with him. You want something to drink? I think I'm going to have an Amaretto."

"Sure. Thanks"

Angela got up and headed for the kitchen. Phil sat on the bed looking around the room. On the dresser was a picture of Carmine. He wondered how Carmine would feel about him now that he had done it with two of the women in his, Carmine's life. Knowing Carmine he would have hated it, Phil thought. Carmine was very possessive about his women which explained why he never mentioned to Phil that he had seen Angela before they left for Atlantic City.

Angela came back with two pony glasses filled with Amaretto. They clicked the glasses together in a silent toast. Angela sipped hers while Phil downed his in one fiery gulp.

"I'm going to tell you something," Phil began. "I'm going to trust you that this will stay in this room. I think Carmine was delivering money the night he died. The problem is that when they found his body the money was missing. It still hasn't turned up."

"Sorry Phil but that's no secret."

"Really? He was genuinely surprised. "I thought you said you didn't know anything about the money. How do you know about this?"

"I didn't know anything. Like I said, he never mentioned it to me. But, I like to gamble too. I'm in Atlantic City once or twice a week. That's where I met Carmine."

"And Dennis Florio?"

"As I said, I've seen him around. How could you miss him he's so huge. But I don't know him really."

"Well, if you don't mind my asking, where did you hear the story about the money?"

"A dealer I go out with once in a while told me about it. He knew about me and Carmine so he told me about it."

"What did he say?" Phil asked.

"Not much really. Something about how Carmine stiffed the mob. Some people think he buried the money under the Seaside Heights boardwalk intending to get it later."

"That makes no sense whatsoever."

"I know that," Angela said, laughing, "But can't you just picture all those idiots digging holes this summer under the boardwalk?"

Phil laughed. "Let me ask you something. It's obvious now that Carmine knew he was dying. Under the circumstances, he might have given the money to somebody he cared about before he ran his Cadillac into that telephone pole. If he did, who do you think he would give it to?"

"Not to me honey. And, if that's why you came all this way,

you're out of luck." Angela clutched her robe tightly around her neck, wary now.

"Listen to me Angela. I know he didn't give you the money. For one thing, he wouldn't have had enough time. For another, he didn't know he would be making a delivery that night until hours after he saw you."

"So what are you asking me?"

"You knew him. You said you went together for a couple of years. I figured you might know who he would give the money too, assuming the cops didn't steal it from the scene of the accident."

Angela relaxed. "Make love to me one more time while I think about it."

Phil was happy to oblige.

Four hours later Phil was finally alone on the Garden State Parkway headed back to his apartment. He thought about Fred for a moment. Their relationship was on thin ice. Fred thought of them as a couple but Phil knew better. If he had any doubts, his escapade with Angela removed them. The only thing he felt a twinge of guilt over was getting in bed with another of Carmine's girlfriends.

Regardless, Angela had been helpful. He had insisted on taking her out to dinner. Once they were back at her house, sitting in his car and saying their goodbyes, she finally told him what she thought: If Carmine left the money with anybody it would be either his sister Marianne or his second ex-wife Paula, she said. According to Angela, Carmine's sister ran his life. But Angela believed that Paula still had a lock on his heart.

Phil asked Angela about Gloria. "Did Carmine ever talk about her?"

"No. I asked him about her once but he didn't want to talk about her. I thought he was angry with her or something," Angela said.

"Angry about what?" Phil wanted to know.

"Who knows? Like I said, he wouldn't talk about her."

"I was always under the impression they remained friends."

"Maybe they did but he never talked about her to me. When he mentioned Paula though, his tone was always soft. If he left anybody money, it was Paula or his sister who got it."

Phil found it interesting that Carmine never talked about Gloria to Angela. He was sure she had misinterpreted Carmine's silence. As far as Phil knew, Carmine liked and even trusted Gloria even after they divorced.

It was getting late and Phil wanted to head home. He said goodbye to her with a light kiss on her cheek.

"I guess I don't need to ask, when will I see you again?" she said.

Chatsworth, California is probably best known as the porn capital of the world. The pornography industry flourishes in the small town of thirty-five thousand residents. To anyone passing through, it looks like a quiet, suburb with its share of service and manufacturing businesses to support the town. The warehouses look innocent enough but behind those steel gray walls so-called film producers, directors and movie star wannabes make movies that appeal to the desires and perhaps secret perversions of certain twenty-first century males.

When Lisa Falco moved to Los Angeles she had no idea she would wind up in the pornography business. Like so many young men and women, she had hopes of getting into the movies but she wasn't unrealistic about her chances. She took an acting class and found a job waiting tables. She worried her father into giving her an allowance for a few months to give her time to get on her feet. She used the money to rent a small, furnished apartment in Santa Monica with two co-workers, an Asian guy and a girl from the Midwest.

A couple of months later she saw an ad in the LA Times for an office assistant at a film studio in Chatsworth. She had no idea that the studio made pornographic films until she walked into the

Double R Productions office. The posters hanging on the walls made it clear what kind of movies Double R made. Momentarily, she considered turning around and walking out. Before she could decide, she met Riley Rivers. He was a charmer. He quickly reassured her that the films he made were simply a stepping stone to something better. This was a line he used to entice many would be starlets. He told her about well known actors and directors who had started in the porn industry. Lisa had no way of knowing that he was making it up as he went along. He hired her right away, impressed by her good looks and sassy attitude.

When he asked her if she would like to be in one of his movies, she smiled and said, "As long as you're not in it with me."

Within less than a week they were living together. Lisa was a natural at running the office which helped because Riley was unorganized and incapable of focusing on anything for very long.

That was almost a year ago. Until Riley knocked her off the suitcase, she had been happy. Now she was hurt and confused. She had altered her looks and the way she dressed to please Riley. She was in love with him and she felt sure he loved her even if he only said it one time. Of course he apologized when he walked into the bedroom and found her lying on the bed, sobbing. He lifted her gently into his arms and stroked her hair. "I had such a fucked up day today. I guess I took it out you, little Lisa."

Lisa said nothing in reply. Riley lifted her head from his chest and gently kissed her cheek. He could see the fear in her eyes and this pleased him. "I promise that will never happen again. And you didn't do too bad today."

That news brightened Lisa's outlook a little. "Really? Do you mean it?"

"Yeah. It was your first time in front of a camera. It will get easier, you'll see."

"I hope so. I was really wigged out, like all those people looking at me, you know? You'll let me do it again?"

"Absolutely. And we'll get you a bigger part next time baby."

With that news she wrapped her arms around the man who had just knocked her to the floor a few minutes ago. "I love you Riley."

"Show me little Lisa, show me."

Chapter 11

The restaurant was closed Mondays. Since they both had the day off, usually, Phil and Fred would go to a mall, wander around doing mostly window shopping, and then see a late afternoon movie. That was what Phil assumed they would be doing, Fred had other ideas. She wanted to take a ride to New Hope, Pennsylvania to browse the antique shops. They had done that a couple of times but Phil hated it. On their last trip to New Hope, only two weeks ago, Phil finally faced facts about his relationship with Fred. It had been brewing for a while. Her language was often salty to put it mildly. She was very opinionated, which would have been fine with Phil if not for the fact that many of Fred's opinions could not be supported by even the most basic facts or for that matter, common sense. For example, she maintained that the terrorist attacks on the World Trade Center were orchestrated by sinister forces within the United States government to ensure that President Bush's term in office would be a failure. She was also convinced that inanimate objects like a deck of cards could be inherently evil, causing harm to its owner. Since she didn't dwell on such thoughts, usually Phil was able to overlook her quaint views of the world they lived in. Up to a point, she had other attributes that more than made up for these problems.

But the last time they were in New Hope, Fred saw an old lace petticoat resting on a tired looking mannequin. She fell in love with it which was fine except that she was so loud in calling for the proprietor, asking the price, wanting to know if it belonged to a famous actress from the fifties or something, that Phil was embarrassed. And his embarrassment over her behavior made him angry with himself. Who was he to be embarrassed by Fred's behavior?

Nevertheless that was how he felt. He just couldn't live with the tradeoffs anymore. He had grown restless again. Fred was too young and too coarse for his taste and he saw no future with her. To make matters even worse, Fred was putting pressure on him to move the relationship forward. One morning, when they were lying in her bed, she broached the subject openly for the first time. She started out by complaining how high her rent was. Phil just listened without comment. When that didn't work she took a more direct approach. "Why don't you move in with me? We could share expenses and we both would save money." She knew by now that saving money was an idea that appealed to Phil.

"We're not ready for that," Phil said. It was a foolish answer and he knew it as soon as he said it. Suggesting that moving in together was an option in the future was wrong. "Anyway, you're too young for me Freddie," he added.

Fred turned to face him, placing her hand on his bare chest. "What are you looking for Phil? We could have a great life together."

"What am I looking for? Peace and contentment. I'm tired of working so hard. I want to play golf again,"

"That's it? You want to play golf? You're not interested in having someone special in your life to grow old with?"

Phil saw his opening. "That would be nice Fred but I'm more of a realist than you are I guess. I'm growing old a lot faster than you are. When I am an old man you'll still be young enough to want things I've lost interest in."

Fred knew she was defeated, perhaps for the moment, but in the days and weeks that followed, she continued to apply pressure. She wanted more from Phil.

Phil knew he had to break it off with Fred. How to do it? He wasn't sure. One thing he knew was that having to face her every night at Veneto's would be more than he could handle. He knew a clean break was the right thing to do but he wasn't ready. Nor was he ready, after his Sunday with Angela, to spend all day Monday with Fred. Instead, he called Fred and made up an excuse to avoid seeing her. While he was at it, he let her know that he was going to be busy the following Monday too.

He also found himself thinking about Marianne Cifelli. He really liked her. She was attractive and intelligent and she wasn't too young for him. He had spent so much time with Fred since coming back to New Jersey that he didn't take the time to try to reconnect with old friends. Maybe if he had done that he would have had a male companion to help him sort all this out. He made a mental note to look up at least one or two old friends from the neighborhood.

Knowing he wouldn't have to see Fred the next Monday, he spent the better part of the week trying to build up the courage to ask Marianne out for that Monday night. He was beginning to feel like a high school kid playing the field and he liked it.

The one thing that bothered him was whether Carmine might have given the money to Marianne. He couldn't help thinking about what Angela said. Either Paula or Marianne would have the money if Carmine gave it to anybody. And that was his only real hope: that Carmine did give the money to someone. He was sure if he could explain what happened, Marianne would work something out with him. Maybe if he got to know her better, something beyond the long standing family friend status he was relegated to now, he would feel comfortable leveling with her about what happened with Florio.

Of course thoughts like that made him question his own motives. Certainly Marianne had denied that Carmine had given her the money. Why not just believe her and let it go at that? For one thing, there was too much at stake. And, that kind of money could make a liar out of almost anybody, including Marianne. Hadn't she already lied about having one of Florio's men ask her for the money? No, he couldn't simply assume that she didn't have the money. He wished with all his heart that he could do that. The chemistry he felt between them was real, at least to him. He had fun with Fred but he felt more alive just talking to Marianne than he did in bed with poor Fred.

By Friday afternoon he made up his mind. He would roll the dice and give her a call. Maybe she would enjoy a baseball game. Feeling optimistic, he bought two tickets to see the New York Yankees and called Marianne on Saturday morning. He was nervous about making the call. Again feeling like a teenager, he was afraid he would be rejected.

But Marianne sounded happy to hear from Phil, a good start.

"I called you to see if you might want to go to the Yankee game Monday night."

"A baseball game? I haven't done that in years."

"Me either. Want to go?"

"Sure, why not? What time?"

"The game starts at 7:05. I'll pick you up at four thirty. We'll drive over to the stadium and we can eat there."

"Okay, see you then." Just like that he had his date. That was the first time he had actually asked a woman out on a date since Tracy. The weekend before his big date with Marianne was nerve wracking though. He was filled with anticipation. He felt lucky that Veneto's was extremely busy. Friday night's crowd was a lot bigger than usual and Saturday night, for the first time in anyone's memory, people actually waited outside the door, behind patrons standing in the bar waiting for tables. One good rush was considered a decent night on most weekends. These crowds were well beyond the norm. Sunday brought more of the same. Typically, there would be a good crowd between one and two in the afternoon on Sundays followed by a smaller rush beginning about five-thirty. That Sunday felt like one long rush. Everyone, the cooks, the dishwashers the busboys and of course, the wait staff, was exhausted by Sunday night. Usually the cooks prepared one last meal for the entire staff on Sunday nights as soon as the doors closed. No one had the strength to eat at the end of that weekend. Certainly the cooks weren't eager to prepare another meal. Yet, tired as they were, both Phil and Fred were thrilled with their earnings. Phil brought home close to seven hundred dollars for his efforts.

While the two of them did follow their ritual of retiring to Fred's apartment after Friday and Saturday's shifts, they really were too tired to get physical. On Sunday night, Phil was bone tired. He told Fred he was going home, reminding her he would be busy the next day. Fred was too tired to argue. They simply agreed to meet for lunch Tuesday afternoon. More than anything else, Phil was relieved that Marianne wasn't one of the hundreds of customers who ate at Veneto's that weekend. He had been nervous about that. He was afraid that Marianne might say something about the game within earshot of Fred. If Fred heard of their plans and made a scene, only the hearing impaired wouldn't know about her displeasure.

It didn't occur to him until he was lying in bed Sunday night that maybe Marianne wasn't taking any chances either. Maybe she was still seeing her teacher friend. She probably avoided Veneto's to make sure that Phil wouldn't spill the beans, he thought. He fell asleep with a smile on his face.

Phil spent the better part of the day Monday doing chores around the apartment. He woke up that morning wondering if there was any chance he and Marianne might wind up at his apartment after the game. It was a long shot to be sure but he assumed that with her son Ricky living with her it was unlikely they would go to her place. And, if they did go to Marianne's it was a safe bet it would be strictly a matter of coffee and conversation.

No, the better choice would be his place. Then he panicked when he thought about how messy his apartment was. He had been living there for months. He had not dusted the furniture more than a couple of times and he never, not once, mopped any floors. That got him up and moving.

The first thing he did was throw out every bit of accumulated trash. There was a lot: Old newspapers, some Chinese food containers and a few beer bottles plus what he found in the refrigerator that had long since passed its prime. He dusted and waxed the furniture, he vacuumed the rugs and he mopped the floors. He scoured the bathroom too. In the process he really took note of what he didn't have. For example, there wasn't even one picture on the walls. No knick-knacks or personal effects except for a picture of Lisa to give the place a little warmth. As soon as he finished cleaning, he got himself cleaned up enough to be presentable in public and headed out to the nearby strip mall. He spent two hundred bucks on items that to his eye added a little warmth to the place. He found some inexpensive prints, mostly landscapes, already framed. He bought a couple of vases and matched them with both plastic and dried flowers. He also bought new sheets and a few new towels and wash cloths. He felt pretty good about what he had done. It occurred to him that in all these months, Fred had never seen his apartment. Not only that, he was sure he wouldn't have gone to all this trouble if he knew she was coming.

By the time he got all that work done, it was time to take a shower. He needed to put some gas in the Altima and then he could drive over to Marianne's. He got there at ten past four. She was ready for him and she seemed genuinely happy to see him.

"You're right on time," she said.

"A few minutes early maybe. Are you ready to leave?"

"In a minute. I have to leave a note for Ricky. He was really jealous by the way, that I was going to see the Yankees play. I packed us some snacks," she said, pointing to a brown bag with handles.

"It's been a long time since I went to Yankee Stadium. Do you think they'll let us in with all this stuff?"

"Funny you should ask. One of the teachers at school said the same thing today. So I checked on line. It's allowed."

"Okay then. We'd better get going."

Phil opened the passenger door for Marianne. She was about to step in but stopped. "Oh, I think I forgot to lock the side door," she said. "I do that all the time." Once that was taken care of, they were ready to leave.

The traffic on the Garden State Parkway was heavy. It got worse on Route 4 as they approached the George Washington Bridge. With all the extra time Phil had allotted, it still looked like they wouldn't be in their seats with much time to spare. Marianne was rather quiet at first but Phil was genuinely curious about Marianne so once his initial nervousness subsided, he had lots of questions.

"When Carmine and I were driving to Toms River, he mentioned that you were taking an acting class. How is that going?"

"Oh God, that was months ago. Actually, I only went to the first two classes. It was such a hassle to get into Manhattan during rush hour. Well you can see, even going to the Bronx is a nightmare," she said gesturing to the congested road. "Getting into New York is always a hassle, really."

"Did you enjoy the classes you attended?"

Marianne shook her head. She pulled down the visor to check her lipstick in the mirror. "Not really. I was easily the oldest person in the class. I thought it would be fun, something different, you know?"

Phil nodded.

"But the people in the class were dead serious about acting. It was like all of them were hoping to be stars on Broadway or in movies."

The conversation shifted to talk about Marianne's job. "You've been a teacher for a long time. Do you still enjoy it?"

"God I hate to sound so negative Phil. You're asking all these questions and I'm going to sound like a burned out old lady. No, I don't enjoy teaching the way I used to."

"It's understandable," Phil said. "Kids don't want to learn anymore or maybe their parents don't care enough. You get a lot of disciplinary problems?"

"You have no idea," She said.

They continued talking about her job as a teacher. At one point Marianne mentioned that the Newark school system didn't have enough teachers. She said they were hiring college graduates, people who had experience in other fields, something that in the past simply was not done. But they were in desperate need of teachers. This piqued Phil's interest. He wondered if this might be a solution to his current problem. He knew that his life would be a whole lot easier if he could find work someplace other than at Veneto's. He had no doubt that a breakup with Fred would mean he had to find a new job. He was intrigued by the possibility of becoming a teacher. He decided to come back to that topic later. They were getting close to the Bridge and the Stadium wasn't too far off in the distance.

They stuck to small talk until they got into their seats. Phil had been able to get field level box seats just ten rows from the visiting team dugout. The Yankees were playing the Cleveland Indians. The first thing Phil did was get them each a beer. It was only the second day of June but the weather was balmy enough to work up a sweat just sitting in the early evening sun. The game turned out to be exciting. It was a pitcher's dual until the seventh inning. Then Derek Jeter hit a double down the left field line. Alex Rodriguez followed with a long home run. Suddenly it was 2-0 Yankees. After that it was as if both teams were taking batting practice. The final score was 9-8 with the Yankees coming out on top.

On the way home, they chatted a bit about the game and how much they both enjoyed it. The closer they got to Marianne's house the more nervous Phil became.

Marianne had been friendly but Phil didn't sense any romantic vibes. He felt the tingling that signaled strong chemistry but if she was feeling anything she was keeping it strictly to herself. To test the waters, he asked her about going out again.

"I really enjoyed your company tonight Marianne. I would like to see you again. Maybe we could go out to dinner."

Marianne was silent. Phil rushed in to fill the void. "Bad idea?"

"It's not that Phil. I had a good time too. I just don't know how I feel about getting involved with you. We've known each other a long time and you and Carmine were so close."

"Is that something you need to decide right now? I understand why you might have reservations but I have to tell you I don't share them. I am very attracted to you."

Marianne smiled. She touched Phil's arm and said, "Let me think about it okay?"

"Sure. But promise me you won't decide too quickly. I'll tell you what. Meet me for dinner next Monday night, a week from now. I want to talk more about the teaching thing, what did you call it?"

"You mean the alternate route for people who want to become teachers?"

"That's it. The alternate route. Can we meet next week?"

"Okay, but I think you're crazy if you're thinking about teaching at this stage of the game."

Phil dropped Marianne off in front of her house. She didn't invite him in but she did give him a quick peck on the lips before saying goodnight. As brief as it was, Phil felt it down to his knees. As he drove home he remembered that he never got to ask Marianne about Carmine's ex-wife Paula. Maybe it was just as well. He would have something more to talk about when they met for dinner.

Hot weather came early. The temperature hit the nineties on Memorial Day and it never let up the whole summer. Phil suffered through it but not because of the heat. He could handle that a whole lot better than the cold. What made his life miserable was that he was forced to spend the summer working at Veneto's. His relationship with Fred went into a slow, torturous, downward spiral. They were arguing now over little things like where to have lunch or whether she really needed a second glass of wine if they ate out on their day off. He was working six days a week now, Tuesday through Sunday. He did his best to try to put a little space between himself and Fred. He wasn't cold but he was quiet. Of course, from Fred's perspective he was cold as ice. He understood perfectly that they would both be better off if he could just tell her they were finished, like ripping the bandage off hairy skin quickly rather than trying to gently ease the adhesive off. Somehow he couldn't bring himself to say the words. He hoped that his actions would send the message and allow him to forgo the explanations. He was old enough to know that such tactics would not work but tried it anyway.

Finally Fred had had enough of his too tired routine as in, too tired to go home with her, too tired to meet her for lunch, too tired to sleep with her. After work one Thursday night she made sure they walked out the door of Veneto's together.

"You coming over?" she said.

"Not tonight. I'm bushed," Phil said, trying to make his voice sound weary.

Fred didn't say a word. She walked to her car, got in and drove off. Phil knew he should have told her it was over and he would, he told himself. Tomorrow morning he would drive over to her place and tell her they were through.

Fred had other ideas. She went to her apartment and gathered all the things Phil had left there over the months they were together. Then she got back in her car and went to Phil's apartment. He was surprised to see her. She had left his things in her car just in case she was wrong. She half hoped she would find him asleep. Instead she saw, as soon as he let her in, that he had been watching the Yankees. A half bottle of beer sat on the end table next to his recliner. "I thought you were tired," she said.

"I am tired.

"Not too tired to drink beer and watch the fucking baseball

game I see."

"Okay Fred. I guess it's just as well you're here. Here's the thing," Phil began.

"Don't bother. Why couldn't you just tell me you didn't like me anymore? Why did you make me come all the way over here? You could have told me weeks ago. Do you think I couldn't tell something was wrong you dickhead?"

"I wasn't sure until maybe a week ago, really. Anyway, I'm just too old for you or you're too young for me. You can do a lot better."

"Obviously; stay here a minute. I'll be right back." Fred ran down to her car, grabbed the cardboard box filled with Phil's things and brought it back up the stairs. Phil had gone back to his chair and turned off the television. He assumed they would talk things through for a while. He steeled himself to remain firm. This thing had to stop.

Fred walked into the room carrying the box. She was crying but the look on her face made it clear that no further conversation would be necessary. She flipped it upside down spilling the contents on the floor. Then she walked over to Phil and hit him as hard as she could with the box. "Drop dead," were her parting words. Phil sat there staring at the shirts, underwear, sunglasses and Veneto's order pads sprawled on the floor. While Fred was struggling to see the road through a flood of tears, Phil was feeling an overwhelming sense of relief, even joy that he was free. He actually clapped his hands like a kid who was thrilled because school was out and summer had finally arrived.

Of course he still had to work with Fred. He would see her tomorrow night. He knew she would make his life a living hell. And, as he drank another beer he couldn't erase the image of the hurt look on her face even as she was yelling at him. It was his fault. He had no business getting so involved with Fred knowing he wasn't interested in a long term relationship. Fred was a good woman. She deserved better. And then he was shamed by his own feelings of relief. He got out without so much as a scratch. He finished his beer in one long swallow. Then he got up to get another one. He slept in his recliner that night.

Every night at Veneto's was torture after that. Every employee knew about the breakup and no one took his side. Even some of the customers knew about it. A couple of them wouldn't sit with Phil anymore. Fred took every opportunity to make snide remarks about him; his looks, his intelligence, his skills as a waiter. To his credit, Phil bit his tongue. He was sure he would be fired but nothing happened. Then one night about two weeks later, just before his shift was starting, Jerry the owner pulled him aside and told Phil to meet him in his office. Phil figured that was it, he would be fired. Instead, he was surprised to learn that Jerry understood exactly what was happening. He liked Phil and he didn't want to lose him. He told Phil he was thinking about firing Fred because she was so disruptive. Phil suggested another tack. He asked Jerry to speak with Fred. He was sure, he said, that she would listen to Jerry if she knew she might lose her job. Jerry talked to Fred that night and it worked.

Fred stopped being openly hostile to Phil and everyone calmed down after that. Still Phil hated being there. Fred was barely civil. She made him wait for his customer's drinks. Sometimes she still made them weak or deliberately got the order wrong like making a vodka martini with gin. Phil found himself drinking her mistakes but it didn't help much.

CHAPTER 12

What kept Phil going was that he had a plan. Marianne kept her promise and met Phil for dinner to discuss the possibility of teaching in Newark. He picked a quiet spot that was known for its excellent seafood. She explained the alternate route program to him. She was very helpful. It turned out that as a college graduate, Phil could become a teacher. Like many states, New Jersey needed teachers especially in urban areas. The alternate route program was one way of attracting educated people who might want to get into teaching but didn't have the desire or wherewithal to go back to school and take all the course work plus having to deal with student teaching assignments. Marianne explained how he could probably get a job teaching at one of Newark's high schools that fall. North Ward, where she taught was always looking for teachers, she said. He would have to take courses at a local college throughout his first year as a teacher but in about ten months time, if he completed the course work, he would be a certified teacher. Even better, she said, he would earn more than $40,000 and have the summer off. And, just like any teacher, he could be tenured in three years. He would be eligible for pension too if he could manage to last ten years.

Phil found all of this appealing. He was tired of chasing management opportunities in health care. He had way too much gray hair for that. He had continued to respond to ads but interviews were rare. On the phone prospective employers seemed enthusiastic. Once he met them in person, however, their ardor soon melted away. He was confident it wasn't his interviewing skills. Rather, he suspected it was his age. One recruiter he had worked with more or less confirmed his suspicion when she suggested he dye his hair. Neither his experience nor his education helped. He wondered if he could be denied a teacher's job just by virtue of being fifty-eight.

He asked Marianne about this while they shared an appetizer. "Is my age a factor here?"

"Oh no. We have retired cops, retired firemen, you'd be surprised. Don't take this the wrong way but we're desperate for teachers."

"So, do you think I could be a teacher?"

"Why not?" Marianne said. "It isn't so much the teaching. With your background they would probably let you teach a business course or math or who knows, even English. The question is can you handle the kids?"

A waitress brought their entrees, with the usual warning about hot plates. Of course she wanted to know if she could get them anything else. Phil smiled and waved her off. He turned his attention back to Marianne.

"What do you mean, if I can handle the kids?"

"Phil, you have to understand something. It's not like it was when we were kids. It's not even like it was when our own children were in school. These kids are severe disciplinary problems. Most of them come from disadvantaged backgrounds. They don't want to be there."

Marianne went on to describe the typical student body in her school. First of all almost all of them were minorities, either black or Hispanic. Most of the kids, she said came from broken homes. Then she corrected that, saying it would be wrong to imply that many of them ever even lived in a traditional family situation. They were wounded animals, scarred by living without nurturing, no sense of nutrition beyond whatever was available at the moment and unable to visualize a better future.

"Well, they listen to you don't they?"

Marianne rolled her eyes and smiled. "I suppose but it's not easy. Keeping peace is my number one challenge. Teaching them something is a bonus. I have six more years before I can retire. I can't wait."

"It sounds like you think I shouldn't do it."

The waitress was back, wanting to know if everything was alright. "As soon as there's something important to tell you I'll come and get you," Phil said. The waitress wasn't sure how to take it but it must have dawned on her that she was being asked to leave them alone because they didn't see her again until she arrived to take their dessert order.

"I thought about that," she said. She reached for Phil's hand and held it in hers, the first warm gesture she had made that night.

Phil was pleased she was holding his hand. It took some convincing to get her to have dinner with him. When he called her to remind her about having dinner together, she pretended she didn't remember the conversation. She agreed to have dinner with him only when he practically begged her to tell him more about the teaching opportunity. But she insisted on meeting him at the restaurant. He settled for that. He had no choice.

"At first I thought it was a nutty idea. But really, you've always been a professional. You were an important executive at the hospital and all. Carmine said you made a six figure income. Being a waiter is no place for you. You can do better. Maybe teaching will be good for you."

"But you seem to be going out of your way to make it sound unattractive," Phil said.

She smiled. "Maybe it isn't as bad as it sounds. Every year I still feel like I reach at least one kid. That's what keeps bringing me back."

They sat quietly for a moment. "Contact the principal at North Ward High School if you're interested in a teaching job," Marianne said, "His name is Doctor Kelsey Griggs."

Phil thanked her profusely. He had never given serious thought to teaching before but the more he thought about it, he was confident that he could handle it.

The waitress brought coffee. They decided to skip dessert. Marianne mentioned Carmine. His name came up whenever they talked. She really missed him, she said. Phil agreed.

"By the way, speaking of Carmine," he said, "whatever happened to his second wife Paula?"

"Paula? Oh God. Let me think. You know, I think she lives in Florida now. Whatever made you think of her?

"I don't know," Phil said. He wasn't about to bring up the package again. He wanted the chance to rule out Paula as somebody Carmine might have given the money to. If she lived in Florida, that might rule her out right away. "So she lives in Florida. Doesn't everybody move to Florida once in their lives? What part of Florida?"

Marianne shook her head. "I'm not even sure she moved. I just remember a couple of years ago Carmine mentioned that he heard she was moving."

"Carmine had his problems with women," Phil said.

Phil dropped four twenties on the table and they got up to leave. He walked Marianne over to her car. "I went to their wedding but I can't remember her last name for anything."

Marianne stared into Phil's eyes for a moment, wanting to grasp what this sudden interest in Paula was about. "Her last name was Parnell. I'm beginning to wonder about you again Phil."

"What are you talking about?"

"I just think it odd that you would be so interested in one of Carmine's ex wives all of a sudden."

"I'm not that interested. I guess I'm still sorting out Carmine's passing and I wonder about his life. A lot of time passed between when we were kids hanging out on the street corner and when we got to be middle aged men. We didn't spend that much time together. Maybe that bothers me."

Marianne's expression softened. "Okay. But maybe now you can understand why I don't think you and I should pursue anything. At least not now," she said. "I probably shouldn't be saying this but under other circumstances I'm sure I would find you attractive. You're a nice man. The timing is all wrong. Do you see what I mean?"

Phil put his hands up to his chest, palms out. "Not really but I'm a patient man." He reached over and kissed her lightly on the lips. She allowed it.

"It isn't really a matter of patience. Anyway, if you're really interested in teaching, call Doctor Griggs."

Phil stood absolutely still as she got in her car and drove away.

Phil got an appointment with Doctor Kelsey Griggs the following Monday. He wore a suit for his meeting and took two copies of his resume with him. After careful consideration, he decided to leave his Yankee cap in the car.

"Doctor Griggs will see you now." The secretary behind the desk, a young black woman, was strikingly beautiful.

Phil walked into the principal's office. The doctor, a thin black man in his early forties, motioned Phil to a chair directly opposite the doctor's desk. The man wore a well trimmed beard. His head was shaved.

"I haven't been in a principal's office for a long time," Phil said.

The doctor stared at him as if he was trying to get a read on who he was dealing with. "So, you think you want to be a teacher." He had a soft voice, but there was no mistaking the power behind it. He articulated every word with great care.

Phil waited for more until he realized the doctor was waiting for him to speak. "Yes, Doctor Griggs. I want to be a teacher. The timing is right for me, I hope I'm right for North Ward High School and maybe I can do something here to make it right for a few kids."

"So you're not here because you've worn out your welcome in the industry you came from? You feel a missionary zeal all of a sudden. Is that it? Came here to save the black children of Newark?"

"No, I came here because I heard there are openings on your staff. I think I'm qualified and I'm willing to take the courses I need to take to get certified." Phil was beginning to wonder if this was going to work.

"I see. Ms. Cifelli, Marianne tells me you went to this high school."

"I did."

"So did I."

The two men spoke about their experiences at North Ward High, comparing notes about the way things had changed in the years between when Phil was a student and when Doctor Griggs was there. Griggs went on to talk about the alternate route program. He explained that a mentor would be assigned to him and that he, Phil would have to pay the mentor the sum of five hundred dollars out of his own pocket. He told Phil that based on his resume, if things worked out, he would probably wind up teaching American history. He noted that Phil had minored in the subject in college. Then he had Phil walk him through every job he ever had. He was a good interviewer. Phil thought the doctor must have been satisfied with what he heard because he suggested that Phil hang around for a while.

"Mister Falco, if you have the time, I want you to spend the next few hours observing. Here are the room numbers and the teachers' names. Come back to my office when you've finished and we'll talk."

Phil assured him that he had the time and went to look for the first classroom. He found a Mr. Farbman teaching American History in room 204. There were about twenty-five teenagers, most of them black, sitting in the room. All of them looked bored. Farbman was talking about the Civil War, focused on the battle of Bull Run. He asked questions about it addressing no one in particular. Each time he was met by blank stares. He would then answer his own question. It went on like that until he got up to write something on the blackboard. As soon as his head turned away from the students the room changed. The boys began to make guttural noises. Some of them tried to get the attention of a good looking girl sitting nearby. A few gave Farbman the finger, but given how late it was in the school year, that was old hat. Nobody really paid any attention. Farbman studiously ignored the noises. He simply wrote some dates and the key battles associated with them. Then he turned slowly toward them as if to give them time to regain their composure.

"I want each of you to pick one of these battles and write a one page paper about it. I would like to have them on my desk by Thursday."

Some of the students wrote down what they saw on the board. Others looked out the window or down at their desks. Still others, boys and girls, smiled so broadly Phil expected them to laugh.

That was how it went in every class but one. The last classroom Phil walked into was occupied by a well built black man. He had the students sitting around him, their desks moved into a semi-circle. Phil checked his list. This was a math class being taught by a Mr. Cowens. When Phil entered the room, Mr. Cowens said, "Identify yourself sir."

"I'm Phil Falco. Doctor Griggs sent me here to observe."

"Welcome. We are discussing Isosceles triangles."

Phil observed a very obedient class. He couldn't tell whether these kids were simply afraid of this guy or they were acting out of respect.

When the bell rang, Erik Cowens walked over to him and shook his hand. He was a middle aged man, in his early fifties Phil thought, with milk chocolate skin color. Like Doctor Griggs, his head was shaved. He looked every bit as tough as his voice made him sound. Thinking of giving this a go, huh?"

"I am. Tell me something. Why do the kids in your class behave so well? They even looked like they were paying attention."

"First of all, it's an honors class. Second I take no shit from any of them and they know it."

"What does that mean?"

"It means if they give me trouble I might not be able to restrain myself. I might find it necessary to take care of business outside the confines of this school. I'm a retired detective. They figure it won't help them to report me to the police. I am the police."

"They buy that?"

"So far," Cowens said, laughing.

Phil made his way back to Doctor Griggs' office. He hoped he might run into Marianne but she was nowhere in sight. The receptionist smiled when she saw him come through the door of the principal's outer office.

"You still here?"

"Well, I finished my rounds and I think Doctor Griggs wants to see me."

"Oh I know that. Not too many people come back though. One look at our so called student body and they run, and I do mean run to their cars."

Phil laughed. "Still here."

Doctor Griggs was waiting for him. "Marianne said you wouldn't wilt. I have a position available teaching American history to juniors and seniors. Are you interested?"

"I am."

"Okay, pending a background check it's yours. See Keisha and she'll get you an application to complete. Now the choice is yours but Marianne has already offered to be your mentor."

"That will be fine," Phil said.

"I thought so." Doctor Kelsey Griggs smiled for the first time.

Now that he knew what he was going to do, Phil began to relax for the first time in more than a year. He called his daughter Lisa a couple of times but she wasn't home. He left messages but Lisa never returned his calls. Not sure of what to make of it, and uncertain of what to do about it, he let it go. He fell into a regular routine of studying in the morning and working at Veneto's in the evening. Doctor Griggs had given him two text books to read and course outlines for American History I and II. He filled his nights after work watching the tail end of baseball games. After so many years in Florida he was really enjoying the chance to follow the Yankees and the Mets so closely again.

He called Marianne a few times just to chat. She was cordial but she never gave him an opening that might encourage him to ask her out again. He also found Paula Parnell. It had been easier than he expected. Her name was listed in the white pages. She lived in Nutley, just one town over from his apartment in Bloomfield. He had been about to call Angela Dearborn to see if she could give him a lead but then he decided to check the phone book first. He was relieved to find her name listed.

The thought of calling Angela made him nervous. She had called him once after their meeting and left a very suggestive message. He chose to ignore it but he was tempted to run down to Beachwood and see her again. Her connection to Marianne, however tenuous it was, gave him pause. He decided not to risk it.

Phil waited a few days trying to decide how to approach Paula. They had met at the wedding of course. In fact, when he married Tracy, Carmine was married to Paula so she had attended his wedding too.

Finally, without having the slightest notion of what he should say, he picked up the phone and called her. He heard a man's voice.

"Hello."

Momentarily Phil considered hanging up but he realized his name would show up on caller ID. Almost everyone had the service and Paula would probably remember the name.

"Hello. My name is Phil Falco. I was wondering if I could speak with Paula. I'm an old friend of hers and her former husband, Carmine."

"Paula's not here."

"I see. Are you her husband?"

"Her boyfriend. What's this about?"

"Carmine died recently. I'm just contacting some of the people who were close to him."

"What for?"

Phil could see this was going nowhere. "I'll tell you what. If you would please tell her I called I would appreciate it."

"I'll tell her."

Phil wasn't surprised when he didn't hear from Paula. After a week went by he decided to call her again from the restaurant. This time she answered the phone. Phil acted as though it was the first time he called.

"Oh sure, I remember you. Didn't I go to your wedding? How is your wife doing?"

"We're divorced. I live in New Jersey now."

"I'm sorry to hear that. That you're divorced I mean."

"Thank you. Paula the reason I called was to ask if you would meet me to talk a little about Carmine. I know you and he had a difficult breakup. Just the same I would appreciate a little of your time."

"That was a difficult time in my life. I'm not sure I'm comfortable revisiting that."

"I understand and I'm not trying to intrude. I may be way off base here but I'm under the impression that you and Carmine stayed in touch after your divorce."

"That's interesting. Where did you get that impression?"

"From Carmine and a friend of his." As soon as Phil said that he knew he made a mistake. Just then one of the waiters walked up to him, announcing in a loud voice that his party sitting at table A-4 was looking for him. Paula overheard the remark.

"Are you at work Phil?"

"Yes."

"Please don't tell me you're working at Veneto's." Her tone could not have been more condescending. "Did you take Carmine's place?"

"Temporarily, yes." He was grateful for the diversion. "I start a teaching job in the fall."

"Will you be working with Carmine's sister - what's her name-by any chance?"

Again Phil answered in the affirmative.

"How cozy. So Phil, did this so-called friend shed any light on how or why Carmine and I might have remained in contact?"

"Not really. Listen, if it's too much of an imposition we don't have to meet. The thing is that there are a few unanswered questions about Carmine's last days. If you were in touch with him, you might be able to ease my mind."

"How could I do that?"

"I don't know. Maybe you can't but I won't know that until we talk."

"Isn't that what we're doing now?" Paula asked.

Phil's patience was wearing thin. "Will you meet with me Paula?"

"This is certainly mysterious. How can I refuse?"

They agreed to meet in Paula's real estate office the following Friday morning at 9:30.

On what was supposed to be his next to last night as a waiter at Veneto's, a very busy Thursday night for the restaurant, Dennis Florio walked back into Phil's life. To be precise, the Mafia don walked into the restaurant to have dinner. Phil was in the kitchen placing an order when Florio walked in. Even in the kitchen though, he became aware that somebody important had walked into the restaurant. There was a discernable buzz coming from the dining room just like the night the actor, Joe Pesci came to Veneto's.

Before he could even walk to the door and look through the little windows into the dining room to see who it was, one of the busboys busted into the kitchen and said, "The Godfather is here."

"And that would be?" Phil asked.

"Dennis Florio," the busboy said, pleased with himself that he was in a position to instruct the older man about the Mafia boss.

Phil listened patiently while the kid explained who Florio was. He knew he could crush the kid's moment simply by informing him that he not only knew Florio, but they had been friends when they were kids. When the young man finished, Phil simply nodded. He was annoyed by the kid's excitement. He hated the fact that otherwise good Italian American citizens who would have hated such a criminal on sight if he was Irish, Russian or God forbid, black, felt a certain pride in one of their own. It wasn't that he didn't understand the convoluted logic. After all he had grown up in the Italian American culture. He understood that on some level, idealizing the guys in the Mafia was an acknowledgement that there were people with the strength and courage to twist, bend and break society's rules. He understood fully how it was easy to romanticize the life; the idea of a secret society with a strict code of honor that looked out for its own extended family. That the men involved in organized crime lived lives filled with brutality and constant fear of betrayal or the shame of being arrested, was somehow overlooked. To say you knew a guy who was connected was significant. In some circles, it added to your own reputation as a man deserving of respect.

Standing in the kitchen, dreading the inevitable scene when Florio spotted him, it occurred to Phil that these thoughts were not long held beliefs. How could he afford to be critical of the busboy and all those people sitting in the restaurant when less than a year ago he contemplated, however fleetingly, having that hoodlum Bucco give Tracy's boyfriend a beating? No, it had taken personal experience to really grasp the stupidity of honoring these animals. He was angry that he had become a victim of one of these criminals, a guy who had been a friend of his to boot.

Phil took a deep breath and stepped out onto the dining room floor. Florio was seated at another waiter's table, a stroke of good luck. Bucco and another guy were sitting with Florio. Bucco saw him first. He tapped Florio's arm and said something. Florio looked up and called out. "Phil! Phil Falco!"

Phil walked over to Florio's table. "Dennis. You're looking well." He ignored Bucco.

Of course Bucco couldn't let that pass. "You don't remember me Phil?"

"I remember you."

"You work here?" Florio asked.

"Tomorrow is my last night. I start a teaching job at North Ward high in a couple of weeks."

"No shit. Our alma mater huh?" Florio motioned the hostess over. "I hate to bother you honey but can we switch tables? This guy is an old friend of mine."

"Oh that won't be necessary Mister Florio. Phil can serve you right at this table. Okay Phil?"

"Of course." Phil turned to Florio and said, "We're out of everything but escarole and beans."

Florio laughed. "Why don't you eat with us?"

"Thanks, but it's too busy. My station is full."

The hostess, still hovering in the background was ready to help again. "I can take your tables Phil." She touched his arm and in a stage whisper added, "I'll make sure you get the tips."

Florio pulled back the chair next to his and Phil sat down. He removed his bowtie and comber bun and handed them to the hostess. The guy sitting across from him was introduced only as Brains. Brains never said a word during the conversation that ensued. The two men talked about old times. Florio behaved just like he did months ago in his suite at the Brandford Hotel and Casino. He never mentioned the money or the status of the supposed investment Phil had made. Of course Phil never brought it up either. He hated the fact that he was stuck eating dinner with Florio again. At least Bucco managed to keep quiet too. His body language made it clear though that he wished Phil would disappear.

By the time the dinner plates were cleared, the two men were out of old stories about the neighborhood and playing ball together in high school. Phil figured he was about done with these jerks and could finish out the night. He had already decided he wouldn't work the next night. He would turn in his order book as soon as the hostess gave him his tip money, which he planned to take. He was sure she would offer it, confident that he would refuse to accept the money. She was in for a surprise. It would be Phil's way of paying her back for not minding her own business.

But it turned out his dinner with Florio wasn't quite finished. When the waiter asked who wanted dessert, Florio pointed to his two cronies and said, "These two don't want any. They have to get going." As the men stood up to go he added, "Pick me up in half an hour."

When the two men were alone, Florio's tone became serious. "I heard you went to see Angie Dearborn."

"That's right." Phil was wary. He couldn't process where this was coming from or where it might be going fast enough to come up with a clever response.

"I also hear you asked her about the money." Florio squeezed Phil's arm to emphasize the point he was about to make. "Putting other people's business on the street is the kind of mistake that can have dire consequences. Capece?"

Phil shook his head in disgust. Suddenly his mind was clear. "Do you have any idea of what you did to me? Do you think I would be working here or taking a job babysitting misfits if I had my money? We go back a long way. We were friends once."

"We're still friends," Florio interrupted him.

"No we're not. You set fire to my apartment. Remember? I'm a victim who got kicked around just because you could do it. You come in here and act like we're friends but I'm out half a million dollars. Why is that?"

"That is a different topic. In any case you're an investor in a legitimate business. You signed papers to that effect. Remember?

And for the record, I didn't set fire to your apartment. You think you're better than me but you're not. Maybe you had better luck than I did when we were kids. We came from the same streets. And don't think I don't remember that you were there the night we stole that car."

Phil looked at his hands, trying his best not to let them betray what he was thinking. He had done his best over the years to forget that night. Stealing a car wasn't the worst thing they did that night. They had driven the car up to Montclair and then picked a fight with a couple of kids from a rival high school just for something to do. One of the boys was seriously injured. Phil had done his part that night, hitting the boy in the back of the head with a beer bottle. It was the worst night of his life. The kid recovered and neither Phil nor his friends ever got what was coming to them. The police pulled them over a couple of miles from the incident and took them in for questioning. Florio's well connected father got them off the hook. But after that night, Phil never ran around with Florio again.

"That was a long time ago Dennis."

"It was. Now I don't know why you're talking to Angie but I'm telling you for your own good, let it go."

The two men sat in silence for a moment, each taking a sip of their coffee. "How do you know Angela Dearborn?" Phil asked.

"We used to go out, a long time ago. She didn't tell you?"

"That would be putting your business on the street wouldn't it?"

"You know, you're still a wise guy. You should have gone into business with me when I asked you back in the day. You wouldn't be working for tips now if you went in with me. You're too smart for this," he said waving his hand.

"You were selling dope in the school yard. I guess I didn't see the long term growth opportunities."

Florio stared long and hard into Phil's eyes. "I always thought you were the one who told on me. I could have done time if I didn't have the right connections."

"Time out Dennis. Is that what this was all about? You think I ratted you out? With all due respect, you're crazy. First of all I wouldn't have done that back then. In any case you didn't exactly try to hide what you were doing. Everybody in the school knew if they wanted pot Dennis was the guy to see. It could have been anybody. Why did you think it was me?"

"I got a tip."

"You were lied to. It wasn't me.

Florio laughed. "I wish I knew who did it. Even after all these years I would still kick his ass."

There was another silence. Then, "Stay away from Angie."

Now it was Phil's turn to laugh. "Actually, I didn't need you to tell me that. I just figured she might know something."

"You still think you're gonna find that money? You're the crazy one. Believe me pal, it's long gone. I'll give you very short odds if you didn't take it the cops got it." Florio paused for emphasis. "The people in New York don't know nothing about missing money. Keep your mouth shut. Let it go for your own sake. Capece?"

Phil nodded but didn't say anything.

The two men had cheese cake and espresso with a shot of anisette. Ten minutes later, Bucco walked back into the restaurant and parked himself at the bar.

"No hard feelings Phil. And remember, if you ever need something I'll take care of it. We're still friends." With that Florio got up and headed for the door.

CHAPTER 13

Paula Parnell left Phil Falco waiting in her office for forty-five minutes on the morning they agreed to meet. Phil sat patiently in a leather wingback chair and drank coffee. While he waited for Paula, Phil pondered his dinner with Dennis Florio. As much as he hated to admit it, the guy had a certain charisma. He could be very charming when he was in the mood or it suited his needs. He could also display a frightening malevolence when that suited his needs. He had no doubt that if he ever found the missing money, Florio would take that too if he found out about it. He would have to be very careful.

Phil smiled to himself as he thought about the looks on the faces of his co-workers after Florio left the restaurant. They all wanted to know how he knew the big man and Phil obliged but said only that they played ball together as kids. When the busboy pressed him for details, Phil refused, saying only that knowing a criminal was simply a fact, not an accomplishment.

Just as he was finishing his third cup of coffee, he saw Paula pull up in her Lincoln Navigator. She walked in and saw Phil, recognizing him immediately. Phil wasn't sure he would have known who Paula was. He hadn't seen her in years. One thing was certain: She was a lot better looking than either Angela or Fred. She was even better looking than Marianne.

"I remember you. Handsome as ever I see."

"You must have me confused with somebody else," Phil said looking around the room as if she could actually be speaking to another man.

"No, I remember you. You're Phil. You're good looking like Carmine was without his charm."

"That's flattering."

"Hasn't anybody told you Phil? Charm is overrated. Come on into my office. I have about fifteen minutes."

Phil followed Paula into her office. He asked her how business was. They quickly filled each other in on what had happened to them since they saw each other last. Phil talked about his divorce, how he was fired from the hospital and his plans to begin a teaching job.

Paula said that she had married Carmine only six months after a bad breakup. She enjoyed his company and, contrary to Angela's opinion, he was a great lover. The problems began when Carmine became obsessed, as she put it, with casino gambling. What made it particularly bad was that she got the bug too. Their marriage lasted just five years. In spite of some memorable times, great shows at the casinos, expensive wines and gourmet dinners, they never achieved the high roller status they coveted. Meanwhile, their debts were piling up. They had reached the point where they were living week to week. She decided she had had enough when Carmine's car was repossessed.

"That was a wakeup call," she said. "After that I got myself into a rehab program and filed for divorce. Then I went to real estate school and as you can see, everything worked out, at least for me it did."

"How about Carmine?"

"He was your friend. I assume you would know. I didn't see him much after the divorce."

The phone rang. Paula took the call. It sounded like a nervous buyer. Paula calmed the buyer down, her tone friendly but firm. She winked at Phil while she listened to the buyer's concerns. Phil used the time to think things over. He had been too direct with Angela. He realized now he should have taken more time with her. He might have learned about her relationship with Florio had he not been in such a hurry. He didn't want to make the same mistake twice. Paula put the phone down and turned her attention back to

Phil.

"Do you think you will enjoy teaching?" She asked, changing the subject.

"I hope so. I think I might enjoy the challenge. And, it beats the hell out of what I was doing. Waiting tables was hard on my legs and feet."

"Have you considered real estate? You would make more money and I think it's fair to say you'll meet some very interesting people."

"Like you?" Phil said with a smile on his face.

Paula laughed. "You don't think I'm interesting?"

Phil saw an opening. "I'm afraid I would need more time to answer that and my fifteen minutes is about up."

Paula tapped a pen on her desk contemplating something. "I'm sorry I don't have more time to answer your questions about Carmine but I do have to get to a closing. Think about real estate as an alternative, Phil. I'll bet you would like it."

"I'll do that." Phil got up to leave. She stood up with him and they shook hands.

"Call me if you want to talk more about Carmine."

Summer was almost over. Labor Day was only a week away. Phil spent a few days at the Jersey shore in a rental condo a couple of blocks from the beach. He enjoyed the quiet time. He needed time to clear his head. Things were still moving fast; another new job, the breakup with Fred and the seemingly unsolvable mystery of the money Carmine was carrying. He knew he would see Paula Parnell again but already he doubted that Carmine gave the package to her.

He wanted to stay at the beach longer so he could have more time to relax but he was still watching his money carefully. It didn't take long after he left Veneto's for his cash to dwindle. He had put enough aside to allow him to meet expenses for a few weeks without dipping into his savings account but beyond that he would be forced to withdraw funds during September until he got his first paycheck as a teacher. And, he would have to use savings to cover that month's alimony check to Arlene. He was actually already a week behind in making his alimony payment.

In fact, when he got back to his apartment, his time at the beach at an end, Arlene called him. He expected her to harass him about not receiving her check. Instead, it was about Lisa. This time she didn't dance around the issues. She was direct when she told him about Lisa's job. She didn't know that Phil already had a good idea of what was going on or that he believed that he had slowed things down considerably before he left LA. In any case he was dead wrong about that. Riley Rivers had given some thought to what Phil had said. But when there was no further word from Lisa's old man, no visits or even phone calls he felt safe. Rivers figured the old man was bluffing. Then, after he smacked Lisa around, Rivers figured that maybe Lisa would have called her father. She didn't. Just to test her, he hit her again a couple of weeks later. Not as hard this time, but enough to raise a nice welt on her cheek. Once again nothing happened.

So, he made plans to have her act again in one of his films, this time as a full fledged performer. He was practiced in turning out girls like Lisa. He knew from experience that once they submitted to an occasional beating and didn't leave or retaliate, they would do what he wanted. Lisa, still filled with naïve dreams of becoming an actress, was happy about her opportunity to act in a movie. Riley treated her especially nice for the whole week leading up to the shoot. Then he ran into some cash flow problems and he had to delay the start of the movie another couple of weeks. Since Lisa was getting on his nerves, he sent her to Phoenix to visit with her mother. Rivers never met Lisa's mother but he wasn't worried about her either. According to Lisa the woman was so self-absorbed she would barely notice the changes in Lisa's looks or attitude. But Arlene did notice and it upset her. As soon as Arlene saw her daughter, she called Phil.

"Phil, Lisa's in trouble." Not even hello. She got right to it.

"What do you mean she's in trouble, Arlene?"

"Phil have you seen her? She looks like a tramp."

"I saw her about three months ago. Maybe she dressed different when I saw her."

"It's not only the way she's dressed it's her hair, her makeup and all those god awful earrings."

"Phil was silent for a moment. He didn't know what to do. "She's over twenty-one Arlene. What can we do?"

"That's just like you Phil. You measure your obligations in time or money. The girl needs help. You're her father. Do something."

"And you're her mother. What do you plan to do?"

"Fly out here and we'll do it together. This is serious. Please don't ignore me this time."

"I can't fly out there. I'm about to start a new job. What has she told you?"

Arlene took a drag on her cigarette. Her words were very deliberate. "Lisa is making a movie. She said it starts next week. Do you know what kind of movie she's making?"

"I can guess. Has she told you that?"

"Not in so many words."

"How long is she staying with you?"

"A week. She leaves Monday afternoon, Labor Day. Can you come out here?"

"Maybe. I'll get back to you. I might have another idea."

Lisa had always been a quiet kid who listened to her parents. Even after the divorce she never acted out, behaved wildly, drank too much or experimented with drugs. Of course she had become manipulative in her relationship with them, often playing one off against the other to get what she wanted. For Phil, it usually meant giving her extra spending money or paying for a trip during spring break while she was in college. Nothing major, just the post divorce guilt trip she laid on them. By taking her mother's side in the divorce, Lisa soon realized that her father was particularly vulnerable to her requests for money. She would tell him she needed clothes or spending money; whatever it was he would comply.

Still, when she graduated from college, Phil felt vindicated. He had managed to reshape his life without destroying his daughter's. Only now, their daughter was in real trouble. She was headed down a destructive path and there might not be any way to turn back.

He didn't sleep well that night. He tried studying his instructor's copy of the American history text he would soon be using, but he couldn't concentrate. The next morning he dragged himself out of bed and took a long shower. By the time he was dressed and groomed he had made up his mind. He would fly to Phoenix that day if he could and see for himself what was going on with Lisa. Before he went to plan B he owed it to himself to see if he could fix things. Money was really tight so he took a deep breath and called Arlene.

"Arlene, its Phil, I'm coming out there today but I have a problem."

"I'm glad you're coming. What is it?"

"I don't have the money. Can I give you half the alimony this month and catch up next month?"

There was a long silence as Arlene thought it over. "Okay, pay me half and we'll call it even this one time."

"Thank you," Phil said, hardly believing what he heard. Arlene must be really worried he thought.

Even with the break Arlene was giving him, he had to get lucky to find an affordable flight. He managed to find one for just under three hundred dollars through a discount travel service on the Web. He arrived in Phoenix in time for dinner. Arlene and Lisa met him at the airport. One look at his daughter and he knew he had made the right decision. She was wearing a red halter top and white, skin tight jean shorts. Standing in three inch high heeled shoes and wearing more makeup and jewelry than he had ever seen on her before, he was stunned by her appearance. A pale tattoo of what appeared to be a bleeding rose rested on the base of her lower back, plainly visible.

"Hi Daddy. How was your trip? Did you come all the way out here to save me?"

Arlene rolled her eyes, an unintentionally comical effort. It wasn't hard to see the panic in the woman's eyes.

"Something like that," Phil said, giving her a quick hug.

"Isn't it a little late for that?" Lisa asked.

"Not too late I hope," he said. "Should we get dinner somewhere?"

"I made us something. I just have to warm it up when we get home," Arlene said.

Phil took a good look at Arlene. She had been a pretty girl when she was young. Time had not been kind to her. Yet, it was obvious that something was different about her. Then he saw it. She had lost weight and colored her hair. Maybe it didn't make her pretty again but she certainly looked a lot better than the last time he saw her.

"You cooked something? That was nice of you. Let's go," Phil said. He was grateful to her for saving him the expense of dinner out. As they walked to the car he found himself wondering what Arlene saw when she looked at him. Did he look old and tired? Did the fear he felt about the future show on his face?

They had a quiet dinner together. Phil figured he and Arlene would talk first and then decide how to approach Lisa. For her part, Lisa seemed happy to have the three of them together again. She didn't say much during dinner but at one point she took each parent's hand and said, "I never thought I would see us together at the same table again."

Arlene and Phil smiled but they did so separately, not looking into each other's eyes. There was nothing to see.

The next morning Phil was awakened by the sound of activity

in the kitchen. He had slept on the living room couch which was close enough to the kitchen for him to smell coffee brewing. His thoughts turned immediately to his conversation with Arlene the night before. They agreed to ask Lisa to leave California and move permanently to either Phoenix or New Jersey. She could live rent free until she found herself. And, they would buy her a car to get around in. Maybe she could trade the car she was driving for a new one.

While they were discussing this Phil was making plans to go back to work on weekends at Veneto's. That was the only way he could possibly make this work. But then Arlene had another surprise. It turned out she had met someone and they were thinking seriously of getting married. Phil would be off the hook for alimony. Phil's outlook brightened considerably upon hearing the news. In fact after the news sunk in, he laughed.

"What are you laughing at?" Arlene asked.

Phil apologized. "Funny thing is, Arlene I'm laughing at my own reaction. I'm happy for you really. And, to be honest, not paying alimony would make a tremendous difference to me financially."

"And that's funny?"

"No. What's funny is that when you told me you were getting married again I was upset for a moment. I guess on some level every guy thinks a woman who really knows him can never replace him. That's why I was laughing."

"You are an idiot."

Their proposal to Lisa was met with anger and refusal. She let them know immediately that they were not in a position to decide things for her. Arlene and Phil tried to reason with her. Phil felt so much better about his financial future he even offered to sweeten the deal. He would pay for a month at the Jersey shore whether Lisa chose Phoenix or New Jersey. But Lisa was adamant. She was a Californian now and she was going places.

Arlene did her best to call upon her daughter's sense of decency.

How, she wanted to know could Lisa even imagine herself involved with such filth?

But Lisa held her ground. Times were different, she said. She pointed out that both her parents slept with other people even when they were married to each other. As far as she was concerned filming an explicit love scene was no different.

When Phil pointed out to his daughter that they had not done what they did for money, Lisa simply pointed out that she wasn't doing it for the money. She saw an opportunity to be somebody and she was going to grab it, she said.

Phil and Arlene were bewildered by their daughter's attitude. Certainly they had done their best to raise her to be a good person who had been taught and shared conventional views. The young woman that stood before them was a stranger.

Later, Arlene drove Phil to the airport. Both were dejected, feeling the failure that parents feel when a child goes astray.

"Where, exactly, did we go wrong?" Phil said.

"I don't know. That is not our Lisa," Arlene said.

"It's that boyfriend of hers. That guy Rivers is the problem."

"Maybe so but I can't help wondering if she's just rebelling. You know as well as I do she was always a late bloomer. She never really had a chance to be a rebel. You left when she was seventeen and she became my support system. This is a delayed reaction. I'm sure of it."

"Are you saying she won't go through with it?" he asked.

Until our chat this morning I would have said that. Now I just don't know." Arlene was crying.

"We have to do something," Phil said, "It's not like we caught her smoking. This is deadly. Her life will be ruined."

"I don't know what to do," Arlene said.

Both were quiet for a while. As they pulled up to the curb next to the departing flights area, Phil spoke. "Leave it to me. I have an idea."

"What is it?"

"Trust me. Its better you don't know anything about this."

Phil now knew exactly what he wanted to do. There would be no use talking to Lisa. Obviously she now felt she had something to prove. Maybe Arlene was right; that Lisa was belatedly going through a teenaged rebellion at twenty-five. Regardless, they couldn't afford to take that chance. Something had to be done. They were desperate. His first thought was to pick up the phone and call Dennis Florio. He was sure that Florio could use his influence to rid Lisa of the likes of Riley Rivers. Maybe if Riley was out of the picture, he and Arlene could talk some sense into their daughter.

Phil knew he had to act quickly to save his daughter. His flight home was agony. The four and a half hour flight seemed endless. He imagined the conversation he would have with Florio over and over again. He had no illusions about the man. He would agree to do the favor, no doubt. But what would he want in return? Sure the half million Florio stole from him should be more than enough for several favors like the one Phil would ask. But men like Dennis Florio never saw things the way other men did. If he wanted more, Phil would have to oblige.

He arrived at Newark Airport in the waning hours of Labor Day. He decided to go home and try to get some sleep. He would call Florio the next morning. By the time he reached his apartment he was exhausted. All he wanted to do was wash his face, brush his teeth and then collapse on his bed. He walked into the kitchen to get a glass of water. The message light on his phone was lit. He pressed the button. There were three messages. The first was from Fred, asking him to give her a call if he didn't have plans for Labor Day. Next was a call from Paula Parnell. That was a surprise. Her message was brief. All it said was call me, more of a command than a request. The last message was from Marianne Cifelli. She said she was just calling to wish Phil luck in his new job. She said she was looking forward to working with him and she was glad they would get to see each other more often.

It was too late to return any of the calls. Anyway, he had to get some sleep.

CHAPTER 14

On his first day at North Ward High, Phil stood in front of his first class looking stern. He was tall. He had that going for him. Earlier that morning Marianne had warned him to be tough right from the beginning. She said it would go down hill from there. It was useless to try to befriend the students. They would interpret that as weakness and take full advantage.

Twenty-nine students stared back at him waiting for him to make the first chess move of a game that would last ten months. He took a deep breath and spoke. "This is American history for juniors. By the end of this school year you will know some things about this country's history that most people your age don't know. Some of you can use that knowledge to make money if you're smart."

His words were met with a few laughs and some mocking ooohs and aahhs.

He continued on. "I'm new at this but I know the rules. In the past you probably got passing grades from teachers who were just glad to get rid of you. Just so we understand each other, I'll flunk you if you don't do the work. I don't care if you quit school or have to go to summer school. I don't care if you can't play football. Do the work or I'll give you an F." He paused for effect. "Now we can have a good time learning this stuff. It's up to you. We're not going to rush through anything. We start with the early settlers and by the end of the school year we will be through the Civil War. We have a lot of ground to cover. For today, I just want to know who you are. I'm going to go around the room. Say your name and anything else you want to tell me."

The kids looked at each other in disbelief. Was this guy for real? The first kid was a tall black kid, just as tall as Phil. He didn't bother to stand. "My name is mother fucker and I'll fuck you up if you don't give me a good mark."

Phil walked over to him. Standing in front of him, close to his desk, he said, "If you don't do the work, including telling me your name, I will give you an F. Now I'm sure you heard me. I'm not afraid of you or anybody else here. What is your name?" Phil made a point of appearing to read his class roster to verify the kid was telling the truth.

The kid sat there, a sullen look on his face. Finally he mumbled his name. "Rashid Marbury."

"Thank you Mister Marbury. Next."

Phil won round one but he had no illusions about how hard this was going to be. At the end of his first day, after going through essentially the same routine with three classes of third year students, he was bone tired. He was sitting at his desk taking care of a few administrative details when Marianne walked in.

"How did it go?"

"All things considered, not bad." Phil had been too nervous that morning when they met to notice how nice Marianne looked. She had on a pale blue dress and low heels that showed off her pretty legs. She looked younger than her years and while Phil admired her youthful looks, he couldn't help wondering if he looked considerably older.

"Well the first day is often the hardest but remember not to let your guard down. Any special problems I can help you with?" she asked.

"No. I do have a question about one of these forms though."

Marianne explained how to fill out the form. They left the classroom together to head over to the administrative office to drop off paperwork.

"Is there anything else on your mind Phil? Are you having second thoughts?" Marianne asked out in the parking lot.

"Plenty," Phil said, smiling. "But I have a problem with my

daughter that's serious. I'm worried."

"I see. I don't want to pry. Is there anything I can do to help?"

Phil took a deep breath. He decided to tell Marianne the story. "Can we get a cup of coffee?"

"Sure. Why don't you follow me? There's a great bakery on Bloomfield Avenue that serves fresh coffee all day long."

Phil wondered about his decision to tell Marianne about Lisa's situation. Was he using it as an excuse to ask her to have coffee? Maybe he was, but he also hoped that maybe Marianne could offer some insight that might be helpful. On the way to the bakery instead of focusing on Lisa and what he should tell Marianne about her, he found himself thinking of a clever way to ask her out again. He came up empty. He thought back to her phone message wishing him good luck on his new job. He was probably imagining things but to him the tone of her voice seemed inviting. He would have to take his chances and then take his lumps if she said no. They pulled into the parking lot and found spaces right next to each other.

Once inside, Phil ordered coffee and an enormous cream puff. Marianne stuck to coffee.

"Hungry Phil?" Marianne asked, eying the cream puff.

"What can I say? I skipped lunch today. You want some?"

"Thanks but no. Too close to dinner. In fact I can't stay long. I have to get home and start supper for Rick."

"How's he doing?" Phil asked just to be polite.

"Okay. I wish I could get him to go back to school," Marianne shrugged. She was resigned to the fact that her son would probably never go back to school. He had left college after one year.

"They find a thousand ways to break your heart," Phil said. He took a bite of his cream puff and spilled a large gob of cream on his shirt. They both laughed and Marianne reached over with a napkin to help him wipe it off.

"So what's going on with your daughter?"

Phil explained the problem with Lisa's boyfriend Riley Rivers but he offered no details about Rivers' line of work or Lisa's role in it. Rather, he concentrated on Lisa's attitude, telling Marianne how belligerent she had been. He was embarrassed by Lisa's behavior and concerned about what Marianne might think if she knew what Lisa was really doing.

They chatted for a few minutes about the way children, even after they become adults still have a critical hold on the lives of their parents. Marianne didn't offer any specific suggestions. She merely said that young women sometimes got involved with men who were all wrong for them. More often than not she said, they would lose interest once they realized how little such men could really offer beyond being entertaining. As she put it, situations like Lisa's often had a way of working themselves out on their own given a little time.

Phil acknowledged the wisdom of Marianne's words. Then, he abruptly changed the subject. "When are you going to go out with me again?" Phil asked. So much for a clever strategy he thought.

"I thought we had an understanding about that."

"I'm operating on instinct. I think we could have a good time together." She stared at Phil for a moment, not saying anything. "Anyway, you helped me find a job. Let me buy you dinner just to say thank you."

Marianne laughed. "I know I'm going to regret this. When do you want to go out?"

"How about Friday or Saturday night?"

"I can't Friday but believe it or not, I'm free Saturday night," she said, laughing again. "What are we doing?"

"Whatever you like. Really, what would you like to do?" Phil asked.

"How about dinner at Veneto's? We can celebrate your first week on the job as a history teacher," Marianne said.

Phil hadn't counted on that. Every instinct told him that Fred would behave badly if she saw them walk into Veneto's together. "I have a better idea. Let's go to New York. We can enjoy what's left of Little Italy.

"It's a deal. By the end of the school year you probably won't even be speaking to me. I'd better take advantage of this offer now."

Five minutes after he got back in his car, Phil's cell phone rang. It was Dennis Florio.

"Hey, paisan. You called me?"

"Dennis, is that you? Yeah, I called. Are you in New Jersey by any chance?"

"Nah, I'm in Orlando. You need something?"

"The next time you're in Jersey I thought maybe we could have dinner again."

Florio was impressed. His friend was catching on. Obviously he wanted something but knew enough not to ask on the phone. "I'm flying up there Saturday afternoon. How about Saturday night?"

"Is there any other night we could do it?" Phil hated the idea of canceling his date with Marianne.

"Not really," Florio answered.

"Okay then, we'll meet Saturday night. Where do you want to meet?"

"Meet me at nine o'clock at Falzone's. You remember the place right?"

Phil remembered. "I'll be there. Thanks."

Phil disconnected the call and put his phone down. He was thoroughly dejected now. He would have to come up with an excuse for Marianne. After trying so hard to work up the courage to ask her out again, he would now have to tell her he couldn't see her. He tried to come up with a suitable explanation the entire ride home. Nothing. This was infinitely worse than finding a clever way to ask her out, he decided.

That week passed quickly. Phil was completely engrossed in what he was doing. By Friday morning it was apparent to him that he would have to read to his students. Most of them had marginal reading skills. He suspected that a few of them were capable of reading the material but were afraid to appear smart in front of their peers.

He did his best to try to make it interesting for the kids. He stopped frequently to ask questions, mostly to see if they understood what he was telling them. The boys were particularly difficult. Not only were they not interested in learning, the leaders seemed determined to make sure that no one else learned anything. One boy in the class, a smallish Hispanic kid seemed interested in the origins of the early explorers. He actually raised his hand to ask a question.

"Yo, Mister Falco. Over here. Them names you saying are they Puerto Rican?"

"They are Spanish explorers from Spain," Phil said.

"Did they speak Spanish man?" the kid wanted to know.

Before Phil could answer, one of the black kids said, "They're Spics just like you Julio." The boy's name wasn't Julio but the blacks called all the Hispanic boys Julio. In return they called the black boys Homie.

Phil spoke up. "The Spanish explorers spoke Spanish and the English explorers spoke English. Why do you ask?"

But the Hispanic boy was cowed, not so much by the black boy's words but his tone. It contained an unmistakable warning. Phil wondered if there was a way to segregate the kids who wanted to learn from the rest.

By the end of the week he found himself wondering what he had gotten into. He even thought about going back to Veneto's yet again. Every afternoon after his last class he got together with Marianne to review the day. She could see he was struggling but she kept offering encouragement. Phil didn't say a word about Saturday night. He was about to break the news to her when Marianne brought up the subject on their way to the parking lot Friday afternoon.

"Are we still on for tomorrow night?"

"Something's come up," Phil said. "It looks like I am going

to have to meet my daughter in Philadelphia Saturday afternoon. She's flying in at four o'clock. I have to pick her up and take her to her cousin's house. It's the only time I can get to see her. I'm really sorry. Could we get together Sunday instead?"

They were standing in front of Marianne's car. "When did this happen?" she asked.

Phil felt miserable, He really hated telling Marianne a lie. Now he would have to make it worse. "Just this morning. I should have said something to you before classes started but I was hoping I might be able to make other arrangements for her. I'm really sorry."

"Don't worry about it. We'll do it another time," Marianne said. She opened her car door and got in. Then she looked at Phil and said, "See you Monday, Phil."

Phil walked a few rows over to his car, head down. It was going to be a long weekend. As he opened his door he noticed Erik Cowens the math teacher standing a few feet from him, apparently appraising Phil's state of mind. "Erik, have a nice weekend."

"You look like a guy who isn't sure he's gonna make it through the weekend," Erik said.

Phil smiled. "Is it that obvious?"

"As a matter of fact, yes. This job's not gettin' you down already is it?"

"Like I said today at lunch, I am tired."

Earlier that day he saw Erik Cowens in the cafeteria and asked if he could join him for lunch. Cowens, who was sitting alone, simply nodded. The two men didn't say much but toward the end of the lunch period, Phil mentioned that he was surprised by how teaching could be so tiring. Cowens laughed and said something about how Phil would get his sea legs eventually.

"I hear you" Cowens said, "I'm guessing you got issues in the love department too."

Now Phil laughed. "You don't miss much do you? Must be all those years as a cop."

"No, I don't miss much. I was a detective for a long time. You ever want to talk, give me a holler."

Phil fixed a salad when he got home, checked for messages and looked at his mail. Most of it was junk but then he noticed a post card advertisement from the real estate office where Paula Parnell worked. Suddenly he remembered that she had called him. With his worries about his new job and Lisa, it had slipped his mind completely. He picked up the phone and called her.

"Hi Paula. It's Phil Falco."

"Well it took you long enough to call me. Are you playing hard to get?"

"Something like that. What's up?"

"You said you had questions about Carmine but we never really got the chance to

talk about it. If you still want to talk, maybe we can get together sometime."

"Are you busy tonight?" Phil wasn't so tired all of a sudden. He wanted company.

"Are you serious? I always have a busy schedule," Paula said.

"Now who's playing hard to get," Phil said.

"I am available tomorrow night."

Phil shook his head. He could not believe this. "I can't. Sorry. What about Sunday?"

"I promised one of the girls I would cover the office. Someone has to be there to handle the phones and walk-ins Sunday afternoon. How about this: Meet me at the real estate office at 5:30 and we can grab a bite to eat."

Phil said he would be there. He was glad to have a little more time now that he had a moment to think about it. He wanted to figure out what he should say to Paula. That however would have to wait. His first task was figuring out how to approach Florio with his request. He spent a good part of that Saturday morning thinking about it. He thought of the alternatives. He could say Dennis owed

him at least that much considering he had half a million dollars of his money. Or, he could say up front that if strings were attached he, Phil would find another way to take care of his problem.
He soon realized there wasn't anything he could say that was guaranteed to insulate him from being required to pay more money or do some hideous deed. It didn't matter. Lisa's future, her very life was at stake. He would do whatever was necessary, including taking matters into his own hands if it came to that.

Beyond whatever new debt he might owe Florio, Phil was uncomfortable about asking Florio for help in the first place. But what other choice did he have? As he saw it he was forced to do whatever was necessary because there were no laws that could protect him or his family in a matter such as this. He consoled himself with the thought that Riley Rivers was not an innocent person. He had to be stopped. Phil knew his logic was convenient, that what he was about to propose couldn't really be justified but he loved his daughter. That was all that mattered to him at the moment.

He got on the Garden State Parkway just after four o'clock and headed south toward Beachwood. He wondered if maybe Angela Dearborn would be at Falzone's. The way his luck was running she would be there. He imagined he would run into her before Florio got there and immediately she would ask Phil if they could go out that night.

As it turned out he was spared the embarrassment of running into Angela. Florio was sitting at the bar holding court when he got there. He introduced Phil to his cronies, making a point to say they had played ball together in high school. He played the part of the Mafioso to the hilt, dressed in black from head to toe.

Each of the men exchanged greetings and soon after, as if by pre-arrangement, they slipped away so Phil and Dennis could chat.

Phil ordered a glass of cabernet. While he was waiting for the bartender to bring his drink, he told Florio about his new teaching job. Florio laughed long and hard when he heard about the kid who said his name was Mother Fucker. As soon as the bartender brought his glass of wine, Florio motioned for them to leave the bar. Phil turned to the bartender to ask what he owed but Florio, anticipating him simply said, "It's taken care of."

The two men were led to a table in the corner of the restaurant. It looked to Phil like one or two tables had been moved away to give them privacy. A look at the carpeted floor confirmed his suspicion. There were indentation marks where the tables previously stood.

Florio didn't waste any time. As soon as they were seated he said, "What's on your mind?"

"I need a favor." On the ride down the Parkway, Phil had imagined the dialogue he thought they might have. Now that he was here he couldn't remember any of his carefully planned words.

Florio gestured, palm up toward Phil, his eyes asking the question.

"You have a couple of kids right?" Phil asked.

"Two sons. Both good boys. Neither of them working for me."

"I have one child, my daughter Lisa."

"Is she married?"

"No. But she is in trouble."

"You mean she's pregnant?" Florio asked, a smile on his face.

"No, this is worse. A lot worse. Dennis, I'm embarrassed to be telling you this. She's a good kid really. She's just gotten herself involved with the wrong crowd."

"Drugs?"

Phil put his head down. He shook it slightly. "It's worse than that maybe."

"Nothing's worse than that Phil."

"Maybe. She's living in LA, a town called Chatsworth. Does that mean anything to you?"

"Oh Jesus Phil. For real?" Florio knew well what Chatsworth was known for in certain circles.

Phil nodded, fighting to maintain his composure. He took a long sip from his wine glass. "I have to get her out of there. She hasn't been in one of those movies yet but she says she will be in one pretty soon."

Florio shook his head. The waiter walked over and he waved him away. "I know some people out there. What do you want me to do?"

"Can you stop her from appearing in any of those movies?"

Florio thought for a moment. "Maybe. Can you tell me who she's working for or anything like that?"

"Yeah. I'm not asking you to hurt anybody."

"I'll tell you what Phil. Give me some information and let me worry about the details. Your daughter isn't going to be in the movie business, okay?"

Phil thanked him. Florio waved him off but remembering their conversation at Veneto's, he couldn't help saying, "We're still friends, right?"

CHAPTER 15

On Sunday afternoon Phil arrived right on time to pick up Paula. He stepped inside the real estate office just as she was walking around and turning off lights. She was wearing a bright orange sun dress and sandals. Her hair was gathered in the back in a bun. She turned to face Phil when she heard the door open.

"We're very prompt, I see. Your shirt matches my dress. Nice touch."

Phil was wearing tan colored Dockers and an orange Polo shirt "I'm always on time. It's an old habit."

Paula flipped off one more light and waved Phil out the door so she could lock up. "I'm not really hungry just yet," she said as they walked to their cars. "Would you mind if we stopped by my place first? It was warm enough for this sun dress this afternoon but it's getting cool. I don't know what I was thinking when I put it on this morning."

"Squeezing out the last drop of summer?"

Paula drove a red BMW 745, large enough to chauffeur families around looking for new homes. She lived only a few minutes from the office. When they got to her house, Phil was a bit surprised that it wasn't a large home. Paula lived in a modest three bedroom rancher with beige vinyl siding and dark brown shutters framing the windows. She pulled into the driveway and he parked on the street and sat there. Paula stood waiting for him until it dawned on her that he intended to wait for her in the car.

She called him. "Hey Phil! Aren't you going to come in?"

He pulled his key from the ignition and got out of his Altima. "I can do that if you like."

"It's up to you but it does seem silly to have you wait in the car. I'll feel rushed if you do that. Come on in and I'll make you a drink."

Phil was happy to oblige. He was feeling a bit conflicted actually. He definitely had a thing for Marianne but Paula made him wonder. He found her exciting, almost exotic. Marianne was charming and but not the type to keep a man guessing. Paula was mysterious. They walked in the front door and Phil made himself at home on the sofa in the living room. No one else was there.

"What would you like to drink?" Paula asked.

"Do you have a bottle of wine open?"

"I'll check." She opened the refrigerator door and did a quick survey of the contents. "Chardonnay, will that due?"

"Absolutely."

Paula walked in from the kitchen with his wine. "I'm going to get a hot shower and change. Put the TV on if you like."

"Do you mind if I ask you a question?"

"Well that depends now doesn't it?"

"I suppose. Where is your boyfriend?"

"Why do you ask?"

"It just seems strange him not being here on a Sunday afternoon. And maybe I don't want to have to explain what I'm doing here if he waltz's in."

"Fair enough. To answer your question, I don't have a boyfriend at the moment and, I'm not looking for one."

"Go take your shower."

An hour later they were in yet another Italian restaurant, this one, a couple of towns over in Belleville. They chatted for a while. Phil described his concerns about his new job and again Paula suggested he could make a living in real estate if teaching didn't work out. Coffee was being served by the time they got around to Carmine.

"So you and Carmine didn't really talk much after your divorce?"

"No. He was really hurt, and then angry, I'm sure you know the drill."

"Do you know who Angela Dearborn is?"

"I don't think so. Should I?"

Phil shrugged. "She was Carmine's girlfriend for a while. I saw her not too long ago. She seemed to think you and Carmine were still close."

"The only thing I can think of is that Carmine probably told her that. Mutual acquaintances would tell me how he still had it bad for me long after the divorce. So one night after I heard that for what seemed like the tenth time that week I called him. I said why are you telling people this? You know what he said to me?"

"No," Phi said, smiling in anticipation.

"He told me 'it makes me more interesting to women. I'm like a challenge all of a sudden.' Still a jerk, I told him."

"Yeah, but he had a point."

Paula shot Phil a look but she couldn't help smiling.

Phil was back in his apartment by nine o'clock Sunday night. It had been a busy weekend. As he mulled over what had transpired, he decided that notwithstanding blowing his date with Marianne, it had been a productive couple of days. He felt sure that Florio would help Lisa. Maybe that problem was about to go away. That would be a big relief. And, his dinner with Paula had been instructive in a couple of ways. For one thing, Paula convinced him that Angela had been wrong. There was nothing to the idea that Carmine still spoke with Paula on a regular basis. There was no way he gave her the money. However, Paula did confirm that Marianne was her brother's caretaker as she put it. She was also certain that the only woman besides his sister that Carmine had any respect for was his first wife, Gloria. How did she put it? Carmine ran everything by Gloria before he did it, including his decision to marry Paula. That confirmed his suspicion that Angela had misunderstood Carmine's silence when it came to Gloria.

"The bastard even told me about his conversation with Gloria a couple of weeks before we got married. I should have walked away then," Paula said.

Aside from what Paula could tell Phil about Carmine, he witnessed something that obliterated any romantic fantasies he might have about her. They were just finishing their coffee when a man and his wife sat down at the table next to theirs. Paula knew them. Apparently they had bought a home through her. The woman was heavy set and unattractive but the husband was a very good looking guy. It was obvious that the woman wasn't happy about running into Paula. Introductions were made and that was that. At least it was until Paula and Phil got up to leave. Paula took a step up to the other couple's table and put her arms around the man's neck. "You promised to teach me to play golf, remember?"

"I remember," the guy said. His face turned red but he was smiling.

The man's wife broke in. "He doesn't have time for that Paula. I'm sure you can afford lessons on your own."

As if she didn't grasp a thing, Paula responded, "There's no rush. I was just reminding him of his promise."

When they got in the car Phil gave her a look but she ignored it. Phil's interest in Paula evaporated immediately. He knew the type. She reminded him of Tracy.

It was unusually cool in the Los Angeles area for a September afternoon. Riley Rivers arrived at his condo after having spent the morning discussing the scenes they planned to shoot on his new movie later that afternoon. Everything was set. Today, Lisa would make her debut. He told her to get her hair and nails done that morning. He would stop by to pick her up around 1:30.

He opened the door to the condo expecting Lisa to be sitting there, ready to go. When he saw she wasn't there, he called for her but there was no answer. If that stupid bitch overslept again he would really give her a beating this time. Lately it seemed all she wanted to do was sleep. He pushed open the door to the bedroom. He fully expected to see her lying there. He was already fantasizing about yanking her up by her hair to wake her up. In fact he yelled through the door as he grabbed for the knob, "You better be up in there or I'll kick your ass sister."

Lisa wasn't there. Instead he saw two men standing near the foot of the bed. "Who the fuck are you?"

Each man grabbed an arm and flung Riley onto the bed. He struggled to get up but one of the men, still holding his arm twisted it enough to convince him to lie still. "What do you want? Where's Lisa?"

"I'm going to let you up dildo. If you do anything I don't like, your slimy silk sheets are going to turn red real fast. Got it?"

Riley nodded. The man let go of his arm and Riley slowly turned and sat up. "Where's Lisa?" he asked, his voice quiet now.

"Your name is Rivers right?"

"Yeah."

"Never mind Lisa. She don't live here anymore. As of right now you never heard of her so you don't care where she is. Understand?"

Riley was catching on. That bitch's father must have been behind this, he thought. "She don't mean nothing to me anyway. Fuck her."

The other guy spoke. "Who you talking about?"

"Lisa."

Now the guy pulled something out of his pocket and put it on his right hand. Then he swung at Riley and hit him on the nose with a force that snapped Riley's head back and knocked him flat on the bed. Blood splattered everywhere. "I thought you understood. You don't know anybody named Lisa."

Riley was too scared to say a word. He just nodded.

"Now listen to me dickhead. If this girl you never heard of should call you, hang up. If she comes to see you walk the other way. I hear you like to beat up on girls. We like to beat up on jerks like you. Just give us an excuse. That nosebleed you got is only a warning. Next time I'm going to aim lower." He squeezed Riley's crotch hard. "We on the same page now?"

Again Riley nodded. The men left. Riley laid there, blood running from his broken nose and mouth for what seemed like an hour. It felt like his entire head was swollen. Finally he got up, cleaned himself up a little and checked for Lisa's things. Not one thing was left behind. He drove himself to the emergency room to get his nose fixed.

Earlier that day, Lisa had in fact been up in time to make her appointment. She was fixing her hair when she heard a knock on the door. She opened it to find two men and a woman standing there. "Can I help you?"

"We need to talk honey," the woman said. "Can we come in?"

Lisa wasn't sure what to do. She opened the door a bit wider and the three of them barged in. The two men went into the bedroom. "What's going on?" Lisa asked, frightened now.

"It's okay. We're taking you away from here. There are people behind the movie business you're in that don't think you're right for these movies. You could even get hurt if you don't do what they ask."

"Hurt? By who? Where's Riley?" She was in a complete panic now. "What is going on?"

"Don't worry about Riley. The men I came in with will explain everything to him. We're going to give you some money and put you on a plane this afternoon."

"Where? Where am I going? I don't understand."

The woman, who was about forty, had a very soothing and reassuring voice. She simply told Lisa that her job in the movie industry wasn't working out, that executives behind the scenes didn't think she was right for the business. "It happens all the time honey, really."

The two men worked fast. They found a couple of suitcases and filled them with Lisa's clothes. They got a makeup bag and put all her toiletries in that. They were very thorough.

"Who are you people? You're scaring me."

"I know, honey," the woman said, "but we are your friends. Don't be afraid." She spoke to Lisa like she was a child but Lisa was far too bewildered to notice.

"Where am I going?"

"That's right, you asked me that before. You have a choice. You can go anywhere you want as long as you leave LA. I hear you're from New Jersey. Maybe you should go back there."

Forty-five minutes later Lisa and the woman, who said her name was Joyce, were in a black Cadillac SUV headed for the airport.

"I don't understand. How can you do something like this? Am I being kidnapped?"

"No, not at all. When we get to the airport I'll drop you off. I have some money for you, two thousand dollars to get you started. Just don't go back to that condo. It isn't safe. And for your own sake, forget that jerk you've been living with."

True to her word, the woman dropped Lisa at the Burbank Airport. All she said was, "Good luck honey."

Lisa sat in the main terminal with her bags trying to figure out what happened. After a while, she tried calling the condo but no one answered. She had no idea what to do. She felt completely alone. The funny thing was, as much as she hated to admit it; a small part of her was relieved.

She hung around the terminal trying to understand what happened. That was beyond her. She went into the ladies room and counted the money. Two-thousand dollars, Joyce had told the truth. By five o'clock she decided she would fly to New Jersey. After spending time with her mother and meeting her new boyfriend, she knew she would be uncomfortable living there. She assumed her father wouldn't be much help either, but until she could figure something out, he would have to do. She bought a ticket and checked her luggage for a flight leaving at six that would get her into Newark at 6:30 the following morning. Just before it was time to board, she decided to try the condo one more time. Riley answered. His voice sounded muffled.

"Riley, its Lisa."

All she heard was a click. The line went dead.

By the middle of his second week of classes, Phil was beginning to feel a bit more relaxed. He found that a few of the kids were actually interested in American history. He spent as much time as he could, trying to relate what had happened three hundred and fifty years ago in a world that bore little resemblance to the one these kids inhabited. He kept it simple. Given how little these kids really knew he was less concerned about what they might remember about Jamestown and Plymouth Rock. Instead he focused more on day to day activities then versus now. He pointed out how much easier their lives were than the pioneers who settled the country.

At first, most of them scoffed at the thought that life might have been more difficult in earlier times. So he asked them to list the things they thought the Pilgrims had to work with. He was astounded by what they said. Some of them thought the Pilgrims had electric lights and radio. One kid insisted they had model T cars. When Phil asked him why he thought that, the kid responded by saying he had seen a movie once where one of the characters living in those times had a car.

Phil pointed out that what he saw was either science fiction or comedy, not reality. At least he was engaging them rather than sitting there reading while they slept or passed notes back and forth. Marianne was impressed. She was surprised, she said, by how quickly Phil was catching on.

Only a week before that Phil was sure teaching was a mistake. Now he was feeling optimistic. And, he started taking classes himself that week. He had enrolled in the teaching certification program at the Rutgers University campus in Newark. He also joined Erik Cowens, the math teacher for lunch every day. Erik introduced him to Bill Clarke, another retired cop who taught English. He enjoyed their company. As former cops, they always had good stories to tell. He didn't bother to ask Marianne to have lunch with him because she had made it clear that she had a regular group she ate with. There were three women, she said, that had been teaching at the same school for years. He got the message.

Although he realized it was still too soon to know for sure, he felt like he had finally turned the corner after his divorce and loss of all that money. He had no intentions of giving up on finding the money Carmine was carrying that night, but he didn't feel so desperate now that he had a meaningful direction. And, he felt in time he could build a relationship with Marianne. He wasn't interested in marriage but he wanted the companionship of a woman. At this stage in his life, he felt Marianne, or someone like her, would be right for him.

He was feeling so good about things he decided to ask Marianne out again for Saturday night. He didn't see her Thursday morning so he decided to wait until classes ended. He would give her his regular progress report and then ask her to go to a movie Saturday night. As it turned out, he didn't see Marianne because she called in sick that day. Later, he would realize he caught a lucky break. Had she said yes to his offer, again he would have had to cancel. This time Lisa really was the reason.

CHAPTER 16

As soon as she arrived in Newark, Lisa called Riley again. She heard his voice and said, "It's Lisa. Don't hang up, please."

He didn't hang up but he didn't say anything either.

"Riley?"

"Don't ever call me again, understand?"

"Why?"

There was a pause. Then the line went dead. That afternoon Riley Rivers would have his phone numbers changed. He wasn't taking any chances.

Lisa's next call was to her father. He was happy to hear from her and even happier when she told him she was at Newark Airport. Phil had been ready to do a little food shopping. Now he headed for the airport to pick up his daughter. They could shop together so he could have a few things she liked while she was visiting.

When he picked her up at arriving flights and saw the suitcases and duffel bag he was elated. "Looks like you're on your way somewhere for a long spell," he said after they kissed and hugged at the curb.

"Hoping I can stay with you for a while daddy."

"Really? Are you through with the movie business?"

Lisa gave her father a long look. "It looks that way. Did you have anything to do with that?"

Phil returned his daughter's stare. One day he would tell his daughter the truth. At that moment he felt it would be counter productive to do so. "If I had that kind of power you would have been out of that business long before now. Anyway, I'm glad you're here." Of course Phil knew that Lisa's film career was over. He had received a message on his cell phone that simply said, "I think your problem in California is solved." He recognized the voice as Florio's. He knew better than to call him right away. He would have to thank him in person.

"So can I stay with you a while?" she asked.

"Of course. Does your mother know you're here?"

"No, not yet."

They shopped for groceries and then headed to the apartment to drop off her things. He showed her around the apartment, including an empty bedroom that would be Lisa's room. "Where will I sleep?"

Phil smiled. "We need to do a little more shopping I guess. Call your mother and then we'll get going."

They went to a nearby furniture store to buy a bed, dresser, lamp and night stand for the bedroom where Lisa would stay.

At first Phil was delighted with the prospect of getting reacquainted with his daughter. It wasn't long though before he saw the downside of their living arrangement. Lisa liked to sleep late and go to bed well after midnight, exactly the opposite of Phil's routine. That wasn't so bad but Lisa didn't have her car so she couldn't look for work or go very far from the apartment unless she got up early to drive Phil to work. By the time she was there two weeks, they were fighting because Phil would have to practically yank her out of bed on the mornings she wanted the car. Then she would be late, sometimes more than an hour late, picking him up after school was out.

He considered buying her a car but he really couldn't afford it. Instead, he arranged to have her car, which was still parked at the apartment complex in Chatsworth, shipped to New Jersey. It was expensive but nothing like the cost of buying her a reliable car.

Aside from these little skirmishes, Lisa was good company for her father. They talked for the first time as two adults rather than parent and child. He told her about his new job and the teenagers he was trying to teach. In turn, Lisa offered a small glimpse of her life with Riley. She admitted that Riley hit her on occasion.

When he heard it, Phil could barely contain himself. He kept his comments to a minimum but promised himself he would one day pay Rivers a personal visit to settle the score once and for all.

One night they got into a discussion about her childhood. Her observations surprised him.

"You weren't around that much daddy. I was always afraid it was because you didn't like me."

"What do you mean? I was home every night."

"True but you kind of kept to yourself, you know? Mom always said you were a man that lived life just for himself."

That shook Phil up. "I never realized you felt that way kid. I don't remember being aloof. If I was I'm sorry."

"It's okay now daddy, I'm just saying how it was. Anyway you're not like that now."

After that night Phil tried even harder to spend time with his daughter. He noticed that she often complained of not feeling well. She said her stomach hurt at least once a day. Phil finally insisted she go to the doctor. That night she said she felt better; that the doctor had given her something mild for the pain. Phil just said he was glad to hear it.

During the time Lisa lived with him, Phil put any thoughts of seeing Marianne on hold. He wasn't sure how long Lisa would stay and he wanted time to be with his daughter. He was certain he wouldn't get another chance with Lisa. In spite of their differences, they got along reasonably well. Most nights she made him something to eat. She wasn't much of a cook but she tried. He took her to New York a couple of times, once to see a play and another time to walk through museums.

Then, after just six weeks of living together, Lisa told him she was going to Arizona after all. Phil said he was sorry to hear it but in one way, he was relieved. Lisa hadn't really made any effort to make friends and her job hunting efforts were sporadic at best. He knew that soon he would have to put some pressure on her to get her life moving again. He dreaded the thought. They would be at odds again and knowing Lisa, she would probably make things unpleasant.

In spite of his concerns about Lisa, when she left they were on better terms than they had been for a long time. One thing that really made him happy was that Lisa didn't ask him for money. She accepted it if he offered, but she never asked for a dime. A couple of days before she left, Phil gave his daughter five hundred dollars. Lisa would be driving out there. If he could have taken the time off Phil would have driven out to Phoenix with her. He called Arlene and let her know Lisa was on her way. Arlene, who was married by this time, was thrilled to have her daughter back. She thanked Phil for whatever it was he did to extricate Lisa from the horrors of what Arlene referred to as the movie underworld. Not certain of what Arlene might say to Lisa, Phil pretended not to have any idea why their daughter left the movie business. To her credit, Arlene caught on quickly.

"Don't worry," she said, "At this point the less Lisa knows the better."

Phil kissed Lisa goodbye and for the tenth time made her promise to call him every night until she arrived safely in Phoenix. Lisa kept her word. Phil watched the World Series every night with the phone in his lap.

He felt like he had his life back. Teaching was getting easier. Like Erik Cowens told him would happen, he now had his sea legs. He was comfortable in front of his students and he had managed to identify a couple of kids in each class that wanted to learn. He focused on them but did his best not to ignore the others.

One thing he hated was the cynicism of the other teachers. A lot of them were there for the paycheck. The hours were good and it was easy money with summers off if you didn't care. Phil tried not to be unrealistic about the kids and their chances of doing something useful with their lives. He knew a lot of them would do prison time, some would become prostitutes and too many of them would get into drugs. They would have trouble finding and holding onto jobs. Although the curriculum was designed to provide the same type of education the kids in better neighborhoods and wealthy suburbs got, he could see that what these kids really needed most of all was basic reading, writing and math skills. American history, for example was in many ways irrelevant to the world they lived in. He did his best to find ways to make history fit something relevant to his students' lives. More often than not his imagination failed him.

Yet he was able to earn his students' grudging respect and perhaps more important to him, Erik Cowens treated him with respect. Phil was a bit surprised that it mattered to him what Cowens thought. But the more he thought about it, he realized he had always worked hard. He was the type that needed the approval of others around him in the work place. In Phil's opinion, Cowens was one of the few teachers that was trying. Certainly Marianne was doing more than going through the motions, but her heart was no longer in it.

Phil and Erik developed a friendship of sorts, driven by their mutual interest in sports but limited by the fact that the men inhabited very different worlds. Both men had been around too long to completely overcome the racial barrier between them. Had they been born a generation later, it might not have mattered. But these men came up at the dawn of the civil rights era. Neither man had much experience with interracial friendships. Still, they did manage to go beyond simply having lunch together almost every day. Sometimes they met after work and shared a few beers. One night Erik mentioned that he had a part time job refereeing high school basketball games. This was just before the season started. He told Phil he was making an extra two-thousand a year as a referee.

"How did you get that job?" Phil asked.

"I applied for it. I'm a member of the IAABO, that's how."

"That's all there is to it?" The idea was immediately appealing to Phil. What better way to earn a few extra bucks, he thought. But that idea died a quick death when Erik gave him the details.

"The International Association of Approved Basketball Officials, the IAABO, puts you through a strict training program. You got to take classes, pass a test and everything. Takes two to three years before they let you do varsity games."

Phil thought that over for a few seconds. "Maybe I'll come watch you work some night," Phil said. The two men laughed. There was no way Phil wanted to take more courses. He was working hard on his teaching certificate as it was. Phil had begun looking forward to those nights spent eating Buffalo wings and drinking beer. Once basketball season started, it sounded like Erik would be too busy for that.

As soon as Lisa left for Arizona, Phil was ready to give Marianne another try. Just one day after Lisa left he called Marianne to ask her out for dinner. He reminded her that they were supposed to go to New York. Marianne was polite but she turned him down. She said she had just started seeing somebody and didn't want to complicate things. With Lisa gone Phil was really feeling lonely. It was only his sense of fair play that kept him from calling Fred again.

With the baseball season ended, he had more time on his hands. He decided he would make one last all out attempt to find out what Carmine did with the money. So far his efforts had been clumsy and he had learned very little. His failure made him reluctant to dig further. He was torn between wanting to move on and wanting his money back. He found it impossible to forget what happened. Thanks to Carmine, he was now teaching and going to school at night when he should have been coasting toward retirement. Now, he wasn't sure when or if he could retire. He realized that it might be easier to let go had there been a reasonable explanation for what happened to the money. If Carmine's car had burned in a fiery crash, for example, maybe he could live with that.

Instead, he was left to ponder the alternatives. Did Marianne have the money? Maybe Florio had recovered it and didn't tell him. Perhaps, as Florio had suggested, the cops took it. And, of course, he had to consider whether Carmine had in fact given it to one of his ex wives or a girlfriend Phil didn't know about yet. But the more he thought about it, the more Phil believed that neither Paula nor any of his other exes's had the money or knew where the money was. If for no other reason than to close the loop, he decided to talk to Carmine's first wife Gloria. It was a long shot that Gloria knew anything about the money of course, but there was no harm in asking.

As much as he hated to admit it, he still suspected that Marianne had the cash or knew where it was. Based on what Angela and Paula told him, Marianne was the most logical candidate. Well, if she had the money how could he persuade her to part with it?

He considered telling her the whole story but he was reluctant to do that. Since she insisted she knew nothing about the package Carmine had been carrying what good would it do to tell her what happened? True, he had given Florio almost half a million dollars to keep himself and Marianne out of harm's way. But what did that matter? According to Carmine, Marianne had been screwed royally by her ex husband. The guy left her nearly penniless didn't he? She needed the money as much as he did. And, she probably felt entitled. Her brother was dead. And why would she suddenly turn around and admit she had the money now? Most likely all she would say was how sorry she was and she wished she could help him out. Besides, admitting she had the money now after all her denials would make her look bad unless she offered the money to him.

No, he was on his own. It bothered him that there was no way to separate his romantic interest in Marianne from his quest to find the money. Certainly he didn't want to believe that the money was influencing his desire to see her, but he had lived long enough to know he could not be absolutely certain about his motives. His only hope was that he was wrong. Maybe Carmine did something else with the money. Maybe Marianne was telling the truth after all. On that basis he could try to build a completely above board relationship with her.

Phil decided to do two things. First he would talk to Gloria. Then he would take Erik Cowens into his confidence to see if he might be willing to use his connections on the police force to help him get more information about the accident.

Finding Gloria Cifelli was easy. He remembered that she told him she lived in Millburn at Carmine's funeral. She had never remarried and she had held onto the Cifelli name. He found Gloria in the phone book and wrote the number down. Just to be cautious, he decided he should talk to Marianne to see what he could learn about Gloria before he approached her. The next morning when he met Marianne for coffee he asked her about Gloria.

"You ever talk to Carmine's first wife?"

"Gloria? Sure. We talk. Why?"

"I was just thinking about how she never changed her name or got married again. It seems odd I guess."

"I don't see why. They had a good marriage for a long time," Marianne said.

"Why did they split up?" Phil asked.

"I think maybe Carmine liked to play the field too much."

Phil nodded. "Were they close after the divorce?"

"Not right away but over the years I think Carmine came to rely on her for things he couldn't do for himself."

Phil smiled. "Like what?"

"Oh, you know, he always needed help doing the little things we all have to do. She would do his income taxes for him. She took his car to inspection sometimes. Just little things he hated to do."

"And she did all that for him. He had charm you're brother did. You know that?"

"Unlike me huh?" Marianne said.

"Where did you get that?" Phil asked.

"Forget it. I'm just a little sensitive these days."

Aren't we all?"

Phil called Gloria Cifelli that night. She wasn't home so he left her a message. The following day Phil had a harrowing experience at work. He was on cafeteria duty when a fight broke out. Apparently two boys got into it over a girl both of them liked. It started out as a fist fight. Then one of the boys, Rasheed Marbury, the big kid who had given Phil lip on the first day of school, pulled out a plastic knife that had been honed razor sharp. Phil got there just as the kid pulled out the knife.

"What you gonna do with that fuckhead?" the other boy said.

"Stick you mother fucker."

Phil stepped between them. He pointed at Rasheed and said, "Drop the knife on the floor now." He didn't yell. In fact, he kept his voice low and steady.

Rasheed stared at him for a moment, calculating the odds. "Maybe I should stick you dumbass."

Erik Cowens showed up but on some instinct he stood there not saying anything.

Phil looked at the boy's face. He looked to be near tears. "Don't break my heart kid. You try to stick me I have to defend myself. You're going to get hurt. Please don't make me do that."

Rasheed was searching now for a respectable way out. Phil could see his words were wrong for the situation. He glanced over at Erik.

Erik spoke up now. "Rasheed. Put it down. This man didn't do nothing to you. He's only trying to help."

The kid thought that over and made his decision. He put the knife back in his pocket and started to walk away. By then an armed guard who patrolled the school had arrived. He signaled to another guard and together they quickly handcuffed the boy and took him out of the building. Phil would not see the young man again until he testified at a hearing about the boy's behavior two weeks later.

After his last class, Phil walked down to Erik's classroom.

He was sitting at his desk grading a math test. "Mister Phil. You alright?"

"I fucked up didn't I?"

Cowens acknowledged the truth of Phil's statement with a smile. "Live and learn."

"Thanks for your help. Can I buy you a beer?"

"I don't see why not."

Erik Cowens arrived at the bar about fifteen minutes after Phil got there. It was only two short blocks from the high school. Phil waved him over to the stool next to his. He was already working on a draft beer. The two men chatted about the day's events. Erik went out of his way to reassure Phil that he had good instincts; that more experience would serve him well in crises to come.

"You did right in not yelling. You remained calm and showed no fear. A lot of teachers wouldn't get that. You would have made a good cop."

"I wonder if being a cop would have been easier. These kids are too much."

"In some ways it was easier," Erik agreed.

"You have any connections still on the force?" Phil asked, trying to sound casual.

"Sure. You need a ticket fixed?"

"No, no, nothing like that. There is something that is bothering me about my friend Carmine's case though."

"Carmine?"

"The friend who died in the car accident near the turnpike back in January. I think I told you about it."

"Oh yeah, you said something about it at lunch a while back. He was your best friend, I think you said. What's your concern?"

"He should have had a package. He did when he dropped me off. But it was never found," Phil said.

"Maybe he delivered it after he dropped you off," Erik said.

"Possibly. But I don't think so. I think he was planning to deliver it the following morning," Phil said.

"What was in the package?"

Phil anticipated this question. He had wrestled with the answer he should give. He thought Erik was a straight shooter but what if there was a chance, slim though it might be, that the package was sitting unclaimed in police custody? The mans could retire in style if he got his hands on that kind of money. It would tempt anyone. And, if he went ahead and told Erik it was money, that would lead to even more questions. He didn't want to lie to him so he decided to keep his response vague. "I think it was papers he was carrying for a client. He said he did some kind of courier work."

"For who?"

"He never said who it was."

Erik took a long swallow of his beer. He looked at Phil and said, "Was your friend involved in organized crime?"

"Why would you think that? Because he was Italian?"

Erik shook his head. "Nothing personal Phil. Over the years I've heard it all. So, was he mobbed up?"

"I don't think so. He liked to gamble and didn't know his limits but that's about it."

"I see. So you want me to ask around? See if the investigating officer found a package and maybe kept it?"

This wasn't going the way Phil planned but now that it was out there, he decided he might as well go for it. "Yes. I'm not looking for anything official. I just want to know off the record if anything was found."

"I'll see what I can do. Give me the full name of your friend and the date of the accident."

Phil gave Erik the information and thanked him. Then he said, "I doubt I'll ever have a chance to do something for you but if the chance comes, I'll be ready."

Erik shook his head again and finished his beer.

Phil wasn't in the mood to cook that night but he was hungry. As he drove up Bloomfield Avenue toward his apartment, the

Veneto's sign caught his eye. He hadn't been there in weeks. He gave in to the impulse, his desire to get a glimpse of Fred, and pulled into a parking space. He was determined to get a quick meal and be on his way. He would sit at the bar and talk to Fred, he told himself, but he would keep his distance. He missed her in bed but that was it.

As it turned out he had nothing to worry about. Fred treated him as if she never met him before. She handed him a menu without a word. "Would you like a drink?" she said, her tone curt.

"Sure. How about a glass of Cabernet?"

"Whatever."

One of the waiters walked over to him. "Long time no see Phil."

Phil chatted with the waiter, relieved to have someone to talk to.

"Not for nothing Phil but Fred took the breakup hard."

Phil just nodded. He couldn't think of anything he could say that would make sense.

Fred walked over with his glass of wine. "Ready to order?"

Phil looked at her and said, "I changed my mind. I think I'll just drink my wine and get going."

Fred turned and walked to the other side of the bar.

"Looks like I have a party. Nice to see you again Phil," the waiter said, "And don't feel too bad. I think Fred met another guy. She'll be okay."

Phil took a quick sip of his wine. He pulled out a twenty and dropped it on the bar. He would eat Chinese.

When he finished eating his shrimp lo mien, Phil decided to give Gloria another try. He sat in his living room, a bottle of beer in one hand and the phone in the other. Again there was no answer. He put the phone down and turned his attention to the TV. An hour later she called him.

"I was wondering when you would get around to calling me." Gloria didn't bother to say hello.

"Well my caller ID says I'm talking to Gloria Cifelli. What I want to know is why you haven't called me. I've been back in

Jersey for months."

She laughed. "You know, I guess old habits die hard. All those years ago I wanted to call you but never did."

"You did the right thing."

They talked for a few minutes about old times. Whenever he came home from college, especially summers, Phil spent a lot of time with Carmine and Gloria. Almost every weekend Carmine would take Gloria down to the Falco's summer house to spend the weekend. Sometimes, if Phil had a date, they double dated. When Gloria mentioned Carmine it gave Phil the opening he was waiting for.

"I miss him too," Phil said. "Living here now, I forget sometimes that he's gone. I think about giving him a call to get together and it always brings me up short. I wanted to talk with you about Carmine. Did you know I was with him the night he died?"

"I heard that. He took you to the airport or something."

"Right. Anyway, maybe we could get together and talk. Would you mind?"

"No not at all. Maybe it would do us both some good to have a chance to talk about old times and maybe even fill in a few blanks about him," Gloria said. "We should get together. Where would you like to meet?"

Phil hadn't thought about that. He didn't really want to take her out to dinner or anything like that. He just wanted to ask his questions and let it go at that. "I don't know. Do you have any suggestions?"

"You could come to my house. My mother lives with me but she won't be a bother."

Phil hesitated but he couldn't think of an alternative. "Sure. How about tomorrow night at 7:30?"

CHAPTER 17

After her divorce from Carmine, Gloria kept to herself for two full years. Once she started dating though, she had plenty of suitors. She got engaged twice but in both instances she had second thoughts. Now, at fifty-five years of age she was often lonely but at the same time grateful that she wasn't trapped in a relationship with a man she didn't care for. Besides, her mother, a seventy-five year old woman who loved playing the slots and sometimes a little black jack in Atlantic City's casinos, was usually good company.

Gloria was excited that she would get the chance to see Phil Falco again. She thought he looked tired, almost worn out when she saw him at Carmine's wake but Marianne told her later that the man had recently been through a divorce. Gloria simply assumed that was why Phil look haggard. Once she heard that he had moved back to New Jersey, she fought the impulse to call him, biding her time instead. She was sure their paths would cross sooner or later. Now she congratulated herself on her patience. Maybe it would pay off if she played her cards right. Phil's instinct about Gloria had been right way back then when they were young. She did have a thing for him, for a while at least. It didn't stop her from marrying Carmine of course. He had his strong points too.

The closer he got to Gloria's Millburn home the more uncomfortable Phil felt. He was beginning to feel like he was living Carmine's love life now that his best friend was gone. First it was Fred, then Angela and now he would spend time with Gloria. It wasn't that he was expecting a sexual encounter. But, in the back of his mind he remained aware of the chemistry between them all those years ago. Paula had been a close call, at least in Phil's mind. They had flirted shamelessly with each other. Nothing happened of course and as it turned out her style didn't appeal to him. Even his attempts to develop a relationship with Marianne had an eerie feel. She insisted on treating him like a brother. He was playing Carmine's role with her too.

Unable to get his mind focused on the real business at hand, he wondered what made him chastise Gloria for not calling him. Once again he had behaved flirtatiously. Most likely he set the wrong tone for their conversation. Was he subconsciously trying to get even with Carmine, a dead man for goodness sake? He shook his head as if to reorganize his thoughts. He willed himself to concentrate on what he would say to Gloria.

He was having trouble finding Gloria's home. He wasn't familiar with the area. Mostly, Milburn was an upscale bedroom community serving the needs of executives who worked in New York but preferred to live in a quiet suburb. Part of his confusion was due to his expectations. He knew that Gloria's father had been a well to do businessman but they had always lived well below their means. Just looking at the houses as he got closer to where Gloria lived told him that somehow she had transitioned from a girl who lived in North Newark to someone now living in elegant style. As a younger man he would have been intimidated by it.

He finally found the street he was looking for and almost immediately the directions began to make sense. He pulled up to her home and left the car in her driveway. Wide enough to be a side street in the old neighborhood, it lead to a four car garage. As usual, he was on time.

As he approached the well lit front porch, the door opened. Gloria was standing there with her mother. Both women were smiling.

"He looks just like he did forty years ago," Mrs. Milano said.

"Gloria's mother? My God, you look terrific, Mrs. Milano." Phil wasn't just being polite. The woman was the picture of health.

"A glass of wine a day and good Italian cooking is the secret," Mrs. Milano said, "When Gloria told me you were coming, I didn't believe it. Come in, come in."

Up to this point Gloria hadn't uttered a word. She smiled, took Phil by the arm and led him into the house. The house was huge and it was beautiful; a French colonial décor with hints of the Tuscan style, particularly in the kitchen.

Phil got a good look at Gloria too as they followed her mother into the kitchen. She obviously had her mother's genes. In spite of the short but stylish silver hair, she looked younger than her years. That she was carefully dressed in expensive looking slacks and blouse made Phil nervous. He had deliberately chosen to wear jeans and a flannel shirt hoping to signal his lack of interest in anything more than conversation.

The three of them sat at the kitchen table. Italian pastries and cookies sat at the center of the table along with a bottle of Sambuca and espresso cups. They made polite conversation for a while. They caught up on what had transpired over the years and what was going on in their lives now. Phil learned that Mr. Milano had died of a heart attack five years ago. Gloria worked part time at the Milburn library for something to do she said. Mrs. Milano mentioned weekly bus trips to the casino. Just to test the waters he asked if they remembered Dennis Florio. They did but other than a quick exchange of glances between the two women, nothing more was said.

Mrs. Milano got up and made the espresso. When it was done she filled their cups and excused herself, taking her espresso and half of a cannoli with her.

"Your mother looks great," Phil said once Mrs. Milano was on her way up the stairs to her bedroom.

"Thanks. Do you think it runs in the family?"

Phil smiled and nodded his head in the affirmative. "This is a beautiful home you have."

"I know. Who would have thought? It's a long way from that

two family house I grew up in that's for sure."

"You and Carmine lived rather modestly too as I recall," Phil said.

"We did. We had no choice really. Once he got the gambling bug it was a constant struggle. You know I could have lived with his running around but not knowing if we could pay the electric bill was too much for me."

"I thought the gambling fever came later, after you and he split up."

"Well it got a lot worse later on but he liked to play the horses and bet basketball games almost as long as I knew him. After seventeen years, I couldn't take it anymore."

"Are you saying you left him?"

Gloria shook her head. "No, it wasn't like that. I probably should have left him but he saved me the trouble when he got involved with that Paula woman. She really got inside his head. He went a little crazy if you ask me."

"I met her not too long ago, Phil said. "Carmine should have been able to see her coming from a distance."

"Carmine? He was a sucker for a good looking blonde," Gloria said, "I even dyed my hair blonde for a while."

They went on for a few more minutes until Phil changed the subject. First he helped himself to an éclair and a shot of Sambuca. "So how did you wind up in Milburn if you don't mind my asking?"

"After my father died we decided to spend some of his money. Remember he had that ravioli company?"

Phil nodded. The old man had made a small fortune over the years making ravioli pasta that was sold under a variety of brand names throughout the northeast.

"Well he made a killing when he sold the business. Still he wouldn't move out of Newark. After he died we moved here. I guess you could say I'm well off now."

"Good for you. Did Carmine know about that?"

"Of course. But if you're thinking he would have come sniffing around to get his hands on any of it you're wrong. He would never do that," Gloria said.

"I know that. That wasn't why I asked. In fact, I was wondering if maybe he left you money after he died."

Gloria laughed. It was a hearty laugh. "You have got to be kidding! I'll bet he didn't have two nickels to rub together. He didn't even own a house."

"Good point I suppose. I guess I was thinking maybe he made a score at the tables or something."

"Carmine never won. He had to do odd jobs for that Florio character to keep the wolves at bay." She said this with sadness in her voice. After all these years she still had affection for Carmine. "Anyway, speaking of making a score, I saw him a couple of days before he died. He was picking you up at the airport to take you to the closing of your parent's shore house right?"

"Yeah."

"I loved that house. Such fond memories of weekends we spent there. Carmine said you would make a bundle."

Again, Phil just nodded. He was tempted to tell Gloria what happened but he knew better. And, now he knew better than to think that Carmine might have given Florio's money to Gloria Cifelli.

It took three weeks for Erik Cowens to get back to Phil about Carmine's accident records. Phil was sitting in the faculty room alone reading the newspaper when Cowens walked in.

"My ass is dragging today Phil. Double overtime last night."

"Is that right? How much do they pay you to be a ref?"

"About sixty-five dollars for a varsity game. Less for JV."

"Well, it keeps you in shape right?"

"Right. Hey Phil, that thing you asked me about?"

Suddenly, Phil was all ears. "You heard something?"

"I wouldn't say I heard something. But I don't think there was a package in your buddy's car."

Phil looked at Eric for a moment wanting to be sure he was getting the truth. "So that was it then?"

"Yeah, pretty much. There was one other thing though. Probably doesn't mean much."

"What?"

"About thirty or forty feet from the car there was a laptop. It looked pretty new. Only, get this, it was smashed. Run over and it looked like it took a few good shots from a hammer or something."

"What do you think that was about? Were they able to tie it to Carmine?"

"Do you know if he owned a laptop?" Erik asked.

"Yeah, I think he owned one."

"Well ask Marianne if she has it. If not, it might have been your buddy's," Cowens said.

"Did the cops try to get anything off of it?" Phil asked.

Cowens laughed. "You kidding me? It looked like a suicide. The thing is probably still sitting where the officer found it. It wasn't even in the report. The guy I talked to just happened to remember it."

"Jesus."

"Do you think it means something?"

"I have no idea," Phil said. "Carmine always had a temper. He could have just been pissed off because he couldn't get wireless access that day."

"Well that's all I got." Cowens finally sat down. "I hope it helps whatever it is you're trying to do."

"It does. Thanks."

Phil glanced down at his newspaper searching for a new topic. He wanted to change the subject. Then one of the other teachers walked into the lounge and saved him the trouble.

"Well I don't know about anybody else," the teacher said, "but I am counting the days to the Thanksgiving break. These monsters are killing me."

Phil pushed his newspaper aside and motioned for the teacher to join them. She waved them off. "I gotta go have a smoke."

"Speaking of Thanksgiving Erik, I would like to come up with some kind of project for my classes. Is it safe to assume they don't spend the day in a Norman Rockwell type setting?" Phil asked.

"Yeah. That's a safe bet," Cowens said. "You have any ideas?

"I wish. The Pilgrims story seems a bit irrelevant to these kids."

"Are you having Thanksgiving dinner with Marianne?" Cowens asked. In a weak moment Phil had confided his interest in Marianne to Erik. He had been supportive but doubtful about Phil's prospects.

"No. I thought I might get an invitation but so far nothing."

"You ever tell her how you feel man?" Erik asked.

"Yes, I have."

Cowens raised his eyebrow in anticipation.

"She doesn't want to get involved with me right now. I was too close to her brother," Phil said.

"You mean kissing you is like kissing her brother?" Erik was smiling broadly, letting Phil know he wasn't trying to be mean.

"She didn't say that."

"Too polite. She is a sophisticated woman," Erik said. He saw Marianne as a woman looking for a guy with lots of money. Not unkindly, he said, "You don't fit her financial parameters, I'm afraid."

Phil shrugged his shoulders and fiddled with the newspaper. "I do have an invitation from someone else but I haven't accepted it yet."

Cowens smiled. "Getting around a little bit huh? I'm impressed."

Phil waved him off but he managed a smile.

A few days after his visit, Gloria had called him and suggested they meet for lunch. Reluctantly, Phil agreed to meet her at a diner that sat across the street from the school. It turned out to be an enjoyable hour. Phil found Gloria easy to talk to and she seemed genuinely interested in his new career.

"I envy you," she said. "I don't think I would have the nerve to start a new career so late in life."

Phil grinned.

"Oh, not that I think we're old. We're not. I just think you have a lot of courage is all I'm saying."

"I wonder if there is ever a point in life when people just admit they're old, "Phil said.

"I'm never going to admit it. I refuse to even think it," Gloria said.

"Someday you will. And maybe it will set you free as we used to say."

"You're crazy. But maybe, I don't know. Maybe you're right."

As they were getting up to leave the diner she said, "Thanksgiving is coming up. If you haven't already made plans, why don't you join us?"

He put her off saying he might go to Phoenix to spend the weekend with his daughter. He asked if maybe he could let her know the following week. Actually, he was hoping that Marianne would invite him to her place for Thanksgiving. She continued to be friendly toward him during their mentoring sessions. A couple of times after school was out they drove over to the bakery they liked and had coffee. Once he asked her how the new romance was going but Marianne just rolled her eyes.

"I'm waiting in the wings," Phil said.

Marianne patted his hand and said, "Don't be silly."

Phil took that as a bad sign but he resolved to be patient. With the holidays approaching though, he began to fret over spending Christmas alone. He had done that last year in Florida and it had been a miserable experience. In spite of being immersed in his new job and preparation for classes, plus his own course work to achieve certification, this year might be even worse than the year before. In truth, he was often lonely. His friendship with Erik aside, it wasn't like he had a circle of friends he could pal around with the way young men did when they weren't involved with a woman. He was spending a lot of time alone. The thought of spending Christmas alone and greeting the New Year by toasting the walls of his apartment depressed him even more.

And, it looked like he had reached a dead end in his quest to find out what Carmine did with the money. Marianne was now the only one left. It had to be her. Who else would Carmine give the money to? He wondered if that was why she wouldn't go out with him. Maybe it was guilt. But then he realized that made no sense. Marianne didn't know he had given Florio four hundred-fifty thousand dollars to protect them both. Again he contemplated whether he should come clean and tell her what really happened. If she had the money, maybe she would offer to split it with him.

He had yet another thought. What if someone stole the money from Carmine? But who would take the chance? They would have had to know Carmine had the money in the first place. How else would they know when and where to pick it up? Phil made a mental note to ask Dennis Florio about that if he ran into him again. As unlikely as it was that someone would have robbed Carmine, at least it was still another unturned stone.

Thanksgiving week was hectic for Gloria Cifelli. Weeks before that she had agreed to work eight hour shifts at the library Monday through Wednesday so one of the regulars could visit relatives in Tennessee. That would have been fine but then Sunday night Phil Falco called and accepted her offer to spend Thanksgiving with her and her mother. There was house cleaning, food shopping, getting a few good bottles of wine, cooking, baking; the works. On top of that she wanted to buy a new outfit for the occasion. Of course she could have paid someone to handle the cleaning and the shopping but she was old fashioned about things like that. She didn't want other people cleaning her house, so she did the work herself. By Wednesday night she was exhausted.

By the end of that day Phil was tired too. He had finally come up with something for the kids in his classes but it took some doing. He decided to take all of them, three classes totaling ninety students, to a culinary class at the culinary arts college near Atlantic City. In conversation with Gloria she happened to mention that her nephew was attending school at the academy. On a hunch he called them and found out that every Thanksgiving they prepared meals for the homeless, beginning on Monday of that week. He made a few more inquiries and managed to arrange to let his students observe and maybe let a few of them lend a hand with simple tasks.

That turned out to be the easy part. He needed permission from the school system, transportation vouchers and parental consent forms for each student signed by the parents. As it turned out, that made the outing manageable. Only thirty-four students produced the necessary signatures. Then he had to arrange substitutes for the kids who had to remain behind. He did manage to get several of the parents to act as chaperones and make the trip with the class. Tuesday, was the appointed day. They were supposed to leave at six a.m. for the three hour ride to the school. They would spend six hours at the school and then head back, arriving back at the high school by six p.m.

Well, the bus was an hour late. Then one of the chaperones couldn't make it, leaving him one short of the required number. That problem was solved when Marianne, who was scheduled for an administrative day and had no classes, agreed to fill in. Phil was delighted of course.

It turned out to be a long day. The kids were noisy but worse; some of them were so disrespectful to the culinary school's instructors that the visit had to be cut short.   Refusing to do the assigned work was one thing but then three of the boys started throwing food at one another and then at some of the culinary arts students. It was disheartening for Phil. He was particularly angry because the kid who instigated the food throwing was Rasheed Marbury, the same kid who flashed the knife in the cafeteria. He had been let back in school after just a two week suspension. No charges had been filed. When Phil saw that Rasheed had a permission slip to make the trip, he called the boy's aunt to verify that it was her signature. The woman said it was but Phil sensed she was covering for her nephew.

Now the kid was causing trouble again, this time ruining what should have been a nice outing for everyone. Phil could not help noticing that before the trouble started, a couple of his students were taking a genuine interest in food preparation. He suspected that this was exactly what caused Rasheed to become so disruptive. Well, this time he would insist on a longer suspension. He really wanted the kid kicked out of the school. There were several boys and a couple of girls that always seemed to be at the center of trouble. Whether it was disruptive behavior, fights or flat out refusals to do assigned work, the ringleaders were always involved. Phil was convinced that getting rid of these bad apples could do wonders for the other kids.

He talked quietly with Marianne about it on the return trip to the school. She pointed out to him that what he saw was only the tip of the iceberg. "Almost every one of these kids is troubled," she said, "If we get rid of a few of them, others will step up if for no other reason than to get someone's attention."

Phil acknowledged the probability that Marianne was right. They rode in silence for a while. They didn't talk much beyond that, limiting their conversation mostly to teaching and observations about the people they worked with. Phil did remember to ask her about Carmine's laptop.

"You know I have looked everywhere for that. I can't find it," she said. "What made you think of that?"

"I was thinking of buying one," Phil said. He was telling the truth, technically at least. He had been shopping for them on line.

"It's an unsolved mystery I guess," Marianne said.

As they pulled into the school parking lot Marianne said, "I'm so glad we have a long weekend coming up. Jerry and I are going to Cape Cod for Thanksgiving weekend." It was the first time Marianne had mentioned her boyfriend by name.

"Good for you," Phil said. It was all he could manage. He was grateful that she didn't ask about his plans. He was having second thoughts about spending the day with Gloria. Maybe he would be better off with a pizza and a beer parked in front of the TV for the day.

North Ward High's principal, Doctor Griggs, was waiting for the students when the bus arrived. He told the three boys who had been involved in the food throwing incident to wait for him in his office. Then he took Phil and Marianne aside so they could debrief him. Phil wanted to know how he knew about the incident.

"A reporter from the Star Ledger called me. Were you aware the press was going to cover this event?"

"No. Why?"

"I need to be certain that you didn't contact them in an effort to get some publicity for yourself."

"It never would have occurred to me."

"Excellent. I assume it was the culinary college then."

"Is there a problem?" Phil asked.

Doctor Griggs stared at Phil intently. He was trying to decide whether the man was naïve or a fool. "I don't think the story in the morning papers is going to reflect well on this high school."

Phil nodded. He was beginning to catch on.

"Marianne, will you excuse us please?" Doctor Griggs spoke.

"No Kelsey. I won't. I am Phil's mentor. I should hear this."

"Very well." He turned to Phil. "There will be some questions from the school board about the advisability of a field trip with these students. I expect to take some heat. I'm going to suspend the three boys for a few days but I want you to be aware that if any improprieties on your part should be uncovered, you too will face disciplinary action."

"I followed the rules to the letter as far as I know."

"Let's hope the school board sees it that way."

The newspaper article turned out to be a short piece that didn't do a lot of damage. The superintendent of schools asked Doctor Griggs a few questions to ensure that there wouldn't be any repercussions on the school system or the state of New Jersey. Since no real damage was done to the equipment and there were no injuries, the matter was dropped. The officials of the culinary college, embarrassed now by the publicity, were not the least bit interested in adding any fuel to the fire. For his part, Phil was a bit miffed that Doctor Griggs didn't seem to appreciate his efforts to do something beyond babysitting these kids. After all, what other teacher at North Ward put himself out? Most of them behaved as if they were doing the school system and the students a favor just by showing up.

But Phil was wrong about that. Doctor Griggs had gone to bat for Phil in his conversation with the superintendent. He said, "We need more Phil Falco's. He stuck his neck out for these kids. I don't think he realizes it yet, but he cares about their welfare. Unlike some teachers who seem to be simply running out the string to retirement, this man is trying to reach his students with whatever tools he can conjure."

In fact, Phil's thoughts were often focused on retirement. He had counted on the sale of the shore house to help fund it. At 58, he figured he had just four years to go until he could collect Social Security. As far as he was concerned doing something creative for his students was part of the job. He had always looked for ways to be more valuable to his employer. This was no different. By Wednesday afternoon, he felt much like the teacher in the lounge who had been counting the days to the long weekend. He was looking forward to the break. At that moment he could barely stand the sight of North Ward High School or the miserable kids that were sleepwalking through its halls.

CHAPTER 18

It rained hard early on Thanksgiving morning. When it stopped raining it was cold and damp. Phil had planned to attend the annual Thanksgiving Day football game between North Ward and its sister school, South Ward, but when he woke up to the rain he knew he wouldn't go. He was dreading the onset of winter. He remembered well how much he hated the cold. On days like this he would long for Florida.

As he sat watching one of the NFL football games, he thought about spending the rest of the day with Gloria and her mother. He had promised to be there by 3:00 p.m. He asked if he could bring something but Gloria said no. Still, he had gone to the liquor store after school on Wednesday and bought a bottle of Frangelico. If he showed up empty handed his mother would have turned over in her grave. Mrs. Milano would have written him off as a cafone, a low class boorish man.

Before he left, he called Arlene hoping to speak with Lisa. They had only spoken twice since she left. Arlene answered the phone. She was in a good mood. Her new marriage seemed to agree with her.

"Is Lisa around?"

"No. She is out with her boyfriend," Arlene said.

Phil was almost afraid to ask. Arlene sensed his worry. "This is a nice guy Phil. I'll let her tell you about him. Wait and I'll get her cell phone number."

Phil had the number but he wrote it down anyway. Does she have a job?"

"She does. My husband Jack owns an Internet services franchise. They put up Web sites and help small businesses do e-commerce."

"e-commerce?" Phil asked.

"You don't know what that is?"

"I know what it is. I guess I was just surprised to hear you say it."

"A dope like me huh?" Arlene said.

I didn't mean it that way Arlene, really."

"Anyway, Jack gave Lisa a job. In fact that's where she met her boyfriend."

So, everything is okay then?" Phil asked.

"Pretty much. The only thing is she keeps complaining of a stomach ache. She's been to the doctor a few times but they can't seem to find anything."

"That's still a problem? She was complaining about that when she was here with me," Phil said.

"Don't get carried away," Arlene said, "I'm keeping an eye on her."

Phil called Lisa next. They had a nice chat. Lisa sounded very happy. Her tone of voice was an octave higher to Phil's ears. He asked about her boyfriend and she gushed about how wonderful he was. She wanted Phil to meet him.

"Maybe you can come out here for Christmas," Lisa said.

"Maybe I can," Phil said, "It would get me away from the cold weather."

"I hope you do Daddy. You need to meet Nicolas. He's Greek."

Phil teased his daughter a little about the new man in her life. The sound of her laughter brought back memories of much happier times for Phil when they were still a family. He asked her about her stomach problems.

"Oh that. It's not that bad really. I'm just trying to find a doctor that can fix it."

At that moment Phil heard the siren of a fire engine running past his apartment. He waited until it passed before he spoke again.

"How many different doctors have you been to Lisa?" He asked.

"Only a couple. It's nothing really," Lisa answered. "I have to go daddy. See you at Christmas."

Phil decided to let it go. He remembered that Lisa had been to at least two different doctors when she was staying with him. That worried him a little. He was aware from all those years working in the hospital that doctor hopping could be the sign of other problems.

Phil decided to call Arlene the next day and mention his concern to her. No sense in ruining their Thanksgiving dinner. He was probably overreacting.

He drove over to Gloria's house in the rain. He was grateful now that he wouldn't have to spend the day alone. He had been worried that he was making his initial descent into what would become a deep Holiday melancholy. Gloria always seemed to be upbeat. That was just what he needed.

He thought about Marianne and how happy he would have been to spend the day with her. By now she was probably sipping cocktails in a cozy Cape Cod bungalow with her friend Jerry. In spite of not knowing a thing about this Jerry, Phil was convinced that he, Phil, would be a better choice for Marianne. Again he resolved to be patient with her. Maybe her romance with whoever this guy Jerry was would falter.

As he turned into Gloria's driveway, he forced himself to put on a happy face. He knew Gloria was happy that he would be her guest. He would do his best not to be a disappointment.

Gloria's mother must have seen him come up the driveway because by the time he got to the front door, she had it open for him. He was about to step inside when he remembered his bottle of Frangelico.

"Happy Thanksgiving," Mrs. Milano sang.

"Same to you. I need to get something out of the car." Phil walked quickly back to the car, the cold rain and wind hitting his face in spite of the umbrella he was carrying. He silently cursed the weather. By the time he got back up to the front porch, Gloria was standing there waiting. Mrs. Milano was nowhere in sight.

"Happy Thanksgiving Phil," Gloria said. She ushered him in the house giving him a gentle push as if to get him out of the elements faster. Before he could say a word, Mrs. Milano reappeared carrying a towel.

"Use this to dry off," she said.

Both women were dressed smartly. Mrs. Milano had on gray slacks and a colorful sweater adorned with autumn leaves. Gloria was wearing a black skirt and a lavender blouse. She had a cream colored scarf around her neck. Phil had to admit she looked good. Her outfit was obviously expensive and she carried herself very well. She looked elegant, a picture of class.

"Here, this is for you," he said handing the bottle to Gloria.

"Ah, one of my favorites. You really didn't have to do that."

Phil laughed. "Hey, I don't want you thinking I wasn't brought up right."

Gloria smiled. She took his coat and hung it in the hall closet. Then she led him into the family room so they could sit by the fire. Again, Mrs. Milano disappeared. "It's funny how the old country traditions stay with us," Gloria said. They were quiet for a moment. "You look very nice," she said.

"Thanks." Phil was wearing a black sports coat over a gray dress shirt. A red tie with gray stripes complemented his ensemble. He had felt bad showing up the last time dressed like a slob.

"Would you mind making us a drink?" Gloria asked.

"Not at all. What would you like?"

"A Manhattan sounds great. My Mother will want one too but use more ice and less whisky when you make hers, okay?"

Phil gave her a quick thumbs up and walked into the kitchen. Mrs. Milano was busy sautéing mushrooms. She smiled when she saw him.

"I think my daughter's got a thing for you, Phil." Obviously Mrs. Milano wasn't the type to waste time with small pleasantries.

She got right to the point.

Phil was thrown completely off balance but he couldn't help laughing at her directness. "Why do you say that?"

Mrs. Milano rolled her eyes. "She's my daughter. Don't you think I would know?"

Phil thought that one over as he put ice in the rock glasses. He looked for maraschino cherries in the refrigerator, finding them on the door shelf. He decided to have a Manhattan too. "So, Gloria hasn't said anything to you. It's an intuition thing I suppose."

"I remember when you were all kids. You spent some time at my house, you Carmine and Gloria. I told my husband then; she's marrying the wrong one."

Phil poured the vermouth over the whiskey and stirred. "I think she was in love with Carmine at the time. I don't know what happened between them really. Carmine never said too much about it. In any case it's all water under the bridge now."

Mrs. Milano took the mushrooms off the stove and covered the pan. "All I'm saying Phil, is neither one of you is a spring chicken. Open your eyes before it's too late. Do you have a girlfriend?" She waved off her own question. "I guess not. If you did you wouldn't be spending the holiday with us."

Phil laughed. He handed a drink to the old lady. "Let's go in and sit by the fire."

"You go. I'll be there in a little while. I got a few more things to do here. Get to know my daughter again. A lot happens in thirty-five years." She smiled.

As it turned out the three of them had an enjoyable afternoon and evening over a traditional Thanksgiving meal. Phil did his best to be a good guest. He even helped clear the table and put dishes into the dishwasher over the protests of both women. Once the dishes were done, Gloria invited Phil back into the family room. This time she poured the drinks, opening the bottle of Frangelico.

Phil felt relaxed. The day had turned out much better than he imagined. Thoughts of melancholy seemed silly in retrospect. One holiday down and two to go he thought. Gloria was an engaging conversationalist. Over the last five years she had traveled twice to Europe, visiting Italy, France and Germany. She also made a trip to Australia where she met one of her cousins. What made it so interesting she said, was that neither of them knew that the other was in Australia. They ran into each other in a coffee bar in Sydney. Gloria was traveling with a friend who it turned out also knew her cousin. The three of them spent the next couple of days together taking in the sights.

One of the things Phil liked about Gloria was the way she told her stories. She wasn't trying to impress Phil with her exploits. If she stayed in expensive hotels or ate in five star restaurants she kept those facts to herself. She also seemed genuinely interested in what Phil was doing. She thoroughly enjoyed Phil's story about the culinary school. She was tickled that he had come up with the idea because she had mentioned the school to him. Phil noticed the two women exchange glances when he mentioned that Marianne had accompanied him on the trip. Mrs. Milano quietly mumbled something under her breath in Italian when she heard Marianne's name. Phil was about to ask what she said but then he saw a look on Mrs. Milano's face that told him that was precisely what she wanted. He glanced over at Gloria. She was giving her mother a warning look. Phil got up and went to the bathroom. It was the safest place to be.

When it was time to leave, Gloria walked him to the door and gave him a warm hug. He sensed that she was hoping for a kiss goodnight. He had considered it and he might have done it if Mrs. Milano hadn't said what she did. He wondered if Gloria and Mrs. Milano had discussed what Mrs. Milano would say to him beforehand. He had no idea that Gloria would have been mortified had she known about their conversation. In any case, Phil was wise enough not to mention it to her.

They stood on the front porch for a few minutes. The rain was down to a light drizzle. "Do you have a busy weekend planned?" Gloria asked.

"Schoolwork, I suppose. I have to write a paper and I've got some papers to grade."

"Well, thanks again for coming today. Call me. We'll do something."

Phil got back to his apartment in time to watch the news. He took off his shoes and sat in his recliner. He lost interest in the news after just a few minutes and his mind drifted to thoughts of Gloria. As much as he hated to admit it, he liked Gloria. She was attractive. Unlike Fred, she had interests beyond looking for ways to entertain herself for the next few days. Fred lived day to day. Gloria was trying to embrace life fully, even if she was getting a late start. She had acknowledged that inheriting money freed her to explore. Now she was taking advantage of her good fortune.

The next two weeks were uneventful. Phil called Arlene immediately after the Thanksgiving weekend was over. She listened to his concerns about Lisa. Surprisingly, she didn't dismiss Phil's worries. Rather, she fueled them by saying exactly what Phil had been thinking. Was their daughter shopping doctors to get prescriptions for pain medication? She promised to do what she could to check on Lisa.

"That's all we need now," she said.

Phil and Gloria spoke on the phone a couple of times but their conversations were brief. He knew Gloria was hoping he would ask her out and he was tempted, if for no other reason than to have someone to spend Christmas with. But then he also realized that it would be a selfish act. Perhaps it was too late in life to do him much good, but he was finally coming around to the realization that maybe Lisa had been right. He was often selfish. His relationships with women were no exception. More than anything, he thought, that was why he was alone. He felt his loneliness was well deserved.

Still, the temptation to get something started with Gloria was strong. He hated the thought of spending the holidays alone. Last year had been truly miserable. As insurance against the possibility of another lonely Christmas holiday he booked a flight for Phoenix so he could spend a few days with his daughter during the week between Christmas and New Year's Day. He didn't tell Lisa he was definitely coming. He decided to surprise her. If he didn't make it to Phoenix for Christmas he could always use the ticket later. He had spoken with Arlene once again but she had nothing to report. Lisa seemed to be doing okay.

His students were more wired than usual as the holidays approached. Their attention spans got shorter by the day. Phil wondered what they were really excited about. He assumed that Christmas as he knew it, with gifts under the tree had not been their experience. One day he asked Erik about it.

"What kind of Christmas do these kids have at home?"

"What do you mean?" Erik asked.

"What I mean is do they have a tree, the idea of Santa Claus and presents?"

"You mean "It's a Wonderful Life, White Christmas and the rest?"

Phil nodded.

"You might be surprised. Some of them do have something like that in their lives. Why do you ask? You thinking of an excursion to the North Pole next week?" Erik was smiling.

By now Phil was used to being ribbed by the other teachers about his trip to the culinary school. "Not the North Pole. Siberia maybe. Actually I was wondering why they're so wired. I know when I was their age I was excited because I looked forward to the big holiday meal and, even as a teenager, I had a few expectations about what might be under the tree."

"You forgot midnight mass," Erik said, again smiling, "but I see what you mean. More than anything I think it's the time off. They get about ten days off from school. Didn't you think about that when you were in school? "

"Sure. I thought about it. I'm thinking about it now."

The Christmas break was scheduled to begin at the end of a full school day on December 21st. The day before the break, Phil wrote a list of items on the blackboard. Each item had either some historical significance related to the holiday season or a tradition associated with the season. The birth of Christ, Washington crossing the Delaware, the history of Kwanzaa, the Christmas tree, and the Hanukah bush topped the list. He gave the students a choice. They could pick one item from the list and write a paragraph about it, or they could write a personal remembrance of the holiday. Of course he heard the usual groans but then he told them that as a Christmas present, he would automatically give an A on the assignment to every student who wrote something. He said he would read the best ones aloud the next day.

All things considered Phil got a good response from his students. Most of the students in each class had completed the assignment. Not surprisingly, most of them wrote a few sentences about Kwanzaa. A few had tried to be funny with decent results. One kid wrote:

Mister GW crossed the Delaware to meet his ole lady so he could give her some bling-bling. His men secretly followed him but they got lost and had to duke it out with them Hessian dudes while GW was gettin' some.

One of the girls wrote a heartwarming note about her grandmother's Christmas morning tradition:

My grandma every year write me a letter asking me to do good and study hard so I can be somebody good. She always put money in the envelope. Then sometimes she ask can she borrow some of it back. I think she likes me to feel good about holding the cash for a while. She always borrows it back though. But sometimes there's enough left to buy a little something for myself anyway.

Phil was drained by the time the kids in his last class piled into their seats. To accommodate a student body assembly, classes that day were reversed. His last class would normally have been his first. Later, he would wonder if what happened could have been avoided had the change not been made. As it was, Phil was all that stood between them and their long anticipated Christmas break. They would all be off for a while. As the kids turned in their assignments Phil thought about the holidays. He was happy for the break from work but he was already feeling lonely. As he had suspected, Gloria invited him to dinner for Christmas but he turned her down as politely as he could. Marianne asked him to stop by Christmas Eve and he promised he would. She said she really wanted him to meet her friend Jerry.

Looking out at the student's faces, most of them staring back at him, he could see they were wired. He wondered if any of them guessed that he wanted the class to be over as much as they did. Still he had to go through one more set of paragraphs. While he read through each one, just as he had done with the other classes, he told them to pull out their history books and read pages 104 to 109, a brief discussion of the French and Indian War. He said he might just give them a quiz if they didn't behave. They groaned and their were some 'fuck you's' muttered just loud enough to be heard over the general buzz in the room but most of the kids placed their book on their desk and pretended to read.

Phil went through the paragraphs as quickly as he could, forcing himself to read every word. One of the submissions impressed him so much that the hair on the back of his neck stood. It was a poem written by Kelvin Cherry, one of Rasheed's sidekicks. Like Rasheed he seemed to be one of the enforcers who used mockery and threats to discourage the other kids from trying. Kelvin was, in fact, the kid Rasheed had threatened in the cafeteria during the fall. Phil had written the young man off as hopeless but here was this poem that suggested that maybe Phil had misjudged him.

Christmas Eve
> Christmas Eve is a wonderful night
> With all the stars out shining bright
> And on the ground the new fallen snow
> Gives all the world a beautiful glow

Phil put the poem aside and finished reading through the stack. It never occurred to him as he picked it up again to read to the class that he had not seen Kelvin actually hand the paper to him. In fact, as he would later discover, one of the girls handed it in for him.

CHAPTER 19

The ambulance pulled away slowly, the driver being extra cautious not to bump into any of the onlookers, police officers or school officials as he made his way out of the school parking lot. It was snowing but not hard enough to amount to anything. It probably wasn't going to be a white Christmas in Northern New Jersey.

For Rasheed Marbury it wouldn't be much of a Christmas no matter what the weather was. He was barely conscious. Another inch to the left and he might well be dead. Initially, the emergency medical technicians were concerned about his chances for survival but extensive experience in such matters gave them reason to hope for the best. If there were no complications, Rasheed would probably live.

When Phil read Kelvin's poem aloud to the class, the room was silent, as if the classroom was empty. When he finished reading, Phil asked if anyone could guess who wrote it. One of the girls raised her hand. She had turned in the paper for Kelvin. "I think it was Cherry Tree." That was his name to the other kids.

Rasheed, who was sitting right next to Kelvin Cherry in the back of the classroom, laughed and said, "No fuckin' way. He ain't no fool."

Phil looked over at Kelvin. He seemed nervous. "I didn't write that shit."

"Well, your name is on the paper, Kelvin."

"He gave it to me just before we got here," Tamika said.

"Yo, pussy!" Rasheed said, "What the fuck you doin' man?"

"Fuck you Rasheed," Kelvin said, in a low voice.

Phil stood frozen for a moment trying to interpret what was

going on. There was usually a lot of trash talk between the boys but this time Phil sensed something different in the tone of voice each of the boys was using. By the time all this registered with Phil it was too late. As he walked down the aisle to get between the boys, who by this time were loudly hurling insults at each other, Rasheed had jumped up. His supremacy challenged, he took a swing at Kelvin. He was at least a foot taller than Kelvin who seemed to anticipate Rasheed's intentions. Pulling his hand out of his pocket he reached up and stabbed Rasheed in the chest with the same type sharp plastic knife Rasheed had displayed in the cafeteria. The force of the blow, combined with the forward momentum from Rasheed's swing facilitated the knife's entry into Rasheed's chest. Still moving forward, he fell flat on the ground. Breaking off most of the plastic handle that stood on the outside of his chest. He uttered a loud groan. By now Phil was standing next to Kelvin. Everyone was screaming which brought other teachers, students and security to the room.

Kelvin was standing over Rasheed saying, "I told you mother fucker you ain't hittin' me no more."

Feeling like he had to do something, Phil grabbed Kelvin and pushed him to the front of the room. Doctor Griggs stepped in and quickly ordered everybody out of the room. He instructed Erik Cowans to take Phil's students to the library. He then told one of the other teachers standing around to get the school secretary to broadcast an announcement instructing the rest of the students in the school to proceed directly to the large assembly hall. He looked at Phil and told him to stay in the room with Kelvin. The school nurse was trying to help Rasheed, who was having difficulty breathing. It seemed like forever before the emergency squad arrived but actually they were there less than ten minutes.

As soon as the hallway was cleared of students, Doctor Griggs told Phil and a security guard to escort Kelvin Cherry to his office.

The emergency medical technicians did everything they could to stabilize Rasheed Marbury before bundling him up and getting him into the ambulance. Doctor Griggs, who had also instructed his assistant to contact Marbury's aunt and the superintendent of schools, walked beside the stretcher carrying Rasheed and waited until he was in the ambulance and on his way to the hospital.

Only then did he walk back into the building, heading straight to the assembly hall. Doctor Griggs was in complete possession of all of his faculties. He knew that to show any weakness at that moment would be disastrous. He strode up to the lectern at the center of the stage and waited for the murmurs to die down. The rumor was that Rasheed was dead. When he spoke he made full use of his deep and commanding voice. He was not a man given to simplifying his vocabulary when addressing his students. He believed they were very capable of understanding his words and spoke accordingly.

"The first thing I want to tell you is that the student who was injured is stable and should be fine in a matter of days." Kelsey Griggs paused for a moment. "I know not whether any of you are religious. If you are this is the season to reflect on your lives and resolve to respect one another. You are here to learn. You are expected to graduate from North Ward High School as responsible young adults. The world you will live in after you leave this school will not tolerate violence. Nor will I tolerate any act of violence in this school. I am going to send you home in a few minutes to spend the holiday break with family and friends. When you return to school, you will all behave in strict accordance with this school's code of conduct. Is that clear?"

Doctor Griggs swept the room with is eyes, his face stern, to make certain that everyone understood. Any further incidents or acts of reprisal would be dealt with severely. To underscore the point he said, "There is a young man in my office that is in very serious trouble. An hour ago he was just minutes away from a long and relaxing break. Now, it will be a long time before he can relax. Would any of you want to be in his shoes now?

"One last thing: If as a result of these tragic events today any of you feel the immediate need to speak with a counselor, you should proceed directly to the nurse's office. If, when you return to school after the break, you would like to speak with someone, discuss it with your guidance counselor who will schedule a session for you. We will now prepare to leave the assembly hall. You will return in an orderly fashion to the classroom you were in before the incident occurred. Pick up your things from that room and proceed directly to your homeroom. You will sit quietly in your homeroom until instructed to leave. There are police officers on campus in addition to our security guards. I am sorry their presence is required. Obey them as you would me and you will be on your way shortly."

For once the kids in Phil Falco's American History class were quiet. In fact, they sat in the library without saying a word. Most of the girls and even a couple of boys let tears roll down their cheeks. Phil wasn't sure what to say. He was pretty sure that Rasheed was alive and would recover but he thought it might be a mistake to say anything. He was grateful that none of the kids were asking questions.

Phil was angry with himself. He kept replaying the scene in his mind trying to see if there was something he missed that he should have seen. A more experienced teacher probably would have known better than to read Kelvin's poem aloud, he thought. Certainly a more experienced teacher would have grasped the implications of the words the two young men exchanged and the manner in which they delivered them sooner than he did. He should have moved faster. He could see that now.

When he heard noises outside the library, shuffling feet, kids laughing and carrying on, his mood brightened a bit. Probably after today he would be waiting tables again but the sounds in the hallways gave him hope that the kids had been given good news about Rasheed's fate. At least that was something. Now he would have to worry about the other kid, Kelvin. Whatever happened to him would in some way be partly his, Phil's, fault. Kelvin would have to pay for his inexperience as a teacher.

Another long ten minutes later Doctor Griggs walked through the doors. He nodded at Phil as if to say I'll take it from here.

"Listen up ladies and gentlemen. The good news is that Mister Marbury is expected to survive and recover. What is important at this moment is that you do exactly what I ask you to do. In a few minutes police officers are going to arrive to speak with each of you. They will ask questions about what you saw and what you heard. Do not make the mistake of thinking you can protect either Mister Marbury or Mister Cherry. You are to tell the truth.

"When the officers are finished with you, you may return to your homeroom pick up your things and go directly home."

Doctor Griggs signaled for the librarian to bring the police detectives in. There were two of them. They set up desks and chairs in opposite corners of the library and began interviewing students. One of them took Phil's statement.

Doctor Griggs waited patiently for the detective to wrap up with Phil. As soon as he saw they were done, he motioned for Phil to follow him to his office. Phil's stomach was in knots. He felt a strange mix of shame, anger and bewilderment. He was truly relieved when he heard that Marbury would probably make it. When they got to Doctor Griggs' office, Kelvin was sitting in the outer office in handcuffs, sandwiched between his mother and grandmother. A uniformed officer stood guard. Doctor Griggs asked the boy's mother to join him and Phil in his office.

"I am truly sorry that your son finds himself in this situation, Mrs. Cherry."

"Carson. My name is Louise Carson," she said, a deep sadness in her voice.

"Ms. Carson this is Kelvin's history teacher, Mister Falco."

Phil did his best to explain what had happened in the classroom. He told the woman about how excited he was about the quality of Kelvin's poem, how it suggested that Kelvin was bright and wanted to learn. He quickly referenced the reading of the poem and then went on to describe how the boys began fighting and apparently, Kelvin stabbed Rasheed.

"Apparently?" Mrs. Carson said, her eyebrows raised.

Phil was about to respond when doctor Griggs' phone rang. Doctor Griggs picked up and listened. "I see. Would you hold one moment please?" Griggs looked up and said, "Mister Falco would you please escort Ms. Carson to my outer office? I have to take this call."

Phil willingly complied. The look on Doctor Griggs' face was disconcerting; more trouble, no doubt. Five minutes later, Griggs opened his door and motioned for Phil to come in. Louise Carson got up to join them but Doctor Griggs assured her they would be with her in a few minutes.

The worst had happened after all. Rasheed Marbury died in the emergency room. An artery had been punctured and he bled to death. The emergency medical technicians at the scene had missed it. The boy was gone. Doctor Griggs, a man who always appeared to be in control, was shaken by the turn of events. Phil was heartbroken. He found himself wiping tears from his eyes. Saddened though he was by the news of Rasheed's death, he understood that his tears were as much a reflection of his overwhelming frustration as they were about Rasheed.

The inevitable inquiry would take on an entirely new dimension now. A lot of questions would be asked. Certainly community leaders and politicians would demand answers to unanswerable questions. And of course the criminal justice system would grind Kelvin Cherry into dust.

It was another two hours before Phil was finally able to leave the school. He spoke again with the detectives and he also met with the superintendent of schools. Kelvin Cherry was taken away in handcuffs. One of Rasheed Marbury's relatives had arrived at the school thirty minutes before Phil left, screaming, cursing and issuing threats. She blamed Doctor Griggs, Phil and the City of

Newark for the fiasco. It was an ugly scene.

Later that night, alone in his apartment Phil continued to replay the events in the classroom. He realized that once things began to unfold, he might have been able to intervene had he walked down the aisle sooner. He understood that he was too inexperienced to really grasp what might happen once the boys got into it but that didn't make him feel any better. He wished he was taking drink orders at Veneto's and had never heard of the alternate route program for teachers.

Phil received four phone calls that night. Gloria called to console him. The tragedy was the lead story on the evening news, made all the more compelling by the media's decision to play up the Christmas season angle. They spoke only briefly. Gloria again asked if he might reconsider and join them for Christmas dinner. With everything up in the air, Phil wondered if maybe he should relent. He asked Gloria if he could get back to her in a day or so.

Of course Marianne also called. She invited him to come over to her place if he wanted to talk. "Such a tragedy Phil. I'm so sorry it happened."

"I can't make any sense of it," Phil said. "I keep asking myself why I didn't see it coming."

"Don't do that to yourself. No one could have predicted it. These kids are tortured souls."

"You're my mentor, Marianne. Where do I go from here?"

"I can't answer that question for you. Only you can do that. I hope you do know that everyone has been really impressed by your performance since you came to North Ward."

"Thanks. And thanks for inviting me over but I'm tired. Maybe tomorrow."

"Sure. Just call me," she said.

Erik Cowens called too.

"You doing all right?"

"Not really Erik. I can't believe any of this happened. I never saw it coming."

Erik let out a long sigh. "I know."

"Did you talk to the kids when you took them to the library?"

"Yeah, I talked to them. Let me ask you something. Did you know that Cherry didn't actually turn in the paper himself? Erik asked.

Now it was Phil's turn to heave a sigh. "I don't know. It might have crossed my mind but I didn't think anything of it."

"I see," Erik said.

"How's that?"

"Look man, I'm not blaming you but guys like you got no business in a classroom with inner city kids." Erik too was frustrated. "That kid wasn't ready to surface as a student. Not by a long shot. A more experienced teacher would have known enough to play it cool," Erik said. "Damn it Phil, understand I'm not blaming you. I know you're trying man. That alternate route thing is probably okay in the suburbs but the issues here are a lot more complicated."

"How come you never said anything before?"

"Like what? What could I say? Nobody listens anyway."

"I feel like shit. Two lives ruined. One's dead and the other might as well be. And there's not a damn thing I can do about it," Phil said.

"True, but you are in it now my man. You got to move forward."

"What does that mean?"

"You still want to teach at North Ward?" Erik asked.

"I do but I'm afraid I'm doing more harm than good. Anyway, it's probably not my decision," Phil said. "Nobody said anything but maybe I'm out the door regardless."

"Not unless you say it," Erik said, "they won't ask you to leave because of this."

"Why not?"

Another long sigh from Erik. "If they fire you how many people like you going to try doing this job?"

"What do you mean, like me?" Phil asked.

"You give a damn about these kids is all I'm saying."

"But you said I didn't belong in an inner city school," Phil said.

"You don't. But there just aren't enough people willing to work hard like you've been doing."

"Well, if I'm not fired, I'm not ready to quit either. That's about the only thing I know for sure. That kid Kelvin? He actually tried today with that poem. First time since school started." Phil had to stop. He could feel himself begin to choke up. He took a deep breath. "I guess I got excited about it and didn't think." He paused again, his mind blank. "I need a drink."

"You do that," Erik said. "One more thing Phil. Maybe it would be best if you don't go to Marbury's services. It could be risky."

The last call Phil got was a surprise. He was lying in bed hoping the exhaustion he felt would overwhelm the tape player running in his head, playing the same scene over and over. Maybe sleep would come. He almost got there but the phone made him jump.

"Phil? You recognize my voice?"

"Dennis Florio?"

"Are you alright Phil?"

Phil told him essentially the same thing he said to Erik Cowens. Then he mentioned that Erik had discouraged him from attending the services.

"Do you want to go?" Florio asked.

"Yeah. I have to go."

"Your buddy Erik, he's an ex-cop right?"

"Do you know him?" Phil asked.

"I know him. Look, he's probably right but if you really want to go I can fix it so you won't have a problem. There's a loud mouth reverend, a real ditzoon, that runs that neighborhood. Don't repeat this but he's on my payroll."

"Repeat what?" Phil said, embarrassed he could laugh.

"Right. Anyway, when you get there I'll make sure he's waiting for you. He'll be your personal escort."

"Thanks Dennis."

"You see? You're investment is still paying off." Dennis said.

Phil didn't laugh.

CHAPTER 20

The funeral services were held just two days later, only two days before Christmas. Phil arrived at the church with Erik Cowens at his side. Erik picked him up and drove him to the church that morning. The sun was shining but it was a bitter cold morning. Most of the school's teachers, all the kids in Rasheed's class, and of course Doctor Kelsey Griggs were there.

Doctor Griggs must have pointed Phil out to the reverend because he walked over to Phil right away. The reverend put his arm around him and thanked him for coming to the service. There was a lot of crying and a good deal of posturing by a couple of local politicians that got up to speak. But the reverend, on Florio's payroll or not, spoke with true passion. He held the mourners in the palm of his hand when he spoke about Rasheed's despair. His final words before the procession:

"No young man in America of any color should fear his future. And make no mistake: It was fear that got this young man killed. He was afraid to try because he believed that in trying, the deck stacked mightily against him, he would look the fool, feel the fool and be the fool for trying to abide by rules that were never meant for his kind.

That other young man committed a horrible act out of the same fear. He was afraid. Afraid that Rasheed and the other children would see that he dared to risk all, that those who mattered most would consider him a fool. Such a tiny step toward believing that there might be something more than the ghetto in his future. He wrote a simple yet beautiful poem. Now Rasheed no doubt, knew it was good. He understood and that frightened him. The applecart was upset. Only one way to right it in a world ruled by fear. One life over and another life ruined. Heartbreak brothers and sisters, heartbreak all around.

When will it stop? Who will stop it? Rasheed Marbury's death must mean something. Kelvin Cherry's sacrifice must stand for something. I beseech you to overcome your own fears and step up, step out and stand tall. In the eyes of God, in his house two days before the coming of the Christ child, resolve to believe in your future, your children's future. Fear it no more. No more wasted lives. This year for Christmas, give your children hope. Let them know it is okay to dream of a better future. Let them know it is okay to strive for something more. Let them see you reach for the stars, unafraid of failure and believing in yourselves. There can be no better gift. There can be no better way to honor Rasheed's memory"

When the services ended, Phil did his best to walk slowly toward Erik's car. More than anything he wanted to get away from the scene. Still he walked deliberately, hoping none of his students or their parents would speak to him. He was spent. Tired from not sleeping and tired from answering questions posed by various school board members and police officers. When they reached Erik's car he felt a tap on his shoulder. He shuddered, not knowing what to expect. He turned slowly, resigned to the possibility that some irate family member of Rasheed's might decide to take out the family's frustration on him. He was ready for it, prepared to accept it if necessary.

But it was Marianne. "Want to ride with me?" she asked. Then turning to Erik she said, "I can get him home. You live in the opposite direction."

Erik hesitated for a minute. Then he looked at Phil and realized that Phil wanted to ride with Marianne. "Just to be sure, let me take him a few blocks and then we can switch."

Erik drove Phil out of the neighborhood. Marianne followed

them. Phil thanked Erik for his help and wished him a Merry Christmas. The two men shook hands and agreed to find some time to get together during the Holiday break. Then Phil got into Marianne's car. They drove up South Orange Avenue together in silence for a few minutes, headed to the Garden State Parkway. They passed the old Pabst Blue Ribbon factory where the giant brown beer bottle crowned the top of the building facing the Parkway.

"No matter how many times I see that bottle I never think of it as the Pabst bottle," Phil said, just to have something to say.

"Really?" Marianne said. "What do you think of?"

Phil turned and looked at her. "Do you know what it was before it was a beer bottle?"

"No. What else could it have been?" she asked.

"It was a soda bottle. Hoffman Soda built it in the Thirties. It used to be green."

"I never knew that. I don't really remember Hoffman. I do know the building and the bottle are supposed to come down," Marianne said. "Riding down the Parkway won't be the same."

"Nothing is the same," Phil said.

"Are we talking about buildings and soda bottles or are we taking about Rasheed and Kelvin? You're really taking this hard aren't you?"

Phil shrugged. "A seventeen year old kid is dead; my fault that it happened. I should have stayed in Florida."

They rode in silence again for a while. They got onto the Parkway headed north. In a matter of minutes they would be at Phil's apartment. He glanced over at Marianne and saw what he always saw, a pretty face with keen eyes. She didn't miss much and Phil correctly assumed she knew how he felt about her.

"You still want me to stop by tomorrow?" Phil asked, remembering Marianne's invitation.

"Sure. Why don't you come about 11:30? I want you to meet Jerry."

Phil smiled. "I really can't wait."

Marianne poked him in the ribs. "I'm serious Phil. He's a very nice guy. You'll like him."

"Why do women say things like that? Do you really expect me to like him?"

"I have no desire to hurt your feelings, Phil, honestly. But it would never work out between us. You and Carmine were too close. It would always seem funny, you know?"

Phil nodded. Now it was really out in the open. He would never have the kind of relationship with Marianne he had once hoped for. While the reality was a blow to his ego, he recognized that there was something liberating about the certainty of his fate. Still, he took one last shot.

"We never gave it a chance though. Who knows what might have happened between us."

Marianne shook her head. She gave him a sad smile. "Phil, I have never gone wrong by trusting my instincts. There are some things you can tell about without having to test them. You're a wonderful man but we are not right together. Anyway, you have other options from what I hear."

Phil was about to ask what that meant but thought better of it. He had a pretty good idea of what Marianne was driving at. They pulled up to his apartment and he got out of the car. "I'll see you tomorrow. At least I don't have to shop for the perfect gift."

They both laughed.

Home and finally alone, Phil slumped comfortably in his recliner. It was still early, not quite two o'clock in the afternoon. He felt a sense of relief. Having done his duty by attending the funeral service, he could relax a little. He felt bad about Rasheed and Kelvin of course but he wasn't from their world. Whether he might have been able to save the two boys from catastrophe was a moot point. The preacher's words resonated with Phil. He found them comforting. What mattered now was the future.

Everyone had to move forward. A few minutes after the service the preacher had approached Phil. He put his arm around him and said, "I checked you out. I hope you can find a way to get past this brother."

It was time for Phil to think about his own future. And now that Marianne had finally put her cards on the table, he could do it with a clear mind.

He thought about his conversation with Erik Cowens. Erik had been right. He did care and that had been a surprise to Phil. He took the job thinking it would be easy, certainly easier than waiting tables. Not only did he want to continue teaching, he now wanted to find better ways to reach more kids. The reverend's words gave Phil hope. No more wasted lives. He said this aloud, mimicking the reverend. He pulled himself up out of his chair and headed to the kitchen.

The message light was lit so he punched the button. There was a call from Lisa wanting to know if he was coming to Phoenix for Christmas. Other than buying a ticket, he hadn't had time to think about it. He would call her the next day and let her know he was indeed coming to Phoenix. He was still worried about her. Now he was determined to see for himself if she might be having a problem.

The second message was from Gloria. "Oh hi Phil. I must sound like a pest but I did want to give you a call and see how things went today. Call me when you get a sec."

Phil stared at the phone for a moment. He thought about Marianne again and how she couldn't see them together because of Carmine. Yet, here was a woman that had been married to Carmine and she didn't see a problem. The thought made him grimace. On impulse he picked up the phone and called Gloria.

He pulled into that long driveway wondering for the fiftieth time if he was crazy. His conversation with Gloria had been short. He glossed over the details of the funeral and said he had to go to the mall.

"Feel free to stop by when you're done," Gloria said, "But I should warn you that my mother is staying at her sister's, so don't expect to be pampered if you come."

Phil did a little shopping. He got a few things for Lisa and a tie for her boyfriend. He also picked out a pale blue and yellow scarf for Marianne. She was fond of wearing scarves and he had seen enough of them to know the one he picked would suit her taste.

Now, taking the long walk up Gloria's driveway to her front door, the cold weather made him think of Carmine and the last time he saw him. He never imagined he would submit himself to a winter again but here he was. He wanted to be angry with Carmine but he was out of steam. Poor Carmine was dead and that was that. Well, he had lived a hell of a better life than Rasheed. That Carmine had made Phil's life difficult was another story. Anyway, just thinking about Rasheed's miserable, short life put things into perspective for him. He stopped about three-quarters of the way up the drive. At that moment he forgave Carmine. He walked up to Gloria's front door and rang her bell. "Fuck you Carmine," he said, but he was smiling.

Gloria acted surprised to see him but considering the way she was dressed, an expensive looking ensemble of white wool slacks and an emerald green blouse, it was obvious she expected he would come. They sat on opposite sides of the couch by the fire just like they had done on Thanksgiving. He teased her a little about how huge the house was, saying that his entire apartment would easily fit into the sitting room they were in. The room was really decked out for Christmas. A large and colorful manger occupied one corner of the room. Another corner had a fifteen foot tall Christmas tree decorated with expensive ornaments. Phil complimented Gloria on her taste in decorations. She thanked him, adding that her parents had always made a big deal about Christmas. She reminded him how years ago her father used to put so many lights and Santa Claus characters outside that people would drive by constantly during the holidays just to see what he had done. They chatted on about the holidays for a while until Gloria changed the subject.

"I'm really sorry about what happened to that boy, Phil. I hope you won't give up on teaching. You seem to like it so."

"I'm not giving up."

"That's good. From what I've read and seen on TV, it wasn't your fault."

Phil brushed some imaginary lint off his sweater. "I'll tell you something. I was there. I saw what happened. I keep replaying it and it always comes out the same. No matter how I try to imagine a way to fix it, Kelvin manages to stab Rasheed. I imagine myself running down the aisle between the desks as soon as Rasheed starts acting up. Somehow, I don't know, maybe I turn my head for a split second and it happens anyway."

"Do you think maybe if you did stop them from hurting each other in the classroom that it might have happened later on, perhaps in the school yard or on the school bus?" Gloria asked.

"Anything's possible."

"I'm sure this will sound trite but the important thing now is to move forward. I'm so delighted you plan to keep teaching. You're doing a wonderful thing."

"These kids, they get the short end from the day they're born. It's hard to describe the feeling you get when just one of them shows even a small sign of beating the odds."

They sat quietly for a moment, staring into the fire.

" Would you pick a wine and have a glass with me?" Gloria asked.

"Why not? I think I remember where you keep it. The palace seems especially quiet with your mother gone."

Gloria followed Phil into the kitchen. "I know. My aunt wanted me to spend the night at her place too. I'll pick mom up tomorrow night after dinner."

"You're not having dinner with them Christmas Eve?"

"No. I know it sounds silly but I prefer the solitude to keeping two elderly women company," Gloria said, "Oh listen to me. I sound pitiful."

Phil looked at her. He put down the corkscrew and turned to face her. She was good looking; too good looking at that moment to resist. He took a step and a half closer to her and kissed her lips. "As pretty as you are, you can try for pitiful but no one will buy it."

Gloria's eyes shone. "You made my day Mister Falco."

They held each other for a moment until Phil let go so he could open the bottle and pour the wine. They went back into the living room to sit by the fire again. They chose one of the love seats sitting close together this time. Neither of them spoke, hypnotized for the moment by the flickering of the yellowish-blue flames. Phil put his glass down and turned to Gloria. She did the same and they kissed again, this time with passion as if they had been waiting for this moment for years. Of course, in Gloria's case she had been waiting for years.

Once Phil's hands started to roam though, Gloria stiffened and pulled away. "Not so fast Phil Falco. I waited a long time for you. I would be mortified if this turned out to be about the wine, and the moment and nothing more." She smiled.

Phil laughed. "I did get caught up in the moment."

Gloria took his hand in hers. "We have plenty of time to get to know each other. Call me an old fashioned girl but I believe people should be in love before they make love." She lowered her head and looked down at the rug.

Phil cupped Gloria's chin and gently raised her head so they were looking into each other's eyes. "How do you know I'm not in love?"

"I think maybe you are but not with me, at least not yet."

Before Phil could get a word out, his cell phone rang. It was Marianne. She had a message for him. It was from Carmine.

CHAPTER 21

Phil got to Marianne's house as fast as he could. Traffic was light so it didn't take long. Once inside he was greeted by Marianne, her boyfriend Jerry and her son Ricky. They were standing around the dining room table. Marianne introduced Phil to Jerry. He seemed nice enough but Phil was struck by the fact that he was only as tall as Marianne and maybe even a bit shorter. He could not have stood more than five seven and a half by Phil's estimate. He appeared to be younger than Marianne as well.

"Okay Marianne what's this about hearing from Carmine?"

"I didn't exactly hear from him. He sent me a Christmas card. How could he do that? He's dead. We saw his body Phil." She turned to her son. "We saw him didn't we Rick?"

Ricky nodded. It wasn't the first time that night his mother asked that question. He shrugged, showing his irritation now. Jerry put his arm around Marianne to comfort her. She was crying again.

Phil took in the scene. "Where's the card?" he asked in a somber voice.

"I'll get it," Marianne said. She wiped her eyes with a tissue and walked into the kitchen. The three men followed her. The card was in its envelope. She handed it to Phil.

The envelope was blank other than having Marianne's name and address printed on it. There was no handwriting. The cover of the card was a simple Christmas wreath with the words Merry Christmas emblazoned over the wreath. On the inside of the card there was a printed message:

Dear Sis,
By the time you get this I should be gone for almost a year

already. Please don't be mad at me Mare, for doing what I'm about to do. It doesn't matter really because either way I would still be gone by the time you get this. My doctor says I got a stage 4 lung cancer. I don't want to go through what Dad went through and I don't want to put you through it.

I don't have much but there is something I want to leave you and my best friend, Phil Falco. Share and share alike. Sis, you were the best sister any guy could ever hope to have. Phil was always a standup guy especially when it really counted.

I had to think of a good spot for the package. I put it somewhere that Phil will know about. I had to be careful because there are people that will be looking for it. Maybe after a year goes by the heat will have died down and people will forget about it. Ask Phil if he remembers good Old No 7. That's where you'll find your Christmas gift. Don't worry about me Mare. It's better this way.

Love, C.

Phil looked at the back of the card. The card company logo appeared in small print. Universal Greeting Cards.com was imprinted in black.

"Do you have an Internet connection?" Phil asked.

"Ricky does," Marianne said.

Phil followed Ricky to his room. It looked like it had been tumbled dry in the clothes dryer with sheets, clothes, shoes, magazines, dirty plates, cups and glasses tossed together and now waiting for someone to sort everything out.

"Nice room," Phil said.

"Up yours," Ricky mumbled. He led Phil to the computer. In no time Phil found the site and navigated his way through it. All those lonely nights sitting in front of the computer screen were paying off. He saw how, for a nominal fee, anyone could set up an account. They could pick greeting cards for any occasion and arrange to have them sent up to a year in advance. Carmine must have written the card an hour or so before he ran his car into the pole.

Immediately Phil's mind jumped to the laptop that the police found at the scene of the accident. Carmine must have deliberately driven over it to make sure no one would check his whereabouts on the Web. Carmine wasn't taking any chances. Certainly he would have understood that Florio would do whatever he could to recover the money. He printed Universal Greeting Card's home page and returned to Marianne's kitchen. He didn't tell them what he was thinking. He just explained how Carmine managed to send a card after being dead for almost eleven months.

"What does he mean Phil, 'old number seven'?" Marianne asked.

"I'm not sure what that means," Phil said.

"It probably has something to do with Mickey Mantle. He was a Mickey Mantle freak," Ricky said.

Marianne turned to Phil for confirmation. Phil shrugged his shoulders. "Maybe."

"What does it mean though? He seems to be telling us where to find the package." Marianne said.

"Do you have any idea of what it means?" Phil asked.

"I don't have a clue. If you don't know we're sunk," Marianne said.

"Let me sleep on it. Whatever it is has to go back to when we were kids," Phil said, "Maybe something will click after I get some rest. The last couple of days have been unbelievable."

"Oh Phil, that's right. I know how terrible this has been for you with Rasheed Marbury and all. You're coming over here tomorrow morning anyway, right?"

"That's the plan."

Ricky lost interest in the conversation and drifted off to watch TV. That left Jerry, Marianne and Phil standing in the kitchen. "Would you like something to drink?" Jerry spoke for the first time.

"No thanks. I should get going. See you both tomorrow morning."

Phil was happy to have a chance to escape. He could hardly contain his excitement. He knew exactly what Carmine's clue meant. And he was particularly proud of himself for not blurting it out. For once he had played it cool. He wanted time to think. It wasn't that he wanted to deny Carmine's wish that he and Marianne share the money, but he had already put out almost half a million dollars to save their skins. Technically the money was his. He was sure that if Carmine knew what happened he would have seen it that way. Only it wasn't that simple. He had decided on his own to pay Florio off, contrary to Marianne's advice. And unless she married someone with money, she probably would need her share. Regardless, he wanted some time to think about it.

When he got back to his apartment he went right to the kitchen cabinet where he kept his liquor. Although he preferred wine to hard liquor these days, occasionally he still enjoyed Old Number 7. He poured himself a stiff Jack Daniels over ice. He knew exactly where to find the money. The question was when and how to retrieve it.

Phil woke up early Christmas Eve morning. He had a busy day planned. First, he had to wrap the few gifts he bought. He also wanted to stop at a toy store and pick up a couple of gifts he wanted to give to Rasheed's younger brother. Phil figured the kid was about nine, maybe ten years old. He had actually spoken to the young man briefly just before the service. He was sure he couldn't go wrong with electronic toys like a Game Boy. The idea had come to him while he was sipping his Jack the night before.

Then he had to get over to Marianne's house. The money, assuming that was what Carmine had been referring to in his Christmas card, was in Marianne's house in the basement. It was the house she and Carmine grew up in.

He also had promised Gloria that he would stop by to see her that afternoon. That reminded him that he really needed to find a gift for her too. He was pretty sure she would have one for him and he didn't want to get caught empty handed. He smiled at the thought of being with Gloria. He had been surprised when she put the brakes on their make out session. What surprised him more though was what he felt when he actually kissed her. He felt or sensed a chemistry between them that he had always missed before.

After wrapping the gifts for Marianne, Lisa and her boyfriend, he quickly showered, shaved and dressed. He wanted to hit the stores before the crowds became unbearable with people desperately shopping for that one last gift in the final hours before Christmas. As he left his apartment he took a quick look around and saw that he had left Marianne's gift on the kitchen table with the others. He walked over and picked it up. He suddenly realized that he didn't have a single Christmas decoration for his apartment. For some reason that made him sad.

The Marbury family lived on Third Street in the North Ward section of Newark, not far from where Phil grew up. Years ago the neighborhood had been the home of the Dugan's factory. Dugan's was a bakery that had long since gone out of business. As he drove down Abington Avenue he remembered how on hot summer mornings he and Carmine and some of the other boys used to get free powdered donuts just by standing outside the screen door where they were being made. As it turned out, the old donut building was only a few doors down from the Marbury residence.

Phil was nervous standing outside the Marbury's front door. Someone must have seen him because the door opened as soon as he knocked.

It was a man of about seventy years of age. "What you want?"

"Is Ms. Marbury in?"

"In what?"

"I mean is she home."

Before the old man could answer, Rasheed's aunt, Tonya Marbury appeared.

"You're Rasheed's teacher," she said.

"Yes." Phil almost wished her a Merry Christmas but then he realized how inappropriate that would sound. For that matter he didn't even know if the Marbury's were Christian. He glanced down at his packages at the bright red Santa wrapping he had hastily bought and wondered.

"What can I do for you?" her tone far from friendly.

"I have a couple of toys here for Rasheed's little brother."

The woman stared at the bag for a moment. "He's not here," she said.

"Well, would it be alright for me to leave these for him?"

"No. It would not be alright for you to leave them. I think you should leave. You come down here feeling all good about yourself and the spirit of Christmas but you don't have a clue. You like everybody else, just wanting to feel good about yourself. These kids need a lot more than dumb ass toys to play with."

Phil nodded. He was struck by the accuracy of the woman's words. He hadn't thought he was trying to relieve his own feelings of guilt when he decided to buy the toys, but she had a point. Even if she was right though, Phil wondered why she couldn't see that Rasheed's little brother was suffering too. Phil's personal reasons for buying a few toys would be irrelevant to the kid. He would like having them. Perhaps her anger was clouding her judgment, Phil thought.

"Let me ask you something, please," he said.

"What?" she said.

"What should I be doing? What do you think will help these kids?"

"Damned if I know. They need a better education than what y'all are giving them, I know that."

Phil said thank you and turned to go.

"Hey, you leaving those things or not?"

Phil handed her the bag.

He drove back to Bloomfield Avenue and headed to Marianne's house, a ten minute ride. Jerry answered the door and told him Marianne was upstairs and would be down in a few minutes. They sat in the living room. Ricky was nowhere in sight. That gave Phil a chance to chat with Jerry.

"Do you live in the area Jerry?" Phil asked.

"I live in Ridgewood so, depending on how you define area, I guess you could say yes."

Phil asked how Jerry met Marianne and what he did for a living. Jerry was matter of fact in his answers. A mutual friend introduced them at a fundraiser, he said. He went on to explain that he was an attorney, a partner in a law firm that specialized in tax law. It was obvious from the way Jerry talked that he was a man of considerable means. The Mercedes parked outside was no doubt his.

Phil sensed that Jerry was aware that he had been interested in Marianne. Jerry was trying to play it cool. His tone and body language were meant to convey supreme confidence in his position. Phil was amused; Jerry's confident display was overkill. It suggested insecurity rather than confidence. Phil made a silent bet that as soon as Marianne sat down with them Jerry would display his affection for Marianne in some obvious way. As it turned out he was right. When she finally walked into the room she gave Phil a peck on the cheek and wished him a Merry Christmas. Then she sat on the couch next to Jerry. He immediately slid over to get closer, put his arm around her and gave her a kiss. He even gave Phil a little smile as if he was in on the bet.

Marianne looked terrific. She was wearing rather tight jeans and a long sleeved green pullover shirt that had a small white Christmas tree over the left breast. The reason Phil noticed it was Jerry was wearing an identical shirt. As soon as it registered, he looked back at Jerry to confirm his observation.

"Yes I know, twins," she said. "It's too cute but we couldn't resist." Then she leaned over to Jerry and kissed him full on the lips. Phil wondered if the kiss she gave Jerry was a message for him or one of reassurance for Jerry. Maybe it was both, he thought.

He gave her the gift he had bought her. She made an elaborate show of removing the ribbon and the wrapping paper. When she opened the box, her eyes lit up. She genuinely liked the scarf. He was quick to say it was just a token of his appreciation for what she had done for him at work. Then he told her about what had happened when he visited with Tonya Marbury.

"You know, Phil, that woman is right. We aren't doing enough for these kids. But I wonder if she has any idea what we're up against. These kids have no real incentive to do well in school. It's not like they can afford college even if they study hard."

"Aren't scholarships available?" Jerry asked.

"There are scholarships, but not that many. And it's competitive even among the kids living in poverty," she said. "Only the kids who get top test scores and good grades have any hope of getting one and they're not always full ride scholarships. The kids have to come up with a lot of the money themselves."

Phil thought about that for a moment. "I wish I had an answer," he said to no one in particular.

Marianne and Jerry nodded in agreement. Then Marianne suggested they go into the kitchen and have a cup of coffee. She put out a coffee cake and some Christmas cookies.

As they sipped their coffee Marianne asked, "Anything come to you yet on what old number seven means?"

"Only the Mickey Mantle thing," Phil lied. "By any chance, do you still have that stuff? I remember he had a small collection of baseball cards and photos."

"I think so. I'm sure I saved that stuff. I was planning to sell it on e-bay. There's a box down in the basement."

"Can I take a look at what's in it?" Phil asked.

"Sure."

Marianne flipped the light switch on and made her way down into the basement.

She retrieved the box quickly. "Maybe something in here will jog your memory."

"Right," Phil said. He had been hoping to go down into the basement with Marianne and get a look around so he could verify his hunch about where the money was. Then he realized it might be better not to show any interest in the basement. He assumed that Jerry was somewhat suspicious of him and he didn't want to take the chance that he might tip his hand. If Jerry and Marianne decided to rip apart the basement, they would eventually find the package.

They rooted through an old Thom McCann shoe box. Carmine had kept a lot of baseball cards. There had to be at least three hundred cards form the fifties. Phil shuffled through the cards and found three Mickey Mantle cards in excellent condition. There was also an autographed baseball from that period signed by the entire 1958 Yankee team.

"You know, the contents of this box are probably worth thousands of dollars. I wonder if that's what he was trying to tell us," Phil said, floating a trial balloon.

"Maybe," Marianne said. She picked up the tray of cookies and passed it over to Jerry who declined. Phil took a chocolate chip cookie and placed it on his plate. "I was wondering Phil, do you think maybe Carmine did have the money Florio was looking for after all? I feel so silly now after being so dismissive of your concerns. Maybe that's what he hid."

"I thought of that too," Phil said, glad that Marianne acknowledged that she was thinking about the money too. "But I always suspected that either the cops or one of Florio's associates got the money."

"I know," she said, "I just assumed if there was any money, it was lost at the scene of the accident. Somebody got to it before the police, or maybe, it was the police that took it. I knew I didn't have it," she said, a hint of reproach in her voice.

"Well, if Carmine wanted to leave you guys baseball cards, I think he would have said that in his message, don't you? I mean why be mysterious about that?" Jerry said.

Marianne agreed. "It has to be something else. Otherwise why would he say anything about a package that only Phil would know where to find?"

"Yeah, that's right," Phil said.

Just then Ricky came walking through the front door. Before he even got to the kitchen he was talking. "I know what old number seven means," he said.

Everyone turned to stare at him. He was removing his coat, scarf and gloves. It was freezing cold outside.

"What does it mean?" his mother asked.

"I was over at my friend Darrell's house this morning. I said something about Uncle Carmine's Christmas card. Darrell's father was sitting there. He goes, 'old number seven? That's Jack Daniels.'"

Marianne and Jerry looked at Phil. He gave them a blank look in return.

"Look, here it is." He pulled a bottle out of his jacket pocket. "I borrowed a bottle from Darrell's father. Old number seven right on the label."

"Wow," Phil said. "That's something more to go on. We used to get somebody to buy it for us. We drank it all the time."

"Really? Where did you used to drink it?"

"Mostly in the car."

"I'm sure something will come to you," Jerry said, "When it does it might be a good idea for you to call Marianne first so you can search for whatever it is together. That way there won't be any questions or doubts."

"What Questions? Phil asked. "What doubts? Exactly what does that mean?" Phil said, his tone suddenly sharp.

"He didn't mean anything by it Phil. Just lawyer talk,"

Marianne said.

Jerry nodded in agreement. "I'm just saying that's what I would do if I were in your shoes."

For Marianne's sake, Phil let it go. She gently rubbed Phil's arm. "It will come to you. Just give it a little time."

Phil left Marianne's just before noon, promising to call her the minute something occurred to him. He was feeling really lousy now. He knew he sounded defensive when he challenged Jerry. He knew he would wind up sharing the money with Marianne but he was worried about the fact that the money was almost certainly in the basement of her house.

What if her lawyer boyfriend convinced her that notwithstanding Carmine's note, the money was rightfully hers and hers alone? Jerry's remarks gave Phil reason to worry. If Jerry and Marianne, got greedy he could be left out in the cold. Even if he told her he had given the proceeds of his house sale to Florio he had no proof other than a stock certificate in one of Florio's ventures.

No, he wanted to get his hands on the money without them knowing where it had been found. Better they should have to trust him than the other way around under the circumstances.

He drove to the mall and steeled himself for the crowd. He had to find something for Gloria. The problem was he didn't have a clue about what might please her. Obviously jewelry or clothing were out. That seemed too personal. On the other hand, a gift certificate would seem cold. Then he remembered that she had a sizable collection of pitchers, from tiny milk pitchers to large water pitchers, some plain and others ornate. He looked for a store that might carry something like that and found a water pitcher made by one of the famous makers of fine crystal. He had them gift wrap it and then he headed for Gloria's home.

On the way there he wondered if he should have gotten something for Gloria's mother too. Phil marveled over the way his thinking had changed once he and Gloria kissed. This wasn't another Fred or Angela situation; the chemistry with Gloria was undeniable. This could be something special. Again he felt like a teenager but the more he thought about it the more he felt that when it came to romance, nobody ever matured. All romances are high school romances at the start, he thought. He smiled then because a week ago he was trying to avoid Gloria. Now here he was trying to figure out what to get her mother for Christmas. He decided to get the old lady a nice bottle of wine. He noticed that she really liked wine so it would be a hit. He found a liquor store and bought a bottle of Far Niente, Cabernet Sauvignon, expensive but worth it. He was spending money as if he had already found Carmine's stash.

That settled, he now had some time to concentrate on how he was going to get his hands on the money. Marianne had mentioned that she and Ricky would be spending Christmas day with Jerry's parents at Jerry's home in Ridgewood. He was pretty sure he could get into the house while they were gone but the thought scared him. Yet, he couldn't think of a better solution and he thought it best to act fast before another clue surfaced. That was all he needed, some old friend from the neighborhood remembering how Carmine and his friends used to stay up until the wee hours drinking in the basement. Christmas Day would be his best hope and Phil was determined to make the most of it.

When Phil got to Gloria's she was in the middle of preparing an antipasto for her Christmas Eve dinner with her mother and aunt. She was truly delighted by Phil's Christmas gift. As Phil suspected she had one for him too. She gave Phil an expensive button down, gray, alpaca sweater. She said she knew he would look great in a button down sweater because, as she pointed out, against all odds at his age, he still had a flat stomach. Phil was pleased. They kissed and held hands until Gloria broke away so she could finish what she was doing.

Phil also saw that he had been right to get something for Mrs. Milano. Gloria seemed even more pleased that he thought of her mother than she was with her own gift. As he was getting ready to leave so Gloria could get ready to go to her aunt's for dinner, she invited Phil to have dinner with them again. Phil declined, saying he was still tired. They kissed a few times standing in the hallway near the door, not quite ready to say goodbye.

"How about tomorrow then? I'm going to be all alone and so are you," Gloria said.

"That's true," Phil answered. "How about if I come over around two o'clock?" Phil really wanted a place to go Christmas Day. It would be lonely sitting in his undecorated apartment. He was sure it would help in another way too. He didn't want to be alone after he invaded the home of his best friend's sister.

Phil sat quietly through the early part of the evening going over what he would do and more importantly what he would say if he was caught. He figured in the unlikely event that Marianne or Ricky caught him, he would simply level with them and let the chips fall where they may. In fact, the more he thought about it, that was probably the answer no matter who caught him. Of course, if they chose not to believe him then he might be in very hot water.

He realized that his case would be stronger if he could tell his story to someone ahead of time who might verify what Phil was saying: That he planned to share the money with Marianne equally according to Carmine's wishes, that he had been forced to make an investment to protect himself and Marianne and how he was concerned about not getting anything if somehow Marianne found the money first. But really it was too late to burden anybody with that. He decided to write it out, place it in a sealed envelope, mail it to himself and hope for the best.

Suddenly he realized he was hungry. He rooted around in his refrigerator but nothing appealed to him. He berated himself for not doing anything to acknowledge the Holidays. No decorations and nothing special in the refrigerator to give him even a moment's comfort. He almost wished he had accepted Gloria's invitation. The food would have been fabulous. Instead he drove over to Veneto's to have a quick supper. He was hoping Fred would be off work but he wasn't counting on it by any means. Of course she was there. When she saw him walk through the door, she gave him a blank stare. But then, perhaps because it was Christmas, she offered a thin smile and said hello.

Phil walked up to the bar and said, "Merry Christmas. Would it bother you if I sat at the bar and had dinner?"

"That depends. Are you a good tipper?" Fred asked.

"Better than ever," Phil answered.

"I heard you had a little trouble at North Ward. That must have been horrible, Phil."

Sometime during the last twenty-four hours, Phil had managed to stop thinking about it constantly. He shook his head in sorrow. "It was unbelievable, Fred. It's still unbelievable."

She poured him a glass of Cabernet and handed him a menu. "I'm sorry."

"Don't be. Not for me at least. Those kids though. My God what they do to themselves. We live charmed lives compared to these kids."

"Maybe that's their choice though. I mean some of them really seem to go out of their way to be miserable and make other people miserable," Fred said.

Phil understood she was just trying to make him feel better. He also understood there was no way he could explain to her what he saw every day. These kids had little hope and they knew nobody cared. Not about the big things anyway.

"How are you doing?" Phil said, wanting to change the subject.

"Same old, same old, as you can see." Fred waved her hand around the place as if to say, 'still here'.

"Well maybe that's not a bad thing," Phil said.

"Maybe not," she said, "I guess this is where I belong for now at least."

For just a moment Phil wondered if maybe he should ask Fred to join him. She looked lonely and that broke his heart a little bit. He decided against it. Too much history for a dinner invitation to sound innocent.

He ordered his meal and sat quietly while she went into the kitchen to place his order. He thought about Fred's words and how not very long ago he would probably have agreed with her. It occurred to him that for the first time in his life he was seriously interested in something more than his own well being and the fortunes of the New York Yankees. There must be some way to help at least some of these kids, he thought.

He chatted with Fred while he ate. She would be spending Christmas with her mother. As it turned out, she wasn't seeing anyone special. In fact she was avoiding men to give herself a break, she said. He finished his meal quickly and asked for the check.

"You're in a hurry." Fred said her tone somber.

The bill was for twenty dollars. Fred put two twenties on the bar and said, "Have a Merry Christmas Fred. It was really good to see you. I hope things work out for you."

CHAPTER 22

Phil woke up early Christmas morning after a night of intermittent sleep. It would be a busy day and he decided there was no use in lying around hoping for a few more winks. He got up and went through his morning routine quickly. He made some coffee just before he hopped into the shower. Outside it was snowing, already an inch on the ground. For a moment he panicked, worrying that Marianne wouldn't be able to leave the house that day. But then he remembered that the weather report called for a light dusting in the morning, just enough to give sentimentalists a traditional white Christmas.

After breakfast he got a few things together. He found a duffel bag to carry the cash once he uncovered it. He put everything into a shopping bag that would look to any nosy neighbors like a bag of Christmas gifts. He had already decided to go around to the side of the house and try to get in there. He remembered from their one date, the night they went to the Yankee game, that Marianne sometimes forgot to lock the side door. His best hope was that Marianne would forget again. Just in case, he also bought a long slim screwdriver in case he needed to jimmy the door. He assumed she and Ricky would be gone by one o'clock. He knew the route they would take leaving the house. They would head toward the Garden State Parkway. He knew just where to park so that they would be unlikely to notice him but he would be able to see them.

Later that morning he called Lisa to wish her a Merry Christmas. She didn't answer her phone so he left a message promising he would see her in a couple of days in Phoenix.

He watched television, did a little reading and, for courage and good luck, he downed a shot of Jack Daniels. Finally it was time to go. He stopped for gas and headed to his hiding place. Then he realized he forgot his bag. He had to rush back to the apartment and collect the shopping bag. He cursed himself a blue streak for being sloppy. By the time he got to his spot, it was 12:35. He pulled down both visors hoping to make it harder for anyone to get a good look at him. He glanced at the mirror caught his image. For some reason it hadn't occurred to him that wearing his signature Yankee cap wasn't a good idea. Even if someone didn't get a good look at his face the hat could be a dead giveaway. He removed the cap.

He looked at his watch again. He had wanted to get there earlier. Marianne and Ricky might have left already. He really wanted to make sure he saw both of them in the car. He certainly didn't want to break in only to find Ricky lying on the couch. How would he explain that?

Phil thought about riding by the house but he felt that was risky. What if they were leaving just as he drove by? By 1:15, he was beginning to lose his nerve. It was still snowing lightly but the accumulation had stopped. He didn't see Marianne drive by so he would have to drive to her house to see if her car was there. He had no choice. It was now or never. He drove the two blocks to Marianne's and parked in front of the house next to hers. Her car was parked in the driveway but Ricky's car was nowhere in sight. It didn't look like anyone was home. Maybe Jerry picked her up because it was snowing.

He decided to drive around the block again. He grabbed his cell phone and dialed Marianne's home number. If someone was home he would say he called to wish them a Merry Christmas. The phone rang six times before going to the answering machine. He didn't leave a message. He turned the corner and slid the car back into the space in front of her neighbor's house. He opened the door and got out. He was so nervous he was shaking a little.

Phil walked deliberately to the front door, trying not to rush. He rang the bell but there was no answer. After three tries he assumed it was safe so he did a little pantomime for any prying eyes and walked back to the car to get his bag. Then he walked around to the side door, bag in hand. He was actually praying for good luck as if God would give him a hand with a break in on the anniversary of his son's birth.

He turned the knob and the door opened. He almost let out a yell. In fact he wasn't sure he didn't. He entered quickly, closing the door behind him. The side door opened to a landing with steps on each side of it. The stairs going up led to another door that opened to the kitchen. The steps to his right led down to the basement. Now he was in a hurry. He flipped the light switch and headed down the steps. About half-way down, he stumbled and felt himself falling down the remaining steps. He stuck out his free hand to break his fall. As soon as he hit the basement floor he knew he had a problem. His left wrist hurt like hell. It was either broken or seriously sprained. He cursed himself for being so clumsy and then again out loud to acknowledge the pain he felt.

Phil forced himself to concentrate. He had tried his best to remember the cellar's layout when he was making his plans. He was looking for the walk-in cedar closet, about twelve feet by twelve feet that Carmine's father had built at the other end of the basement. That was where they used to store their booze and drink it late at night. There used to be a lock on the door but Phil also remembered that Carmine's father, Mister Cifelli hid the key in an old metal cigar box on a shelf just off to the right of the closet. He was pleased with himself that he remembered it but worried that the door might be locked. Most likely, Marianne would have changed the lock years ago. If the door was locked, Phil would have a decision to make. He was pretty sure he would break the lock and take his chances.

As it turned out he didn't have to worry. The lock was gone. He opened the closet door and switched on the light. The room had four rows of shelves on each side of it. The shelves were filled with old games, cardboard boxes with labels indicating clothing items, photographs, and Christmas decorations, some of which were open and empty. Phil went to his immediate left and saw an old Four Roses whiskey box and pulled it down from the top shelf. He remembered it. It was the same box that was there thirty-five years ago. Behind it was an old Scotch-plaid colored, metal, picnic basket from the forties or fifties. He grabbed it by its handles and eased it onto the floor. He tried to pry it open but with only one good hand available he was having trouble. His wrist was throbbing.

Gloria felt lousy. She had been feeling that way all day. Something she ate the night before disagreed with her. She was hoping it wasn't the clams. She called her mother who assured her that she felt fine. That convinced Gloria that she must be coming down with the flu. She decided to call Phil and let him know in case he wanted to reconsider her offer to get together.

When Phil's cell phone rang he grabbed it after one ring. He had meant to turn it off.

"Hello?"

"Phil? Merry Christmas, its Gloria. How are you?"

"Fine Gloria. Just a little busy right now. Can I call you back?"

"I just called to let you know that I'm seriously under the weather today. I feel lousy. Maybe I'm coming down with the flu."

Phil looked around as if he thought someone else might be listening. He had to get the basket open and get out of there. "Let me call you back, okay?"

"Sure. Do you still want to come over or would you rather take a rain check?"

"No, I'll come over and check on you as soon as I get a few things done."

"I'm glad you're coming but I don't want to give you the flu or anything," she said.

"Don't worry about it. I'll be there soon."

"At least the snow is beautiful. Wait until you see my back yard.

You'll forget all about Florida!"

"I'll bet. I hate to cut you off Gloria but I really have to go. I'll see you later this afternoon."

"Merry Christmas Phil. Oh, I already said that didn't I?"

"Merry Christmas," Phil said.

Phil went back to work. He realized he was going to have to force himself to use both hands to get the lid to open. He did the best he could but his left wrist was purple and swollen now and the pain was brutal. Finally, he managed to open it. Inside there was a package wrapped in brown paper. It looked exactly like the one Florio's flunky had given them that night. There was no note. He pulled the package out of the basket and shoved it into his sack. Then he closed the lid and returned the basket to where he found it. He almost forgot to put the Four Roses box back and probably would have had he not almost tripped on it as he turned to leave the cedar closet. He remembered to shut the light and close the closet door.

Tucking the package under his arm, he headed for the basement steps. He was almost home free. Phil really wanted to open the package just to verify that the money was there but he didn't dare. He started climbing the steps. He was feeling the thrill of having pulled it off when he heard a voice.

"Here it is right on the kitchen table." It was Marianne.

"It wouldn't be Christmas without pumpkin pie right?" Phil recognized Jerry's voice. "Even if we had to drive in the snow on the Parkway we couldn't do without the pie."

Phil froze. He was standing on the third step. He had to get back into the basement or out of the house. It was too risky to try to leave. He stepped gingerly down the steps to reach the basement floor. Then he tiptoed his way to the back of the basement all the way to the other end, away from the cedar closet. He remembered he had switched on the basement light. It was too late to do anything about that. He would have to hope for the best. He heard footsteps and more talking upstairs but at first he couldn't make out what was being said. Then he heard Marianne say in a firm voice, "Jerry we don't have time. Really. Stop," They were both laughing.

"I'll be quick," Jerry said.

"You're always quick," Marianne answered, and again there was laughter. "Come on let's get going. We can do that later."

"What if I'm not in the mood?"

"You're always in the mood."

At that moment Phil would have given anything not to be hearing this. His biggest fear was they would have sex and then somehow discover him in the basement afterwards. But, Marianne wouldn't be swayed. She insisted they wait and nudged Jerry toward the door.

"Oh, I almost forgot," she said. "I want to check the side door. I always leave it unlocked."

Phil heard footsteps and the kitchen door opened. He really had no place to hide. If Marianne saw the light on and decided to investigate he was done for. He held his breath. Marianne climbed down the steps and checked the side door.

"See," she called up to Jerry, "It wasn't locked."

Phil heard her lock the door and turn to go back up the steps. She flipped the light switch as she closed the door. A few moments later he heard the front door close. If his luck held, they wouldn't notice his car sitting in front of the next door neighbor's house. He walked back to the other end of the basement which was at the front of the house. He heard the car doors slam and the car start. Afterward it was quiet. His wrist was killing him. It had to be broken, he thought. He took a deep breath and climbed the steps, opened the side door and stepped out.

Fifteen minutes later he was sitting in his apartment with an ice pack on his wrist. After quickly looking on line he decided that the symptoms suggested a sprain rather than a fracture. Of course he had torn open the package as soon as he closed the door to his apartment. The money was there alright.

Phil took a quick shower, got dressed and immediately put the ice back on his wrist. He took some aspirin too. It was after three o'clock. He had to call Gloria and let her know he would be even later than he already was. He explained that he fell and hurt his wrist and that once the swelling went down a little he would drive over. Then he sat and counted the money. Even though they were all hundreds he knew he wouldn't be able to count them all and still get to Gloria's. For a moment he considered calling her back and begging off, but he really wanted to see her.

He counted out a hundred thousand and quit. He was so excited he could barely think. Finally, he was even. Here were the proceeds of the sale from the house in Tom's River. Once again he pulled out that bottle of Jack Daniels. He had forgotten how fond he was of the smooth Tennessee whiskey. By five o'clock he knew he had to get going. For the first time that day, he was hungry. The last time he really ate anything was the night before at Veneto's.

He put all the money back in duffel bag and took it with him. He knew it was probably safer to leave it somewhere in the apartment. Yet, he also wondered if maybe Marianne or Jerry might get it into their heads to check his place while he was out. Worse, what if Florio had one of his men watching him all these months? No sense taking chances. Under the circumstances being a bit paranoid wasn't all bad but he felt foolish having those thoughts just the same.

Marianne and Jerry had an argument on the way back to her house that night. It had been an enjoyable day with Jerry's family but both were tired now. Jerry started the argument by suggesting that Phil probably knew where the money was. "It wouldn't surprise me," he said, "if it's somewhere in your house."

"That is ridiculous," Marianne said. "Phil would never do something like that."

"Really? You really believe that? That guy wanted to jump your bones so bad and you shut him out. How do you know he wouldn't screw you out of the money just to get even?"

"Please. And it wasn't like that Jerry. He was always very respectful."

"You are so damn naïve, Marianne. I see the way he looks at you," Jerry said.

"You're an idiot. Your jealousy is beginning to wear me out, you know that Jerry?"

The two of them fought all the way home. Although Phil didn't know it yet, Marianne and Gloria were very close friends. She had encouraged Gloria to make a play for Phil, hoping to solve two problems, hers and Gloria's. From what Gloria was telling Marianne, the plan seemed to be working. Marianne explained all this to Jerry but he wasn't convinced. They didn't get to 'do that later.'

Phil arrived at Gloria's house just before 5:30. It was cold and snowing again. More accumulation was expected. She told him she was feeling better and that her mother had decided to stay with her sister an extra night because of the weather. They kissed, a long and passionate kiss, as soon as she closed the door. She said she made dinner for them so they headed for the kitchen.

Phil was in a terrific mood. It had been a long time since he felt this good. He couldn't remember the last time he felt so confident and full of life. In spite of his aching wrist, he was thoroughly pleased with the way he handled everything, from not letting on that he knew where the money was to actually finding it and getting it safely in his possession.

"Hey, you know something?" he said.

"What?"

"I've been to your house at least three times and you've never given me a full tour."

"Later."

"Nah, let's do it now," he said, grabbing her hand and pulling her toward the stairs that led to the rooms upstairs.

"Our dinner will be ruined Phil," she said but she was laughing.

"It will keep," he said.

Gloria put her arm around Phil's waist. He was wearing his new sweater. She finally noticed his wrist. "Wow, that really is swollen. Does it hurt?"

"Oddly enough, not since I saw you."

Gloria led Phil upstairs and gave him a slow tour. She showed him the guest bath, a sewing room her mother used and a music room that nobody used. She led him up to the doorway of each of the guest bedrooms and the master bedroom where Mrs. Milano slept. Finally, they were standing in the doorway of her bedroom. Phil gently pushed past her and walked up to the bed. He was grinning.

"And this was the point of the tour?" Gloria said, still smiling.

"I'm not sure. I do know I wouldn't mind resting my wrist on one of these pillows."

Gloria walked over to him and he took her in his arms. She responded and Phil knew he had guessed right. They fell onto the bed together, Phil being careful not to land on the sore wrist. They kissed for a long while. Phil's hands started to roam and this time Gloria didn't protest. They were soon naked and under the covers. Their lovemaking was slow and satisfying; an experience both of them understood the way anyone who was falling in love would understand.

Later they lay together in bed, their bodies intertwined. They talked about how long it had taken them to get together.

"So, your mother was right about you," Phil said.

"What do you mean?" Gloria asked.

"When I was here for Thanksgiving she said you had a thing for me."

"That's funny she told me the same thing about you. I guess she knew more than we did."

"The thing is I never allowed myself to think of you like

that when you and Carmine were together. Maybe I felt an undercurrent or something between us but I ignored it."

"It was an impossible situation really. I was very fond of you but I did love Carmine back then," she said.

"Did you and Carmine have a good marriage?"

"For a long time we did. But after he turned thirty-five, everything went downhill. He started cheating on me," Gloria said, "And he didn't try very hard to hide it either."

"You know, as close as we were, he never told me that."

"Of course not. He practically idolized you. He could never handle your disapproval."

The two lovers lay quietly for a while. Phil was feeling great. He felt another surge of euphoria over his triumph.

Phil felt so good he told her the whole story about Carmine and the money, how he paid Florio off for Carmine's gambling debts and how he wound up making an investment –Florio's words – to get the mob off his back. Then he brought her up to date, telling her about Carmine's Christmas card and how he got the money.

Gloria listened to the story but she said nothing other than to ask a few questions to clarify things. But when Phil told her about breaking into Marianne's house to get the money she stiffened and then sat up.

"How could you do such a thing?" she asked.

"It wasn't easy. But I didn't want to get left out in the cold. I lost all that money because of Carmine once. I didn't want to lose it again." Phil realized his mistake but it was too late to take it back. He had been talking to Gloria as if they had been together for months or even years. Caught up in the moment, he was flush with excitement over having pulled his caper off. Plus, after a year in limbo he finally had in his possession the money that would even him out. He didn't think before he spoke. The relationship with Gloria was brand new, now he had gone too far.

Gloria was staring at him, not quite in disbelief but wary just the same. "But you were the one who decided to give Florio your money. Marianne didn't tell you to do that. In fact, she told you to do just the opposite."

"How do you know that?" Phil asked.

Gloria got up and put a robe on. The romantic moment was gone. "Marianne told me about it."

Phil thought that one over for a minute. "You and Marianne are good friends?"

"You could say that."

"I know I could but I'm asking you, Gloria."

"Yes. We're good friends. We became friends while Carmine and I were married. Over the years we remained friends. I thought you knew that."

"No, I didn't." Phil was up now getting dressed.

"Does that matter?" Gloria asked.

"I guess not. I probably should have paid more attention though. I assume you also know I wanted to go out with her."

"I was aware of that, yes," Gloria answered.

Phil gestured toward the unmade bed. "So then what was this all about?"

"I was under the impression that you had made a decision."

"Really? What decision was that?"

"Let's not do this, okay? What I still want to know is how you could break into Marianne's home and take that money. Frankly I can hardly believe you told me about it."

"Gloria, the money belongs to both of us, just the way Carmine wanted it. If Marianne was alone, you know, not dating a lawyer who seems to me to be working the angles, maybe I would have played it differently."

They talked a while longer about Marianne and the lawyer and whether he could be trusted. They drifted downstairs to the kitchen. Just as Gloria had predicted, the dinner was ruined. So they had some bread and cheese with wine. Gloria was staring at her wine. Absentmindedly she was rolling the glass's stem between her thumb and forefinger. Phil studied her, not sure of what, if anything, to say next.

Gloria broke the silence. "Now that you have all that money what are you're plans?"

"I don't know really. I guess my perspective on that has changed in the last few months. Six months ago I probably could have told you exactly what I was going to do."

Gloria nodded. "What would you have done six months ago?"

"Moved back to Florida, bought a little condo and found a job that wasn't too taxing."

"That sounds lovely. Why the change?"

Phil knew she would ask that question. He wasn't sure how to put it into words without sounding egotistical. "I believe I'm needed here. For the first time in my life I feel like I'm making a difference in spite of what happened to those two kids at North Ward."

"I see," Gloria said, looking at Phil now. "You think you can make a difference in the lives of the kids you're teaching?"

"I don't know. Maybe. And there's you Gloria, if I haven't blown it."

"What are you going to do about Marianne" Gloria asked.

"I'm not sure. The money has to be counted first, I guess."

"Where is it?"

"It's in the car. Do you want to see it for yourself? It's an impressive sight."

He went out and grabbed the duffel bag and brought it into the house. He opened it and poured the money onto the dining room table.

"Oh my God," was all Gloria said.

Three hours later they had it counted. They did it twice to be sure. It was exactly four-hundred and fifty thousand dollars.

"I still don't know how you're going to explain yourself Phil."

"What would you do? He asked.

"Put it back where you found it. Then tell her you think you know where it is and have her find it with you."

"How can I do that? That's crazy," Phil said.

They sat quietly for a few minutes. Gloria's face looked so sad it broke Phil's heart. It started as a small pout but the corners of her mouth sagged and her eyes went blank.

"What is it Gloria?"

"You don't understand, Phil. I can't be with you if Marianne finds out about this. She's really my best friend in the world. And I don't know if I could be with a man that would do what you've done."

"Come on, is it really that bad? Why can't I tell her I found the money someplace else? When she sees she's getting all that money do you think she's going to squawk?"

"As I said, you don't get it," Gloria said her voice as sad as her face. "Where can you possibly say you found it and make any sense out of that number seven clue? And when she tells me about all this how am I supposed to react?"

"Look, I wouldn't mind putting the money back but how am I going to get in there again? I don't think my nerves can't take it."

"You'll think of something."

CHAPTER 23

Phil did think of something. He called Marianne early the following morning.

"Are you alone?" he asked.

"I am. Are you?"

He ignored her. "I need to see you alone. Can I come over there?"

"Is it about the money?"

"Yes. What time can I come?"

"Did you find it?" Marianne asked, her voice getting excited.

"I'll be there in twenty minutes. Make sure you're alone, okay?"

"Sure."

Phil had decided to level with Marianne. There was little point in a charade now. He had thought it through as he wrestled with his pillow through the night. Gloria had been right. Not about trying to put the money back where he found it. It was too late to undo what had already been done. But, he still had to clear the air with Marianne. She was entitled to the truth.

And, for once in his life he was determined to get it right with a woman he cared about. Handling this situation straight up was the only way he could really make it right with Gloria.

The way he left it with Gloria the night before was that he would sleep on it and see how he felt the following morning. He didn't promise to put the money back. They had an awkward parting. He tried to kiss her goodnight but she turned away. She was visibly shaken which left him feeling off balance.

He drove over to Marianne's determined to explain his actions plainly. He wouldn't sugarcoat it or make excuses. He decided if he saw Jerry's car parked in the driveway though, he would leave.

He wasn't having this conversation with Marianne in front of Jerry. As it turned out there was nothing to worry about. Thanks to their argument Jerry spent the night in Ridgewood. There was no sign of his car or Ricky's for that matter. He took the duffel bag in with him.

"Okay mystery man, what is this all about?" Marianne asked. She was still in pajamas and slippers.

"I found the package: Four hundred fifty thousand dollars in hundred dollar bills." He patted the side of the duffel bag.

Marianne offered a broad smile. "Where was it?"

Phil fixed Marianne with a look. "I want to ask a favor of you."

"Sure, what is it?"

"Is that coffee I smell?" Phil asked as he walked over to the kitchen counter and grabbed a mug. He poured a cup. "I have a story I want to tell you. Let me tell it without interruption, okay?"

"I'm all ears, Mister Falco."

"The night Carmine and I were in Atlantic City, we ran into one of Florio's associates at the roulette table." Phil went on to tell Marianne about their meeting with Florio and his demand that they deliver the package to New York. He glossed over the part about Carmine's gambling debts to spare Marianne's feelings.

"Remember I told you that Florio was pressing me for the package after Carmine died?"

Marianne nodded.

"I gave him the amount that's sitting in this bag to get him off my back and yours."

"Oh God, Phil, you didn't."

"Don't interrupt. You promised."

Marianne covered her mouth but she was shaking her head in dismay.

"I know you thought he was bluffing but what you didn't know was they tore my apartment apart looking for the money and set fire to it a few days after that. They were dead serious. I'm sure you were next. They were so sure we had the money." Phil took a sip of coffee. "Anyway, I had to sign some phony papers as if I was investing in one of Florio's businesses.

"How did Dennis Florio know you had that kind of money?"

Phil didn't anticipate Marianne asking the question. He hesitated before answering. "When we were in Florio's suite, before things got crazy, he asked what I was doing in New Jersey so we told him." It was a white lie really. Of course it was Carmine that spilled the beans but Phil saw little sense in making Carmine look the fool.

"Why didn't you tell me about this before?"

"Maybe I should have. I don't know. What could you do about it anyway? It was embarrassing and it happened because of something Carmine either did or didn't do with the package he was supposed to deliver. Anyway, your brother was dead so why make you feel worse?"

"So why are you telling me now?" she asked.

"That should be obvious," he said, momentarily eyeing the money. "But let me finish my story. At the time I felt like my only hope of having a decent retirement was to find the money. I talked to anybody I could think of that might have a clue about what Carmine would do with the money if he had it. To be honest, I couldn't be sure you didn't have it already."

"Really? Is that what you think of me?"

"All I'm saying is I couldn't rule it out. Put yourself in my shoes, out half a million dollars and feeling desperate."

Marianne sat straight up glaring at Phil. "Is that why you were so anxious to take me out?"

Phil shook his head. That was one question he had anticipated. "Realistically there was no way to completely separate my feelings about you and the possibility that you might have the money. Believe me I tried. On some level I never really believed you had the cash. Regardless, I really liked you."

Marianne relaxed a bit. She got up and filled her cup. She added milk and sugar and picked up a spoon to stir. "Go on."

"People had ideas about what Carmine might do with the money but nobody actually knew anything. I had pretty much given up on getting my money back until we got Carmine's message. When I read the Christmas card I caught on right away. I understood Carmine's clue perfectly. I didn't say anything because I wanted some time to think things over. To be brutally honest I didn't trust that boyfriend of yours."

"What the hell does he have to do with this?"

"Marianne, I don't know the guy. He's a lawyer. Maybe he would insist on you making a claim that you should keep all of it."

"Phil, you're not making any sense here. Where was the money?"

"I'll get to that. Maybe I was being paranoid but without that money I'm practically broke. I wasn't taking any chances. And then he made that remark about making sure you were present when I found it and all. That didn't sit right with me. So, I decided to get the money first. At least then I would have some control."

Marianne stared down at her slippers. "Now that you have it why didn't you just keep it?"

"I thought of that too." Phil said. "Here's the thing, I lost $500,000 just because I was in the wrong place at the wrong time."

Marianne got up from the kitchen table and opened the refrigerator door. She took a quick look inside and closed it. Phil stood up and leaned against the counter, next to her.

"So, why don't you just keep it then?"

Phil took a couple of steps over to the counter again. Carmine's Christmas card was still there. "He wanted us to share it," he said handing her the card.

Marianne opened the card and stared at the message. "Okay Phil, where did you find the money?"

"It was in your basement. I got it yesterday after you left."

"What? You broke into my house?"

"Not exactly. The side door was open. I was in and out in ten minutes."

"What time was that exactly?"

"Sometime after one o'clock. You were long gone." Phil knew she was wondering if he had been in the house when she came back for the pie. That was something he would deny no matter what. Luckily he had left that tidbit out when he told Gloria the story.

"I can't believe you did that. We've known each other for years. Exactly who are you?" Marianne asked.

"I'm not proud of what I did. But I'm trying to make it right now. In any case the one thing I hope you will believe is that I never intended to stiff you. I just wanted to be sure I got my share."

"Do you really think I would do something like that?"

"Money makes people behave badly," Phil said.

"Obviously."

"I'm sorry Marianne. I really am."

Marianne turned to face him. "Phil I don't like what you did but to be fair, I'm really sorry about what Carmine put you through." She put her arms around him and they hugged.

"Carmine wasn't trying to hurt anybody. As far as I can tell, Florio and his crew treated him like shit, no better than a stray dog. Taking the money was his way of paying them off before he checked out."

"Poor Carmine. So now what happens?"

"You get $225,000. It's already broken into separate packets. Gloria and I counted it out last night"

Marianne's eyes widened. "Gloria knows about this?

"Yeah. She found out about it last night. She insisted I tell you everything."

"I see." That Phil had told Gloria everything made Marianne feel better. Maybe Phil did behave badly but at least the guy wasn't a total loss.

"I'm really sorry Marianne. I should have handled this thing a lot better."

"I guess I can forgive you. Did you really give Florio $450,000?

Phil nodded, his face weary.

Marianne sat quietly for a while. "Maybe you should take it all Phil. It's really your money."

Phil smiled. "I have a better idea."

EPILOGUE

It didn't take long for Phil to sell his plan to Marianne. At first she told him she would need the money to supplement her pension once she retired. And, while she thought his idea was noble, she had doubts about whether they could pull it off. She changed her mind on New Year's Day. She called Phil in Phoenix where he was visiting with his daughter to tell him about her change of heart. Of course, Phil was delighted. When he asked her what changed her mind she couldn't wait to tell him the news. Jerry had proposed the night before. They were getting married on Valentine's Day. Since Jerry was a wealthy man, money was no longer a concern. Jerry had even supported Phil's idea and agreed to help with any legal paperwork that certainly would have to be done.

Six months later Phil and Marianne opened the not for profit Rasheed Marbury after school program for North Ward High School students who demonstrated an interest in furthering their education. At first they tried to work with the City of Newark and state officials but there were too many regulations and political roadblocks and too many people with not so hidden agendas.

Tiring of the games, Marianne suggested they just find office space near the high school and open their doors to any North Ward student wanting extra help. Phil readily agreed. Enrollment was small but Marianne and Phil were hopeful they could entice more needy kids into the program. The program was staffed by unpaid volunteers, a few of whom were teachers like Erik Cowens. The majority of the instructors were business men and women who had a desire to give something back to the community. Most of what they taught was remedial writing, reading and math. They planned to offer more advanced programs as students made progress.

To entice students they decided to offer special vouchers as awards for improved grades. For raising a grade in a key course from failing to passing from one marking period to the next, the vouchers had a dollar value accepted by fast food restaurants, clothing and electronics stores. Some of the stores that agreed to participate in the program, also made contributions to the after school program. Students could also earn points, similar to airline membership programs that would cover some of their college expenses if they raised grade point averages and maintained them throughout the school year. Graduation from North Ward was good for a thousand dollar voucher called the Carmine Cifelli award. And, if they chose to go to work instead of college, they could use the vouchers toward the purchase of a reliable car or any other purpose approved by a committee established by the program's finance committee.

Although the expense involved with opening the school and getting it running was high, Marianne and Phil still had some money left to help fund their retirements. Plus, it didn't take long for the program to get the attention of the media. Eventually, it was copied in other cities around the country. Phil and Marianne appeared on several of the local and then national morning news shows. Time and Newsweek ran stories too. Marianne didn't enjoy the spotlight but Phil enjoyed the recognition.

He became an eloquent spokesperson for the program, raising more funds in the process. He even got Dennis Florio to make a nice donation. Of course, Florio insisted on a scholarship fund in his name that would go to the Marbury student that got the highest SAT scores.

Phil was thrilled by the chance to do something useful. Getting his personal life in order was another story. Phil and Gloria had a good run but in the end, the fact that she had once been married to Carmine eventually made them both uncomfortable. They managed to part friends and Gloria helped out with the administrative details at the school.

Then it turned out that Phil had been right to worry about Lisa. When he saw her during the Christmas holidays he confronted her about his suspicion that she might be abusing drugs. She steadfastly denied it. Two months later though, the young man she was dating called Phil and expressed his fears. Again Phil flew out to Phoenix. This time Lisa confessed. She was abusing pain killers. She had to spend time in a rehabilitation program. For several months Phil flew to Phoenix on weekends, going through family counseling with Lisa and Arlene. The process healed some old wounds and improved his relationship with his daughter.

Two days before his sixty-first birthday, Phil had a heart attack. Motivated by the work he was doing, he recovered quickly. As soon as he was back on his feet he took one of the nurses who had taken care of him to a Yankee game. Life was good. The Yankees won 11-7.

Acknowledgements

Thank you to my friends who agreed to read *Back to Newark* and offered helpful insights. John Anderson, Heather Anusbigian, Candy Barone, Joanne Mayfield, Mary Ellen Palmeri, Frank Riley. Thanks to my brother Steve and Art Warner for the very helpful technical assistance. And I want to thank my wife Nancy for her tireless editing and constant support.

Made in the USA
Lexington, KY
02 December 2010